SEASONS OF PLEASURE
WINTER & SPRING

By Anya Bast

SEASONS: WINTER & SPRING
An Ellora's Cave Publication, January 2005

Ellora's Cave Publishing, Inc.
1337 Commerce Drive
Stow, Ohio 44224

ISBN #1419950533

Cover art by Syneca

Warning:

The following material contains graphic sexual content meant for mature readers. *Seasons: Winter & Spring* has been rated E–rotic by a minimum of three independent reviewers.

Ellora's Cave Publishing offers three levels of Romantica™ reading entertainment: S (S-ensuous), E (E-rotic), and X (X-treme).

S-*ensuous* love scenes are explicit and leave nothing to the imagination.

E-*rotic* love scenes are explicit, leave nothing to the imagination, and are high in volume per the overall word count. In addition, some E-rated titles might contain fantasy material that some readers find objectionable, such as bondage, submission, same sex encounters, forced seductions, etc. E-rated titles are the most graphic titles we carry; it is common, for instance, for an author to use words such as "fucking", "cock", "pussy", etc., within their work of literature.

X-*treme* titles differ from E-rated titles only in plot premise and storyline execution. Unlike E-rated titles, stories designated with the letter X tend to contain controversial subject matter not for the faint of heart.

Also by Anya Bast:

CONTENTS

WINTER PLEASURES: THE TRAINING

Chapter One

Sienne glanced up, then lowered her eyes as was proper, but in that moment she memorized the visage of the man who would be her temporary keeper.

A long fall of onyx-in-shadow hair framed a face that was close to handsome, but not quite. His chin was strong and his features well crafted, his body muscular in the way of warriors. This was no weak-limbed nobility seated before her on the dais. That alone worried her. One of his huge hands could probably span her pelvis; break her neck with just a little extra pressure. She hoped he knew his own strength. Some of the large ones didn't and would subject her to pain without realizing it...or realizing it.

But it was not her place to complain. Never that.

"My lord, the winters here in Nordan are long and without distraction. I have brought this tribute to you to entertain you and warm your bed over the long months ahead." Cyrus pushed her forward into the circle of nobility and retainers that had grievances to air before Lord Marken's court.

Sienne glanced up. She could not determine the color of the gaze that rested on her, taking her in from her battered slippers to her thread-worn kirtle.

Cyrus had dressed her in what he deemed finery, designed to display her "assets." The gown was a peach-flesh color. A necklace of pale green stones, to match her eyes, hung around her throat, a crystal the size of her thumbnail rested in the hollow between her collarbones. The gown dipped low in the front to show the swell of her breasts and clung tight to her hips. The sheer fabric outlined her breasts and dark areolas, and the patch of red hair between her legs when she moved just right. It was designed to tantalize—whet the appetite.

She was Cyrus's choicest morsel, trained for the last three years in the sexual arts. Her current keeper intended to gift her to this lord as a peace offering, from Cyrus's country of Sudhra to Marken's homeland of Nordan.

It was a well-known fact that open sexuality abounded in Lord Marken's court. Some said that here the nobles copulated freely, the lord took any woman in full view of others, and sexual games were rampant.

Sienne could not believe such a thing possible. Sex was not a game. Sex was not a pleasurable thing to be engaged in at a whim. For a man, yes…but not a woman. A woman never enjoyed the act. It was a simple unpleasant fact.

"Lord Cyrus of Sudhra, I acknowledge the generosity of your gift," came Lord Marken's deep, reverberating voice.

Sienne shivered. It was like heated chocolate on a cold winter's day. It was nearly sin the voice that came from his throat. But no matter how nice his voice, he'd be a cruel keeper.

They all were.

Out of the corner of her eye, Sienne saw Cyrus bow deeply, likely inordinately proud of the praise from one of the most powerful lords of Nordan. "She is educated and speaks your tongue, my lord."

Marken raised a dark brow, his eyes sweeping over her with renewed interest. Sienne looked away out of respect.

"Look at me," Marken commanded.

Confused, Sienne kept her eyes averted.

"Look at me," he repeated.

Cyrus gave her push on the shoulder. "Your new lord and keeper has given you an order. Obey it."

But it was such a strange one! Never did her keepers wish to look into her eyes. She raised her head. "Yes, my lord."

"What is your name?"

Her eyes widened. "My lord wishes to know my name?" she asked in halting Nordanese.

"You do have one, do you not?"

She averted her eyes. "Yes, my lord, my parents gifted me with the name Sienne."

"Sienne." He rolled her name around in his mouth like it was a choice sugared raisin. "I am pleased. Cyrus, she is a true beauty with those light green eyes and that dark red hair. I see the rest of my court is also pleased to have such a fine woman join us for the cold season."

Sienne glanced around. Many of the men had their eyes on her, their gazes heated and intent. She knew all too well a look of desire. Apparently, she'd quickly become an object of fascination to the Nordan noblemen. Cyrus would be pleased.

"Take her to my chamber, Cyrus. Talyn, the captain of my guard, will lead you. Leave her there alone."

A tall, muscular man who Sienne surmised was Talyn stepped from the crush of nobles lining Marken's court.

His long dark brown hair was caught in a thin leather thong at the nape of his neck. His chocolate colored hair framed a well-made face with vibrant green eyes and full lips.

"I shall return for her in the spring when the passes melt clear of snow," replied Cyrus.

Marken waved a hand. "Come back then and we shall share a glass of spiced wine and discuss trade opportunities between our peoples."

Cyrus bowed. "Yes, my lord."

Talyn led them from the court into a corridor with stone walls and a cobblestone floor. Thick naarbranch rushes crunched under Sienne's feet and sent up a scent of spice. Wordlessly, the warrior Talyn led them up a flight of stairs and down another candlelit corridor. Unsmiling, Talyn halted in front of an ornately carved door, flicked a glance at Sienne that spoke of pity mixed with a touch of lust and left them there.

Cyrus pushed the door open and pulled her into the room. A huge see-through fireplace dominated the center of the chamber, driving out the chill so prevalent in the castle. An enormous bed stood across from the fireplace, heaped with soft blankets and pillows. Tapestries depicting spring-tide hunts covered the walls. A table stood to the left of the bed, scattered with papers and books.

Sienne considered the books and wondered if her new keeper was a learned man. She'd been fostered in a scholar's family and they'd taught her much of philosophy, art, and languages. Her skill in Nordanese was rare in a slave and one of the reasons Cyrus had selected her for this errand.

Cyrus yanked her hard toward the four-poster bed and tied her to one of the posts. He slipped his hands to the neckline of her gown and pulled it down, so that the very top of her breasts showed and the fabric lay right above the nipple. He brushed his thumb over one, causing her to flinch, and then brought his hand to her chin, tipping it up. His brown eyes narrowed and his dirty blond hair fell into his eyes.

"Get what I need from him, Sienne. If you don't, the price will be your life. And, in case you don't care about that, know I'll hold your foster family accountable for your ineptitude. Believe me, I'll make them hurt before they die."

She winced and looked away. Her foster family had been as kind to her as possible under Cyrus's constant threat. She had no wish to see them harmed.

Cyrus had placed her here to get as much information as she could from Lord Marken, about Nordan politics, military positions...and weaknesses. It was amazing what a man would reveal to a woman when comfortable, warm, and sated with sex.

Most men wanted to talk of their intelligent, strategic plans, of their conquests and political maneuverings. They didn't think a woman would understand their ramblings. Talking to a woman of those things was safe, and they believed built them up in a woman's eyes to God-like status. Sienne knew all of the correct things to say to encourage their bragging; just as she knew what to do to their bodies to keep them satisfied and wanting more.

When she looked back Cyrus was striding to the door, his black cloak swirling around him and his boots clicking soundly against the polished stone floor.

She shuddered and glanced around at the books that lined the shelves of the room. Her mind worked, trying to think of all manner of ways to get close to Lord Marken, to get him to confide in her, to believe she was safe. Every man in power needed someone safe. She'd learned that long ago.

Footsteps of a different cadence than Cyrus's sounded at the door and Sienne jumped.

Lord Marken closed the heavy, gold inlaid door behind him. Sienne twisted in her bonds, her stomach tightening low in sudden fear. Although something deep and dark within her always thrilled at the prospect of a new man to please with her skills. Even though she was a slave, she had power in some things, and she'd learned to exploit it.

And this one was far from displeasing to the eye. His black hair reached the middle of his back. Eyes the color of the river in winter, a cool blue-green, peered from a well-sculpted face. His best feature by far was his lips. Full and sensual, they looked perfect for tracing with the tip of her tongue.

Maybe she could get what she needed from this man if she proceeded carefully.

Marken crossed the floor like one of the big jungle cats of Sudhra, taking in her appearance. She knew how she looked, her hair free over her shoulders, her gown clinging to her curves, her nipples, tight from the cold, showing through the sheer, flesh-colored fabric.

He stopped in the center of the room, his gaze intent. His leather jerkin was open halfway down his chest, showing an expanse of smooth, sculpted muscle. His leggings fit tight over powerful looking thighs. She shivered in fear spiced with the slightest pinch of desire and looked away.

"Look at me, Sienne. You are forever looking away."

Her gaze snapped to his. "Yes, my lord."

"You are not here of your own free will, are you?"

She let out a laugh of derision. "My lord sees me secured thus and asks such a question?" She bit her tongue on the last word, not believing she'd had such impudence.

She waited for a cuff, but only got a bemused smile. "Ah, so there is some fire left in you after all. They haven't beaten it all out of you yet."

"Forgive me, my lord. I shall endeavor to be more submissive."

"Oh, now what fun would that be?"

He walked near her, so close she could smell the heady mix of sandalwood and citrus, the soap he must bathe with. He drew his dagger and raised it. She closed her eyes and tensed, waiting for the bite of the blade into her flesh. Only the sound of fabric slicing met her ears. Her arms went lax—suddenly freed.

"I do not abide slavery, Sienne. I know it is a practice in Sudhra, but not here in Nordan. I have no wish for a sex slave. I did not tell Lord Cyrus this because I had no wish to offend him and because it gave me an opportunity to set you free."

She looked up at him with what she knew was an expression of shock on her face. "My...my lord?"

He picked up a pouch from a drawer near his bed. He threw it at her and she caught it. It clinked heavily with coin. He turned and motioned toward the door. "Go. You are free. If you hurry, you will beat the first snowfall. If you would like, I will send men to accompany you to the nearest town."

She stood, stunned...and free. For the first time since she was five years old, she was free.

The pouch lay heavily in her palm. She looked toward the door and realized she didn't have the slightest clue what to do!

And besides that, Cyrus would track her down and punish her. He'd kill her and her foster family for not fulfilling the duty with which she'd been set. Cyrus's reach extended to the ends of Aran. There was nowhere for her to go, no one she could trust.

Her next question quavered in her throat for a moment before she could force into the open air. "But...what will you tell Cyrus, my lord, when he comes for me in the spring?"

Marken shrugged. "Lord Cyrus is a greedy man. I will give him gold enough in recompense so that he will not think of you again."

She walked to a chair and sat down, turning her head so he could not see the sudden tears that pricked her eyes. She held the pouch loosely in her hands. He was actually willing to pay gold for her freedom. Her life meant something to him. She took a deep breath, held it, and then let it out slowly.

It only made what she had to do that much more difficult. She had to fulfill her obligation to Cyrus or her foster family would suffer for it, but she could not reveal that information to Lord Marken.

She turned toward him. "Does my lord know I have been trained these three years, since my eighteenth birthday, in all ways to please a man?"

"The women who come to my bed, come of their own free will and I have plenty of partners. I do not need another." His eyes flicked down her body and her nipples hardened in response.

Sienne wondered at her reaction. Perhaps kindness was an aphrodisiac...or maybe she was simply cold.

"No matter how comely she might be," he finished.

She lowered her eyes and looked up through her lashes. She knew well the different paths to seduction. Lord Marken was a protector. That was more than apparent. She could easily play the role of one needing protection. It was no guise, after all. "My training goes beyond that of the ordinary women who warms your bed, my lord."

"Are you trying to convince me to keep you? I just gave you enough money to begin a new life and set you free."

"If it pleases my lord, I shall go, but I have no location to which to travel." She didn't hide the genuine quaver of fear in her voice.

He turned. "Do you not have family somewhere?"

She shook her head and dropped her eyes. "They've all been killed by Cyrus and his thanes." She looked up. "I am good at what I do, my lord. I can please you, make your body never wish to give me up."

"I'm sure you could. That is not in question—"

"I've known nothing but servitude since I was five years old, my lord," she said quickly. "I don't know what I would do out there alone." She let tears shine in her eyes.

Marken turned and paced the room, then whirled with anger drawing harsh lines on his face. "How can you not wish for freedom, Sienne?"

Her lower lip trembled. She fell to her knees in front of him, making sure the gown dipped low enough that Marken had a view of her bare breasts, and averted her eyes in respect, looking at him sidelong. "Please, my lord. I...I would perish, surely."

Marken pushed a hand through his thick mane of ebony hair. "The chains are no longer around your wrists, but in your very mind. It is more difficult to loose those."

He dropped his gaze to her breasts and hips. "I've no doubt of your skills. But know if you stay, you stay of your own free will. You can leave whenever you choose it."

She left the pouch on the floor, scrambled to her feet and instantly dropped low into a curtsy. "Thank you, my lord."

"First thing, Sienne. Raise your eyes when you speak to me." His voice dropped a notch and infused with heat. "You've lovely eyes. I would like to see them."

Hope sprung within her so fast and so hard it hurt. Maybe he did want her. It would make the task set before her so much easier if he did. She raised her eyes and took several steps in his direction. She wanted to prove her worth quickly, so he would not send her away. It was a bold move and she half-expected to be rebuffed, but he didn't move as she walked toward him.

She placed her hands on his powerful chest and slid them down, feeling her fingers glide over his nipples to the ties on his trews and beneath, his braies. With deft fingers she undid them.

Marken stood, unmoving and allowing. She freed his already hard shaft and stroked the foreskin down. His was a beautiful phallus. Like everything about him, it was large—long and thick. It was one of the largest she'd ever seen, and she'd seen many in the last three years. The head was shaped like a plum and the length slightly bowed toward his stomach, promising delight to any woman who took him because he'd easily reach the pleasure point deep within.

She went to her knees and licked around the head of his shaft, then took him into her mouth and sucked, letting the head of his cock slip past her tonsils and down her throat. Marken let free a groan and his hands tightened on her shoulders.

Lips and tongue working, she feverishly tried to please him, to let him know how skillful she was and that it would be a mistake to let her go.

She cupped and massaged his scrotum with one hand, while using the other to work the base of his shaft as she brought him in and out of her mouth with increasing speed, letting the head of his cock slide down her tight throat.

She slipped him out of her mouth and ran her tongue just under the head of his cock, licking and sucking at the special place directly below it where she knew men were most sensitive. Then she drew him back into her mouth and down far into her throat once more.

Marken's body tensed, his fingers tangling in the hair at the back of her head. His hips moved forward as he thrust his cock into her mouth. Finally he released himself with a deep groan.

She swallowed every last bit of his seed and fell back on her heels, looking up at him with trepidation in her eyes. "Was that satisfactory, my lord?"

He remained silent, merely redoing his braies and trews. She waited, breathless.

"Very. But did you enjoy that, Sienne?"

"My lord?"

"You're very good at it, but do you enjoy it?"

Such a question had never been put to her. Maybe it was a trick? "My lord, I live only to serve you in any carnal desire you wish fulfilled. I am trained in all manner..." He swept her off the floor and into his arms. She let out a surprised hiss of breath.

He sat down and settled her onto his lap. "I desire a willing woman, Sienne. If you are to stay here under my protection, and you insist on serving me in this capacity, we are going to have to retrain you."

She blinked. "My lord?"

He slipped a hand under the edge of her skirt, drawing it up to the apex of her legs. She obediently parted her legs for him, but tensed every muscle in her body. Working his way around her undergarment, he slipped two of his huge fingers into her. He worked them in and out of her, and she felt her pelvic muscles clamp down, pushing him out. It was an automatic response she could not stop.

Marken withdrew his hand, brought his fingers to his mouth, and licked them. "Mmmm. You taste good, Sienne. But there should be more moisture here. You are not the least bit excited, are you?"

"M...my lord..."

Marken shook his head. "Don't lie. Your body betrays you."

Sienne shifted uncomfortably on his lap, feeling the bulge between his legs where he'd risen for her again. "Please forgive me, my lord. I will try to do better. When can I expect a beating?"

He took her chin between his fingers and cupped her chin, guiding her gaze back to his. "I will never beat you." He trailed a finger down her throat to her heaving chest and lazily circled a nipple with an index finger. "I might pound you with my cock, but never with my fists." His voice was a silken rasp. Sienne could tell he wanted her. "Hopefully, you'd enjoy being pounded that way."

His words had a curious effect on her. She imagined him sliding his long, thick shaft into her woman's passage and stroking in and out of her. She imagined how he'd fill her up and touch that place deep within where sometimes it almost felt good.

Marken circled her nipple around and around relentlessly and gently pinched. Her nipple hardened in response.

His voice lowered and he brought his face close to hers. "I intend to bring you to a place where you're begging me to enter your passage, Sienne. Not out of a sense of servitude, but because you want me moving in and out of you, pleasuring you, bringing you to peak over and over."

"P...peak, my lord?" she asked, disconcerted by the tightening of her loins that was caused by his touch.

The motion of his finger stopped for a moment, then resumed. "By the Goddess's eyes...you really don't know, do you?"

She shook her head and he massaged her entire breast with his hand before returning to her nipple. "I'll show you soon, Sienne."

He worked her nipple, running his finger over it, caressing every ridge, every valley of its distended tip. Her breath caught. "As you wish, my lord," she rasped. What was wrong with her? She felt hot, flushed, and achy. Was she falling ill?

"You've been trained to please a type of man who never cared about your pleasure. But you must understand, the pleasures of my partner feed mine and make love-play sweeter. I know a way we might pass the long winter. I'll use it to train you to pleasure."

Anything! Anything as long as she could stay here and fulfill her duty to Cyrus, ensuring her safety and that of her foster family's. "Yes, my lord."

"Here is the most simple of lessons." His hand twined around the back of her neck and drew her face to wed with his. His lips were soft on hers. He kissed her upper lip, then her lower. The tip of his tongue traced her lower lip slowly. It made things deep in her body pulse and come to life. A shiver ran up her spine.

Then he kissed her harder, more demanding. He parted her lips with his tongue and slipped it within. It was nothing like the crude invasions she'd suffered before. His tongue met hers and asked to dance. Their lengths rubbed and teased as his tongue explored the recesses of her mouth. Sometimes he'd withdraw and fall back to kissing her lips individually before sliding his tongue back between her lips.

He kissed her leisurely and at length, as though his mouth made love to hers. His free hand ever concentrated on her breast, rubbing it with the flat of his hand, teasing the tip with his fingers. She moaned deep in her throat. Moisture flooded her core.

He broke the kiss and pressed his forehead to hers. "I believe I'm going to enjoy your training very much Sienne. It will be harder on me than you, I think. I already want to take you hard and fast. But you are not ready. We will begin our training in private on the morrow."

Chapter Two

Sienne twisted between the silken sheets, and the fabric rubbed against her bare skin. The luxurious chamber she'd been given the previous night made her smile. A huge fire roared in the hearth not far from the four-poster bed in which she now lay. The scent of burning branches reached her nostrils.

The warmth of the fire, combined with the heavy down coverlet on the bed, had chased away every last bit of chill from her bones and left her feeling languid, relaxed, and comfortable — things she hadn't experienced but in the rarest moments of her life. She cherished them now.

She rolled over and noticed that a servant had laid a feast on the table near the leaded-glass window. Thick chunks of salted meat and brown braided bread drizzled with honey met her surprised eyes. The sounds of the servant entering the room must have been what had awoken her.

Someone cleared his throat. Sienne sat straight up, looking toward the source of the sound. Marken stood by the hearth, dressed in a fine black linen tunic and close-fitting black trews. His long fall of hair was secured at his nape with a leather thong. Her fingers itched to release it.

"I thought to send a servant to bathe you, dress you, and bring you to my rooms, but then decided I would enjoy doing these tasks myself," he said.

Her mouth went dry and the blanket slid from her lax fingers to pool at her waist. His gaze flicked down and she blushed, drawing the covers up around herself once more.

"Are you shy?" He laughed. "Many men have seen you unclothed, no?"

She nodded, looking downward. "Y...yes, my lord." Just none who had an effect on her like this man.

He walked across the room and stood by her bed. "Pull the blankets from you," he commanded softly.

She did so, her flesh pebbling in the chill morning air. She was hideous, scarred. Cyrus had encouraged her to only show her body to Marken in the cover of darkness. Here it was clear daylight and she was thus exposed. She turned her face away, looking at him from the corner of her eye.

He reached out and traced one thin white scar that ran down her thigh—made from a whip a year ago. His other hand clenched in a fist, undoubtedly angered that Cyrus had sent him such damaged goods.

"I apologize for being so ugly, my lord," she whispered, suddenly frightened he'd beat her for her marked flesh.

"Sienne, you are beautiful. You wear these scars like you've fought a battle, and indeed, you have. It is only that it makes me angry you have been treated thus."

His gaze roved over her body. "Rest your head back against the pillows and spread your legs for me."

Sienne slid down against the silken pillows and sheets so she lay flat on her back and spread her legs as he'd ordered her.

He took her in from head to toe. Sienne could almost feel his gaze gliding over her skin, rubbing her nipples and between her legs. It was cold in the room but his heated gaze warmed her flesh.

"You are exquisite," he said. "Cyrus was right to take pride in you. It is rare I see a woman with a patch of fire between her legs and such kissable breasts. You should never be afraid of displaying your body."

Flipping his hair over one shoulder, Marken leaned down and kissed her scars one by one, letting his tongue trail hotly down their lengths. Sienne shivered in pleasure as his tongue roved over her skin, leaving a tingling, near healing sensation in its wake.

He reached down to pet her mound, running his fingers through the hair. Then he slipped his hand downward and rubbed his fingertips across her pussy and upward to some spot that made her gasp with sensitivity. Pleasure coursed through her so intensely it bowed her spine. She snapped her legs closed and then cowered, afraid he'd cuff her for denying him the touch of her.

"Easy, Sienne. Know that I'm only commanding you to display yourself to me to make you ready for life in my court. You will find yourself unclothed here more often than not. You must grow at ease with displaying your body for many people at any given time."

It was true. Marken's court was known for its easy nudity. Such things were a part of Nordanese culture. Children were notoriously difficult to get on a woman. Therefore sex often and with multiple partners was an encouraged thing. Normal, in fact.

Such was not the case in Sudhra, although children were equally difficult to beget there. In Sudhra open sex practice was outside religious law, against the rule of the new God. Since sexual expression was thus repressed, the sex slave business was rampant.

Women were considered inferior creatures in Sudhra, below the notice of the ruling priest class. Therefore men like Lord Cyrus, one of the most powerful lords of Sudhra and one of the most successful slave handlers, went unharassed.

Marken tipped his head to the side and his tail of silky hair slid down his shoulder and arm. She wondered briefly how it'd feel loose and brushing over her bare skin. "Does my touch displease you?" he asked.

She looked shocked, she knew, because the answer came easily and was the truth. It was probably the first time she'd answered that question without lying. "N...no, my lord. Not at all." She blushed and looked away. "On the contrary."

"Hmmm...I think you lie. Otherwise, you would not have closed your legs. It is time I began accustoming you to my touch, I think." He leaned over and scooped her up into his arms. She splayed one hand against his chest and wrapped the other around the back of his neck.

He walked over and sat her down in the chair in front of the spread of food. "Eat," he ordered.

It was disconcerting. Here she was the servant, being served by none other than the lord of the castle himself. Sienne ducked her head and ate quickly, but savored every mouthful of the decadent food. She closed her eyes as the honeyed bread spread over her tongue and chewed thoroughly to extract all the hearty sweetness from it.

Marken ordered servants to bring in steaming water and fill the bathing tub in her room, and then he sat down in the chair opposite her and picked up a bit of smoked meat. He dipped it in honey and held it to her lips.

"My lord," she objected, shocked. "You cannot feed me! You are a great lord and I am but a lowly—"

"I enjoy this, Sienne." His voice grew stern. "I command you to allow me to feed you. You are my willing pet for this long winter and I will do as ever I please with you and to you."

"Of course," she acquiesced and opened her mouth. She had no wish to displease him. He slid the bit of meat in, rubbing her bottom lip with the flat of his thumb. A thread of honey fell from the meat and curled around her nipple.

"Allow me," said Marken. He went down on his knees in front of her. That alone nearly sent her into paroxysms from the breached etiquette between slave and keeper. When he spread her legs and took her by the waist, sliding her to the edge of her seat, she nearly passed out from a mixture of fear and unwelcome desire. His mouth closed around her nipple with a little growl that sent a chill through her and he laved and sucked. One hand went to her other breast and massaged.

A sudden perplexing and powerful jolt of pleasure went straight to her loins. She panted once and let loose a long, low moan as his tongue flicked over her nipple, lightly biting at it. The servants continued to bring water in, but Sienne barely registered their presence.

Marken did two things at the same time. He put one hand to the small of her back and moved the other between her legs. He slid a finger into her passage and she tried to back away since she couldn't close her legs, but Marken held her in place at the small of her back. He began to thrust his finger in and out of her, simultaneously rubbing that place of sensitivity with his thumb.

All the nerves from her feet to the top of her head woke up and a strange, hot, tingling pleasure pressure began to build. It was an unnamable sensation. All Sienne knew was that she didn't want it to stop. She tipped her head back and closed her eyes.

He worked his finger within her passage until she moaned. Just as the pleasure seemed to reach some kind of a summit, an impending explosion, Marken withdrew his hand. Sienne lowered her head and her eyes flew open in confusion.

Marken sat back on his heels and put his finger to his mouth, licking at it like a cat with a bowl of cream. "Mmmm...that's better, Sienne." He reached out and stroked her mound. "Good girl."

"Something throbs between my thighs," she said breathlessly.

"Your clit, Sienne. It is a good thing." He smiled. "Training you may not be nearly as difficult as I'd presumed yesterday."

He stood and offered her his hand. She stood and took it. The place between her legs ached for his touch. He led her across the room toward the bathtub. "I am going to bathe you now," said Marken.

"My lord, I am a servant. I do not think this is at all appropriate." She fell to her knees. "Please, allow me to bathe you instead."

Marken forced her to her feet. "Did you not hear what I said about you being my pet, Sienne? You are my willing slave for this season. These are conditions you agreed to of your own will. I desire to see you wet and naked now. I wish to run my hands over your body, inside your body. I want to see you glistening with soap and spreading your legs for me. Do these commands make it easier for you?"

They did. In this sea of unfamiliarity, it was something to which she was accustomed. She nodded once. "As you wish, my lord." She stepped toward the tub.

She reached the edge of the bathing tub and saw they'd strewn the top of the water with lavender. Marken stepped behind her. He'd discarded his tunic and when he pressed his chest to her back she felt his warm flesh smooth and hard against her own.

His arms encircled her and he put his mouth to her ear. "Mmmmm...you feel good against me." His strong hands brushed over her nipples and then kneaded her breasts. He cupped them in his palms, bringing his thumb and forefinger around to pinch the sensitive peaks. Over and over he did this until her breath caught and her core quickened.

Marken picked her up and lowered her into the warm bathwater. Taking the bar of lavender-scented soap in his hands, he lathered them, and then applied his hands to her shoulders and upper arms and rubbed, making his way lower.

Sienne watched him as he moved over her, feeling his powerful hands kneading and massaging with gentleness at odds with his size. The muscled expanse of his chest was exposed to her view. It was hairless except for a thin line of black hair, leading from his stomach past the waistband of his trews. Her passage slickened and the thing he'd called her clit throbbed at the mere sight of him. His cock, long and thick, stood at hard attention, straining against the fabric of his trews.

Marken reached her breasts and ran his soapy fingers over them, under them, cupping their weight, and sliding his finger over the sensitive peaks, manipulating them until her nipples were so stiff they almost hurt. Her clit throbbed harder under his ministrations, her pussy lips infusing with blood and pulsing with pleasure.

She imagined Marken lifting her out of the bathing tub and laying her on the bed, sheathing his magnificent phallus inside her and pumping her with it. She'd never wanted a man like this. Already she grew fascinated with him because of his unbelievable kindness.

Marken dropped a hand from her breasts and trailed it down to her pussy. "Spread your legs for me," he ordered. She complied. Using his index finger, he circled her clit. His wet finger slipped around it easily. It swelled under his ministrations, growing larger and more sensitive. With his other hand, he continued to massage and caress one breast.

She gasped and thrust her hips forward from the combination of sensations. He obliged her by easing a finger into her, first one and then another so she was stretched around him. He moved his fingers in and out, stroking her clit with his thumb and caressing her breast with his free hand.

Sienne closed her eyes and gripped the sides of the bathing tub.

"Do you like that?" he asked.

She nodded. Her body was on fire. She felt the pleasure building once more. She spread her legs as far as they could go, her muscles tensing.

He removed his hand from her pussy and rubbed her labia before pulling away completely. Making a noise deep in her throat in her frustration, she opened her eyes.

He laughed softly. "Not yet, little eager one," he said. "When you come, you'll come hard. I'm going to make sure your first peak is one you'll never forget."

Marken lathered his hands with soap again and washed her thoroughly, from her hair to her toes. Sienne was aroused beyond all conscious thought. She watched the muscles of Marken's arms, chest, thighs, and buttocks flex as he moved. She wanted so much to slip his beautiful, rock-hard shaft into her mouth, see his head fall back with a groan and pleasure him until he emptied himself into her.

He stilled by the side of the bathing tub and looked down at her with a heated gaze. It traveled from her face, down her body to her patch of silken red curls covering her pussy. He bent at the waist and picked her up out of the tub, then laid her on the thick carpet in front of the fire. He left and returned with a small razor in his hand.

"Spread your legs again, Sienne," he said. "I won't shave all those luscious curls away, only those around your pussy lips—all the better to lick you." She swallowed hard at the mental image his words evoked—his dark head disappearing between her thighs...

"Catch your knees in your hands and show me everything," he ordered.

She did as he told her to do, stretching her knees back and up, giving Marken a wide and wanton view of her core. She felt the razor being set to her skin and he carefully, methodically shaved her hair away. When he was finished, he took a vial of lotion and lathered his fingers with it, then applied ir to her newly shaven skin. It was slick and slightly cool. He ran his fingers over her folds and slipped a finger within her. With the index finger of his other hand, he massaged her clit in a circular motion. She tipped her head back and loosened her hold on her knees.

"Stay in the position I commanded you take," he ordered in low, harsh voice. He wanted her. It was no mistake.

He inserted a second finger to join the first and kept up the relentless play with her woman's bud. She moaned and dropped her head back to the rug, arching her back and stabbing her tight nipples into the air. She could feel how wet she was becoming. She wanted him to slide his phallus inside her and slam into her. She wanted to hear the slap of his skin against hers.

A warm tongue replaced his index finger, but still he thrust his fingers into her passage. Marken groaned and it reverberated against her clit. He spoke so his lips brushed it. "You taste wonderful, Sienne."

He laved her clit with the flat of his tongue, then toyed with it with only the very tip. Sienne panted in pleasure. What was wrong with her? She'd never wanted a man like this.

He removed his fingers from her passage and swept his tongue down over her, drawing her labial lips into his warm mouth and sucking at them gently. His tongue played with the entrance of her passage, then thrust within it.

Sienne let out a strangled cry and her body tensed. The pleasure was building, cresting toward some unknown point that could only be the thing Marken called a "peak."

Marken stopped right before she reached it and she tipped her head up, looking down her body at him. He undid his trews and stepped out of them. He stood looking down at her and stroking his cock with one hand. She caught her breath in anticipation.

He knelt and placed the head of his shaft to her passage. The smooth, rounded plum-shaped head pushed at her, teasing her. He slid it up her labia until it brushed against her clit. She whimpered.

He moved his shaft against her, but did not slip inside. "Not yet. I want you crying, begging, for the want of me. I desire it though, Sienne. I want to slide inside you and thrust until you come all over me. I want to feel your muscles clenching around me, your liquid course over me. I want to release my seed into you and watch your beautiful face when you peak."

He rolled to her left side and turned her on her stomach. He slid his left arm beneath her and raised her up, so her buttocks were elevated. "Part your legs," he rasped in her ear.

She obeyed. With her pelvis braced against his forearm, he plunged two fingers of his right hand within her passage from behind, driving her hard and deep over and over.

She cried out, her fingers seeking and finding purchase on the carpet. She lifted up until she was on her hands and knees. Marken plunged into her relentlessly with his fingers and her muscles tensed in prelude to the elusive peak.

Marken ceased and rolled away.

She let out a half moan, half whimper of frustration. Her clit throbbed and pulsed. She turned her head to watch Marken raise himself to his knees, his cock looking painfully erect. A whimper caught in her throat. She wanted him to take her hard and fast and slake her desire. This game he played was too cruel.

She remained on all fours and dug her nails into the thick carpet, thrusting her hips upward. "Take me, my lord, please. I beg of you," she sobbed, near tears. "Ease this torture. Ease the throbbing of my loins. Please, my lord. I beseech you."

She glanced up through the still damp tendrils of her hair that had slid down across her face. Marken looked pleased. He clenched his fists and his jaw at the same time, as though trying control himself and not fall upon her like a ravening beast.

He knelt down and inserted two fingers into her passage once more from behind. He did not thrust, but let his fingers stretch and fill her. She spread her legs wantonly to give him room to rub her clit with his other hand.

"Yes, please," she sobbed out through a constricted throat. She was half-crazed with wanting him.

His voice was thick with desire when he spoke. "You've done well, Sienne. For that, you deserve a reward." He began thrusting in and out. He took her clit between two fingers and rubbed it back and forth. Her peak came hard and fast. It washed over her in an explosion and she cried out from the force of it. Waves of pleasure flowed through her, stealing her breath and making her gasp.

"That's it, Sienne. Drench my hand. Good girl," Marken crooned.

Her muscles clenched and released around his fingers and she felt the liquid of her passage flow out of her. The spasms racking her passage made her vision go black and she nearly passed out from the force of it.

She collapsed to the ground, spent, her legs still spread. Marken petted her sopping pussy and crooned over and over, "Good girl, good girl." His voice was strained with need.

It was clear he was barely hanging on to his incredible control. Sienne knew she had but to push him a little further and she would get what she really wanted—his cock within her. She moaned and wiggled her backside, enjoying the feel of his hand stroking her.

That was all she needed to do. With a growl, he flipped her over and picked her up. He took her in two strides to the bed, laid her down and spread her legs wide. The head of his thick shaft pressed against the opening of her passage.

"Yes, my lord," Sienne panted. "Please."

Marken slid his cock into her pussy and slid in an inch, then withdrew and slid in a bit farther. Sweat broke out on his forehead as he apparently endeavored not to injure her with his length. Inch by inch she took him. He stretched her like she'd never been stretched, filling every bit of her. She gasped and then moaned deep at the exquisite pleasure of it.

"Sienne, your passage is so slick, sweet, and tight," he bit off. He withdrew nearly all the way and took her by her hips. In one smooth, hard surge, he sheathed himself inside her to the hilt, making Sienne peak instantly with white-hot intensity. She cried out as the spasms racked her a second time. The muscles of her passage pulsed and squeezed around his shaft like a ravenous mouth consuming him. Marken threw back his head and groaned low and deep.

Then he began to move.

Sienne saw stars as the thick, ridged length of him pistoned in and out of her. He held her by her waist, and his hips hit her inner thighs with every inward stroke, making a slapping sound of flesh on flesh.

On the heels of her second peak came her third, as hard and intense as the last two.

After her third peak had subsided, Marken slowed and, without withdrawing or stopping his thrusts, gently took her left leg and wedded it with her right, so she laid on her side. Then he helped her to her knees, so she was once again on all fours and he was working her passage from behind.

She gasped not only at the sensation of her pussy turning around his shaft while he thrust it within her, but at how deeply he penetrated her in this position. He brushed her womb with every inward stroke.

The little bit of pain mixed with the pleasure nearly drove her insane. She moaned wantonly, uncaring that the whole castle should hear her. Her fingers clenched and released the bedcovers and she spread her knees even further apart, giving him complete access and free rein over her passage. His cock rubbed her pleasure point deep within. With every thrust he stroked it exactly right.

He reached forward and took a breast in each hand, kneading and massaging. He tweaked the nipples between his fingertips. Her fourth peak hit her hard. She sucked in a breath and let it out in a cry. The muscles of her core milked his cock.

Marken called her name and she felt him explode within her, his shaft pulsing as it released its seed to bathe her womb.

"Sienne," Marken crooned as he stroked her backside. "Your passage was undoubtedly fashioned for my cock alone by the hand of the Goddess."

Sienne smiled, pleased that while she'd been far too beside herself to use any of her pleasuring skills upon Marken's body, that he was happy with her nonetheless.

She expected him to withdraw from her and leave. However, he pressed her down beneath him on the bed and pulled out from her passage. Then he shifted to her side and pulled her close, laying feather-light kisses on her lips, cheeks, and forehead.

Marken closed his eyes and his breathing deepened to that of sleep. Sienne snuggled into his hard, warm chest. Laying her cheek against a pectoral muscle, she sighed.

A strange, but pleasant, light, fluttery sensation began in her chest, teasing her heart and rising into her throat. She smiled. Was it happiness? She'd felt it fleetingly throughout her life, mixed in among the heavier, more frequent emotions.

Yes…it was true. She was happy. Marken had caused that.

The thought at once pleased and perplexed her. How could she betray this man who was so generous in lovemaking, so passionate, and who made her happy?

Her thoughts returned to her foster family and she knew she had no choice. A tear rolled down her cheek, followed by several others and finally she cried herself to sleep.

Chapter Three

Marken awoke with Sienne's small head tucked under his chin and one of her arms thrown over his waist. He glanced down at her body. She was such a tiny little thing...and exquisite. Cyrus had not lied about that. Her body was slight but shapely with nicely rounded hips, a narrow waist, and beautiful breasts.

Her mouth was a heaven to which he couldn't wait to return. She intrigued him, this little one. It had been a long time since a woman had aroused him like she did. Even now, looking down at her supple body, his cock grew hard. It was easy to grow jaded when women all around you only wished to give you pleasure, and rare indeed that one in particular should so fascinate him.

Perhaps it was the fact that although she'd coupled many times, she'd never had pleasure. It was as though she'd been a virgin when she'd come to him. She'd peaked for the first time with him. It made him feel a special bond with her for some reason, a connection. It made sex with her more than just simply an act that provided a climax, or a way to conceive a child.

Cyrus would not get her back. He'd see Sienne freed come spring-tide, mind and body. Not only would he teach her to take pleasure from sex, which seemed to be proving an easy task, but he'd try his best to take those chains from her mind so she could live as a free woman and make her own choices regarding her future.

Sienne muttered something in her sleep, then moaned softly. Not a moan of pleasure, but of torment. "No," she whispered once. Then louder, "No!"

Marken shook her. "Sienne, wake up. You dream badly."

Sienne roused, her pale green eyes came open. "My lord?" she asked drowsily.

"You had a nightmare."

She pressed her fingertips to her temple and sighed. "The same one I have every time I sleep."

Marken tightened his arms around her. He could imagine the hell she'd been put through in her life. It made him angry and protective of her. Odd he should feel that way, but she was different from the women of his realm, who were, for the most part, pampered and bold, concerned with their looks and the state of their coffers.

"What do you dream of, Sienne?" he asked her.

She shuddered. "Of things best not said aloud." She went silent for a long moment and then, with a jolt, sat up and bolted from the bed. The cold air pebbled her milky skin and made her nipples stand at attention. Marken's cock stirred. "Why are you still hold me after you take your pleasure, my lord?" she asked.

He chuckled. "Is there a reason I should not?"

She glanced toward the window, blushing. "It is simply that…I am not accustomed to having a man I service so attentive to me, especially not a great lord such as yourself. It is disorienting for me."

"You will have to grow accustomed to it, for I will have you near me often this winter." Marken stroked his hardening cock. Having her stand there naked before him was making him hungry for her again.

He reached over and took the black night wrap that lay across the head of her bed. "Put this on, Sienne. You will grow chilled without it."

She slid it over her narrow shoulders and looked down at herself. The material shifted over her erect nipples. "It is nearly transparent, my lord, but still warms me!" she exclaimed.

Marken nodded. "It is a material made here in Nordan. So that men might admire the beauty of their women during the cold months, it's warm as wool and as transparent as gauze."

Sienne stroked the material covering her forearm with a look of awe on her face.

Marken stretched out on his side with the blankets covering the lower half of his body and braced himself on his elbow. "Where are you from, Sienne? Your Nordanese is accented strangely and I can't place it. It is not Sudhraian, I hear."

Sienne looked up at him in surprise. "My lord has an excellent ear. Cyrus took me when I was five years old, from Sorance. That is the accent you hear."

"Ah. Sorance is a small farming country to the east of Sudhra, no? How did you come to be a slave?"

She looked away and when she spoke, her voice was hard. "Cyrus raided my parents' farm and killed my family. I was fostered until age eighteen by a family in Sudhra, always with the knowledge one day Cyrus would come and take me to train as a sex slave." Her voice held a note of resignation.

"You accept your fate."

She shrugged. "What else is there for me to do, my lord? Rail against it? To what end? I have known since childhood that I would one day be a slave. I have had time to accept the idea."

Marken nodded his head thoughtfully. "Sensible...but sad, Sienne."

"Perhaps so. But was it not Hark'an who said, 'Those who fight the hands of fate, but struggle to tighten their bonds.' It is true, no?"

"The philosopher Hark'an? You've read him? You can read?" He could not keep the excited surprise from his voice. Most women had no interest in reading. It was his passion.

She reached out and drew a finger down one of the bed posters. "Aye, my lord. My foster family was that of a scholar's. I have read all the great Nordanese poets and philosophers, as well as the Sudhraian."

Marken leaned forward, pleasure suffusing him. Perhaps he'd found someone to talk to. He watched Sienne wander over to the hearth, where a servant had laid a fire, and toy with the pieces on the *boyant* board. He wondered briefly if she played. "Are you familiar with the works of Gol'an and Mistr'al?" he asked.

She shrugged, examining one of the intricately craved game pieces. "Of course, my lord. Gol'an studied the social impact of slaves in Sudhraian society. Mistr'al was one of the first feminist painters of Nordan." She looked up from the game piece. "What is this for, my lord?" Curiosity shined in her eyes.

"It's a game of strategy called boyant. If you would like, I could teach you to play."

She smiled and it lit her face. He realized then it was the first time he'd seen her smile. It was a beautiful sight.

"Yes!" Her face fell. "That is, of it is not too much trouble for you, my lord."

"I would enjoy having a partner."

She turned toward him. "I am interested in such things as strategy and also affairs of state. I would like to hear sometime about your system of governance here, my lord, about your military."

A woman interested in such things? How uncommon. "I will talk with you of anything your heart desires, Sienne. Your intelligence and curiosity arouse me more than you can know," he said softly. "Come to me now," he ordered.

She set down the boyant piece and walked to the edge of the bed.

"Drop the wrap to your hips," he commanded.

She slid the wrap from her shoulders and it slithered to her waist, revealing her lovely breasts. He lazily wrapped an arm around her waist and suckled a nipple, flicking at it with the tip of his tongue. She let out a contented sigh.

He loved her breasts. They were so full and fitted perfectly to his hands. He palmed the other as he licked. He wanted to take her again, but wouldn't. His goal now was merely to excite her. He wanted to keep her in a state of constant sexual longing.

The wind blew outside and snow buffeted the windows of the room. Winter had begun in earnest. Marken raised an eyebrow as his tongue explored every bump and valley of her nipple. It was going to be an interesting season. This girl had quite a few pleasing surprises in her.

He slipped a hand to the apex of her legs, found the edge of the wrap and entered, his fingers seeking her clit. He rubbed it back and forth between the callused pads of his fingers, knowing it provided more friction. He teased and rubbed until it grew, blood coursing into it. She moaned, long and low.

"My lord, you make me..." Her words trailed off into a moan and she parted her legs further.

He lifted his mouth from her for a moment. "Yes, Sienne? I make you what?"

"You make me hot, achy."

He slid his fingers to her pussy lips and ran the tip of his finger over them, in between her folds, then slipped one finger within her passage, followed by a second. "What do you what me to do to you, Sienne?"

She groaned and ground her pelvis down on his fingers. One of her hands found the bedpost, the other his shoulder. "I want you to take me, my lord, hard and fast."

She looked so delicious standing there with her legs apart and his fingers sheathed inside her to the second knuckle. Her head was thrown back, her eyes closed. Her cheeks were flushed and her mouth was in a silent 'O' of ecstasy. Perhaps he'd allow her to peak.

"Feel my fingers sliding in and out of you. Feel them stroking your pleasure point deep within."

She moved up and down on his fingers, seeking release. With his other hand, he stroked himself as he watched her. She moved up and down and moaned out her pleasure.

"That's it, Sienne. Good girl," he encouraged her through clenched teeth. He wanted to throw her down on the bed and slide his cock into her, but it was important she learned that a man could give her pleasure and ask for nothing in return but the sweet sight of her.

"My lord," she cried.

He let his thumb brush her clit on every downward stroke and her moans grew louder. Finally, she broke and her sweet liquid flowed over his hand as she found her climax.

He withdrew his fingers and stroked her once. "As I said before, this task I set myself is not nearly as difficult as I'd presumed it would be," he whispered. It made her blush.

"You are not like other men, my lord," she murmured.

"No. I am not like the Sudhraian pigs who think of women as chattel. No, I am not." Anger suffused his voice. "It's their God who drives them to that. I will leave them their God, but question their love of pressing females into slavery."

Marken rose and donned a pair of trews against the chill. His cock was hard and aching, but he would wait to find his pleasure.

The fire in the chamber's enormous hearth raged, but it only bit a fraction into the Nordanese winter that filled the room. He went to the window and looked past the glass. "Snow falls and hems us in for the season," he observed.

"Can you not venture out during winter, my lord?" asked Sienne, who'd come to stand beside him.

"Nay. The snow makes travel impossible. We can trudge across it using drapshoes. They have very wide bottoms that distribute a man's weight and let him walk over the drifts, but it is difficult to travel thus and we do not do so on a regular basis."

Marken reached out, drew Sienne in front of him, and wrapped his arms around her. His cock nestled between the cheeks of her bottom and her head fit just below his chin. They were like two pieces that fit together perfectly. It was as though she'd been made to fit him and he for her. Odd such a thought should come to him. He chided himself inwardly for such fancifulness.

"We gather much food in the autumn-tide, much meat and fruit and vegetables," he continued. "We cure the meat so it will keep and we have preservation processes for the other. We do not have want here. We simply lock ourselves in and await the melt. It's a lazy season. Hopefully each winter season I can find a woman like you to occupy my time."

"Just one woman, my lord? I would think many women clamor for your bed."

He shrugged. "Aye, many women are willing enough to please me in my bedchamber." He laughed. "Indeed just about anywhere. At times a specific woman will fascinate me, hold my attention. You, Sienne, are such a one."

"I am happy to please my lord."

"As I am happy to please you."

She glanced up at him and bit her lower lip. "I hope I will not disappoint you, my lord. I fear I have not used many of the things I learned in my sexual training upon you yet. You make me forget myself," her voice faltered. "You make me forget my place."

He smiled. "Good, I am glad I can drive you to forget yourself. I am pleased to hear it. The only place you have for this season is in my bed, around my cock."

"I am happy to have the honor, my lord."

She sounded so subservient, as though nearly all her fire had been dowsed by her hard life. "Sienne? Why will you not tell me of your nightmare?"

"My lord would not be interested in it."

His arms tightened around her. "But I am."

Sienne drew a breath and stared out the window at the snow-covered world. Marken fancied she believed the white glare would banish the images of the nightmare from her mind. "I dream of the men who've taken me without care. I dream of their hands upon my body, squeezing, invading, taking. I dream of their fists against my face, my stomach." Her voice broke. "I dream…"

"Shhhh, Sienne. I would not have you relive it for my benefit." His voice held barely masked anger.

He released her abruptly. "You will dress for the evening meal now. The hour grows late. Tonight is special, for Annia, a woman who resides in the castle, has conceived. Tonight we celebrate a hard-won new life. I will send servants to you. They will lead you to the dining hall."

She straightened. "Yes, my lord."

Chapter Four

Every male eye in the room was on Sienne when she entered. She wore a gown of pale gold, made of the same flax-cloth—the nearly translucent but incredibly warm material her night wrap was made from. It hung to her ankles and the sleeves reached to her wrists, where they flared out into angel wings that wrapped around and were secured at the small of her back with a small golden clasp. The dress supported and lifted her breasts and held her tight around the waist. It left little to the imagination. Even from a distance, Marken could see her dark areolas and the patch of fiery hair between her legs.

Her long dark red hair had been left loose, so long it brushed her narrow waist, but a long caplet of thin gold chain of equal length had been placed over it.

Marken could feel the sexual interest of every man in the room heighten when she came in. It was palpable. They wanted her. He could feel it. The question was— would he let them have her?

It was no question Sienne was one of the most beautiful women in the castle. She was probably one of the most intelligent too, Marken mused. To him, it was a heady combination indeed.

Marken sensed the ability to have real conversations with her, unlike the other women of the castle, whose minds were only on pleasing him in bed and convincing him to take them to mate as mistress of the castle. As a Lord of Nordan, he would be expected to make such a match, though not necessarily a monogamous one, and take one of the few children produced by the castle's women to foster as his heir, were his own mate unable to conceive.

All the women of the castle desired the mate position, as well as provider of heir, but Sienne had no such designs upon him. Her responses to him were natural, honest. It was refreshing.

He motioned to her and she walked toward him, gliding over the spice-scented rushes strewn over the stone floor and winding her way through the maze of long tables where men and women sat, engaging in the evening meal. She did not look at them, but kept her eyes carefully cast down.

She passed Haeffen, his chief advisor, at one of the tables. Haeffen raised his rheumy eyes and his long white hair shifted over his shoulders. He watched her progression through the room, lifted his gaze to Marken, and smiled. Haeffen missed nothing. Marken was sure the old man recognized something special about Sienne…just as he did.

She reached the dais and Marken rose and took her slender arm, helping her to climb the steps. "Sit, Sienne," he said, indicating the chair beside his.

She looked shocked. "My lord, I…I cannot."

"You can and you will, Sienne, because it pleases me. You will get over this ridiculous notion of class difference you have from your homeland. I am lord of this castle, but I will eat with those whom I wish to eat, no matter their rank. Think on the texts you've read of Gol'an, Sienne, and sit." He drew the chair out from the table.

She stood looking at him for a long moment, and then dropped into a low curtsy, "As you wish, my lord."

Sienne sank into the chair. Marken took his own seat. The nobles at his table eyed Sienne with interest, undoubtedly recognizing her from yesterday, when Cyrus had presented her at court.

Ilyanna, a beautiful woman with hair the color of blackest midnight leaned forward, a territorial gleam in her eye. It was always so when he showed preference for a particular woman. She lowered her eyes and looked up him through her dark lashes, silky as a cat. "So this is the sex slave from Sudhra, my lord?" she asked. "The one the nobleman brought yesterday to entertain you this winter?"

Sienne kept her eyes downcast and did not speak.

"Yes, Ilyanna. Her name is Sienne. But sex slave she is no longer. I will buy her freedom from Cyrus when he returns in the spring, whether or not the lady wishes it."

Sienne's head shot up and her gaze found his. It was filled with hope mixed with apprehension. His heart squeezed a bit at the sight. He'd do his best to banish that apprehension over the coming months.

"But sex slave she has been her whole life, no?" continued Ilyanna. Her shapely lip curled. "She cannot be of much use in bed, my lord. Is she as much like the whipped dog she appears?"

Sienne looked down again, blushing. Marken set his hand upon her thigh and rubbed in an effort to calm her.

Marken leaned forward and drew a careful breath. He needed to assert Sienne's status now with the other women, so she did not suffer their sharp tongues later. "Sienne has a mouth and throat fashioned by the Goddess's own hand. She can make me come with her tongue and lips like none other. Her passageway is tight and sleek and milks my cock with exquisite care. She is responsive to my touch and eager to please."

All discussion within earshot ceased. Ilyanna's lower lip thrust out in a pout. Undoubtedly, she was sorry she'd initiated the conversation.

"She was made to fit me like a sheath to my sword, a glove to my hand," continued Marken. "Not only is she one of the finest women I've ever bedded, but she is quick of wit and possessed of an eager mind. Aye, this one holds claims to my affections that are stronger than most, and I've only claimed her body but one time." Marken sat back. "So far."

Ilyanna fell silent and after a long, pregnant moment, filled with many looks of interest at Sienne, the nobles returned to their conversations and their meals.

Marken looked at Sienne and saw she was gazing at him with tears shining in her eyes. He leaned forward and kissed her until he heard her breath catch in her throat. He slipped his tongue between her lips and stroked.

When he tipped his face from hers, her eyes were still closed, her lips parted. Marken smiled. "Eat, little one. You will need your energy with this mob. I do not doubt many men will approach you this eve." He sat back, a twinge of regret coursing through him. "Especially after what I've just said."

She opened her eyes at that and looked slightly worried. Then she dutifully turned her attention to the food spread before her on the table. Marken watched Sienne inspect the edible offerings with interest.

He reached out and placed a thick piece of pharing bird on her trencher, along with two slick slices of fruit. A serving woman filled Sienne's goblet with sweet wine, her heavy breasts swinging under her gray silken gown.

A horn blew from across the room and the doors opened. Into the chamber came a woman seated on a raised platform, carried by warriors of the castle guard. Annia was draped in rich fabrics and would be waited upon by a male contingent of her own choosing while she carried her child.

It was a grand thing, her pregnancy, a rare thing. All precautions would be taken to ensure Annia carried the child to term and the child was born healthy. Indeed the pregnancy made Annia's fortunes, for she would want for nothing as payment for the gift she gave their world.

Everyone in the room cheered and applauded. The men carried the platform to the dais and helped Annia to the table, where she sat on Marken's opposite side. Marken stood and aided her into her chair.

"My friends," Marken said loudly. The din in the room fell silent. "Tonight we drink and eat in celebration of Annia and the life pulsing within her womb. Let us give thanks to the Goddess above for blessing us." He raised his goblet. "Eat, drink, and make merry in the name of the Goddess, the name of Annia, and in the name of her unborn child!"

A cheer rose from the crowd and Marken sat down once again. Servants attended to Annia, loading her trencher with the choicest bits of meat and filling her goblet with fresh, sweet water.

"Thank you for the words, my lord," whispered Annia. Gently, she squeezed his forearm.

He patted her hand. "It's my pleasure. I hope there will be many more women to congratulate at the close of this winter."

"As do I, my lord." Annia winked one amber-colored eye. "I hope it's your child I carry. Your seed is strong and hearty. I would not doubt it took root in my womb."

Marken smiled at the compliment. "Whoever the father of the child is not important. I am simply glad your womb will bear fruit. We will all raise the child as our own."

Marken glanced back at Sienne and saw she'd been listening to their conversation. "It is a beautiful notion, my lord," she said softly. "In Sudhra it is not so. In Sudhra if a babe is born to a lower caste member, it is taken from the mother soon after its birth and given to a family of the highest caste. It is not so here, is it, my lord?"

"Nay, Sienne. It's not so. The mother is an important part of a child's upbringing. When one in the lower class bears a child, she is elevated in status and given land and money. Indeed, it is a thing most women strive for here." Marken indicated her trencher, now heaped with food. "Eat now."

Sienne fell to the food before her. He watched her slide slices of glistening red cappa fruit between her lips and concentrated on the smooth skin of her throat as she drank her wine. She ate the food with an almost orgasmic air, giving her full attention to the trencher. Marken knew well how excellent the food must taste to her slave's palate.

She did not look up until most had finished their dessert and moved on to other activities. When she finally glanced around the room, she gasped.

Marken followed her gaze. It was after the meal and the second "dessert" had commenced. The occupants of the hall openly petted and fondled each other. It was something no Sudhraian was accustomed to seeing.

One fair-haired man had a chestnut-haired woman on his lap, her gown pushed down to her waist and her breasts bared. He suckled her nipple while under her dress, his hand worked. Another woman rubbed and licked a man's phallus, bringing him deep into her throat at times, and eliciting moans of pleasure from the nobleman.

"No…none of these women are slaves, my lord?" she asked. Her voice held a quaver.

Marken noted her uneasiness and decided to ease it. He wound an arm around her thin shoulders rubbed one stiff nipple. "No," he answered. "Here in Nordan we experience physical pleasures openly and without shame. Our women derive pleasure from sex, Sienne. Men have no need to force them to it."

She shook her head as though trying to get her mind around the notion and was failing. Marken reached a hand down and found the slit in her dress. His fingers brushed over the smooth, warm flesh of her thigh to her core. He found her clit and leisurely massaged it. Blood coursed into her cheeks and between her legs. Marken could tell by her body's reactions that although she wished it were not so, she was aroused at the sight of all these people engaged in sex play before her eyes.

Marken placed his mouth to her ear. "Come upon my lap and spread your legs, Sienne. I wish to make you peak in front of all these people."

She closed her eyes and her breath came in hot little pants. Her clit swelled and pulsed under his ministrations.

"I know you are aroused," he whispered darkly. "I can feel the truth of it." He pinched her clit gently and she started, and then moaned as he rubbed it between his fingers.

"I…I'm aroused. It is the truth, my lord. But I cannot bring myself to display my body thusly in front of so many people. The idea is a heady one, but I am not prepared for it."

He put his mouth to her ear and murmured. "It excites me more than I can say, the image of you displayed in front of all these people. I want to hear your moans and cries of satisfaction filling this chamber."

She shook her head. "I cannot, my lord. Bring me back to your chambers and distract me not with your caresses and I will play such music upon your person that you cry out in ecstasy. But I cannot show myself in such a passionate way here in public."

"Very well, I will not push you to it." Marken withdrew his hand and she drew a ragged breath.

"It's perplexing how quickly you've made me desire an act I've detested for so long," she murmured. "One kiss of yours and I am undone. With every pass of your hand upon my body, you erase part of my past."

Satisfaction welled up within him. It was nice to be so valued on such a personal level. He brushed his lips across her temple. "Do you not wish your past to be erased, little one?"

Her jaw clenched. "I wish it to be eradicated." Her voice had the quality of tempered steel, showing the strength Sienne had employed to make it through her life.

Talyn, captain of the castle guard approached the dais accompanied by Carrick, one of his highest-ranking officers. They climbed the stairs and bowed to Marken.

Marken nodded. "Talyn, Carrick. Good eve." He flicked a glance at Sienne. He knew well why they were here. A knot formed low in his stomach and Marken wondered at it. It was not unusual to ask a woman for sexual engagement, after all.

"Good eve, my lord," answered Talyn in his low baritone. "We have come to ask your beautiful companion if she would like to dance with us."

Sienne went tense beside him. Marken frowned and fell silent. He slipped his arm around her shoulders once more and stroked her nipple, which hardened beneath his fingers.

A strange feeling of possessiveness coursed through him. He shrugged it away. True, he had not lied when he'd said Sienne held charms other women did not, but that was no reason not to share her. It was the custom here. It was expected. Talyn and Carrick were following perfect, respected castle etiquette.

Though it was strange Talyn was willing to share. Marken had never seen him do so with a woman before. Talyn was an aggressive, dominant man like himself and did not wish to part a woman's attention.

"Well…that is not for me to say," he answered finally. "Sienne?"

"Whatever would please you, my lord," she said, looking down at her hands in her lap.

"No. I'm asking you what you want, Sienne."

Sienne bit her lip, as though in deep thought, and glanced at him. She studied his face for several moments before answering far too carefully for his tastes. "Yes, my lord. I would desire it."

Marken frowned. Did she truly desire it, or did she merely say yes because she thought he wanted her to say yes?

He removed his arms from her shoulders. "Very well. Go with them." He turned to the men. "But do not take her in public. She does not desire that...yet."

His dark promise made Sienne stiffen beside him. Aye...he'd make her want him to take her in front of an audience before the end of the cold season. He'd make sure of it.

"Of course, my lord," answered Carrick, nodding his blond-haired head.

Sienne stood and Talyn took her forearm. Marken watched them walk down the steps, Sienne in the middle. His misgivings grew.

Why should he feel thus? He'd never been reluctant to give one of his playmates to another before now. It was a part of the culture within his castle, indeed, within the borders of Nordan. Men and women coupled with each other when and where they wished. Rarely, a couple could take an oath of monogamy should they choose it and mate. However, since children were so difficult to conceive, it was a rare thing. The more men a woman had sex with, the better her chance of getting with child.

That was the ultimate goal. No other.

Marken watched the three sink into the crowd with a frown upon his face.

"My lord, it has been a long time since I've felt your stiff length within me," murmured Calliope into his ear.

Marken smiled. She was one of his favorites. She sank into his lap and wound an arm around his neck.

Marken let her kiss him, hard and deep and tried to push Sienne from his mind.

* * * * *

Sienne allowed the man with the waist-length blond hair to twine an arm through hers on her left side. On her right side, Talyn placed his hand around her waist.

"You know me already," said Talyn. He jerked his head left. "This is Carrick. He is my second in command. I am Captain of the Castle Guard."

She nodded. "I am Sienne." She kept her face expressionless, her gaze steady and straight ahead. She'd slipped into the familiar attitude of slave. She accepted that they would take her together. She did not know if she would enjoy it. The men of Nordan were different than those of Sudhra. Marken had proven that thoroughly.

They led her into the center of the room where others danced. Some men and women coupled against the far wall, some in the center of the room. Sienne watched a female sliding up and down on a male's shaft, his hands on her waist, hers on his shoulders.

Talyn pressed her against him from the front and Carrick from the back. Sienne felt warm hands sliding over her skin. She didn't know whose hands went where, but they left no place unexplored. They cupped her breasts and gently tweaked her nipples. They slid between her legs and massaged her clit, her labia, and her anus.

At the same time, they swayed to the music that surrounded them. Sienne closed her eyes, lost in a sea of sensation. She imagined it was Marken who fondled her now, his fingers that found the slit in her dress and then found the slit in her body, thrusting into her gently with them. She moaned, her hands seeking and finding Talyn's hard cock through his trews. It was every inch as large as Marken's and helped her imagination.

"I watched you arrive, Sienne, and drank of your delicate beauty from afar." Talyn spoke near her ear, then dropped his head and ran his lips down her throat, pushing the fabric of her dress down her shoulder. "You looked so helpless standing there with your keeper. All I could think of was drawing my sword and lobbing off his head."

"You would do such a thing for someone like me?"

From behind, Carrick nuzzled her ears and throat. "Talyn does not like to see people caged. Neither do I. Talyn is a good friend of mine and we almost fought over who would get you first. We decided to take you at the same time." He laughed low and nipped at her earlobe, sending her flesh into a fit of goose bumps. "It will be a first for him. And for you, my lady?"

The formal address jarred her. If only they knew how far from a lady she truly was. Memories pummeled at her. She closed her eyes against them and shook her head. "Nay," she answered.

Talyn kissed her deep, his tongue stroking against hers hard. At the same time he found her clit and rubbed at it. "We will endeavor to make new memories to cover the bad, my lady," he murmured into her mouth. He pushed her dress down over her shoulders to pool at her feet.

Her flesh pebbled in the cool air and she whimpered. Being so exposed to so many people aroused her tremendously, but she wasn't ready yet. Not for this. It was too soon.

"Please, not here," she murmured against Talyn's lips. "If you must take me, take me away."

"As our mistress wishes and our lord commanded," replied Carrick.

Talyn caught her hand in his huge calloused one and led her from the room. Carrick followed.

She kept her eyes diverted from the dais, not wishing to see Marken's gaze upon her. Instead she watched Talyn's thick, dark brown hair move across his broad shoulders.

It was pleasurable, to be sure, to have these men actually desire to give her pleasure. But she was doing this for Marken. He wished her to become accustomed to the ways of his court. He'd said as much in her chamber. This was her way of showing him that she could be whatever he wished her to be. She wanted him to be happy with her.

They left the main room and entered a richly appointed chamber, complete with a large, soft-looking bed. Talyn led her to the center of the room and turned toward her. His green eyes had flecks of brown at the edges, she noted, and were heated with a dark look of desire. He dropped his mouth to her collarbone and began kissing her there while he played with her breasts with practiced ease, palming them and tweaking her nipples.

Sienne put her arms around Talyn's neck and let him pull her into an embrace. His lips found hers and parted them, letting his tongue slip in and dance with hers. From behind, Carrick ran his hands from her shoulders and down her sides. "Part your legs," he said.

She spread her legs and he slipped his fingers inside her and thrust. She instantly soaked his hand. "She is eager, Talyn," Carrick said softly. "She is wet."

Carrick found a low footstool and asked her to straddle it. Then he lay on his back upon it, between her legs. "Talyn gets to kiss you there. I get to kiss you here." Bracing himself against the footstool, he brought his mouth up and licked her clit. His fingers slipped inside her as he bathed her pussy with his tongue, and his mouth fastened around her clit, sucking and gently biting.

Talyn stroked and pinched her nipples at the same time. She moaned against his mouth.

Sienne made quick work of Talyn's trews and slipped her hands inside to stroke his long, thick phallus. Pleasing Marken wasn't such a hardship. She was appalled at how quickly she was getting over being expected to always please and never expect pleasure in return.

Talyn and Carrick's mouths and hands worked magic over her. Talyn dropped his mouth to her breast and laved and sucked her nipples each in turn with a tongue that knew well what it was doing. Her fingers knotted in his thick hair.

Carrick nipped at her clit with his teeth while plunging his fingers within her. He growled low in his throat, and sucked hard at her clit. With a sharp cry she came. Pleasure washed over her in intense waves. As soon as they'd ebbed away, her clit swelled insatiably once more, wanting more of the incredible sensation.

"I can wait no longer, Carrick," Talyn bit off.

Carrick extracted himself and pushed the stool away with his foot. He sought a vial of something from a nearby cabinet and came back with it in his hands. He put a little of the fluid on his fingers and gently rimmed her anus with it, while nipping at her neck. The liquid was slick and warmed her skin. "I am going to prepare you for my entry," he murmured. "Though I think you are more than ready." She could hear the gentle smile in his voice.

She tensed.

"Shh...it will feel good," whispered Talyn as he palmed her breasts. "I'll be within your passage and Carrick will be behind at the same time. You will—"

Marken's voice came from the doorway. "Actually, I will be in her passage."

Carrick and Talyn both stepped back, leaving her body bereft of the touch of them. "My lord," they said in unison.

Sienne dipped low in a curtsy. He sounded very displeased. Had she done something wrong in accepting Talyn and Carrick's invitation? "My lord," she greeted him, her voice shaking.

Marken walked toward her slowly. His boots clicked on the stone floor with every step he took. He circled her with a dark, predatory look in his eyes, reminding her of a jungle cat stalking its prey. Heat rolled off his muscular body and his gaze was just as hot as it roved her body, catching at her breasts and the patch of hair between her legs.

"I am sorry, Talyn, to take such a delectable morsel from you. But I fear I have no choice. I have decided I will be the only one to claim possession of her sweet passage for the time she is here. Later, I will make up the loss of her to you somehow. I promise you that, my friend and my captain."

Hope and joy surged through her. She glanced down so he could not see it in her eyes. Marken wanted her to himself.

Marken flicked an annoyed glance at his captain. "Why you would choose to share a woman anyway, is beyond me. It's very unlike you."

"I wanted her my lord. As did Carrick. We did not wish to fight over her so we decided to take her together," answered Talyn.

Marken raised an eyebrow. "Ah." He reached out and flicked one of her hard nipples with his index finger, then leisurely rubbed it with the flat of his thumb. Desire jolted through her. Her passage was already slick with fluid. Now she wept anew.

"Well...she is exceptionally beautiful," said Marken. "And I can see how she would appeal to you, Talyn, with your need to give succor to those oppressed—to free those imprisoned. Everyone knows your history, and I respect your past hardships."

"My lord," answered Talyn. "Your insight is superior." A mixture of complex emotions infused his voice.

Sienne glanced at the brown-haired warrior and wondered about his history.

Carrick cleared his throat. "We could not know she'd laid such a serious claim to your affections so quickly. Otherwise, we would not have approached you."

Marken stopped in front of Sienne and placed a finger to her chin, tipping her face to his. Lightly he tasted her lips. That small contact alone made her knees weaken and her clit pulse.

"Surprisingly…she has," he murmured, "enough to claim her passageway as mine alone for this winter, at least."

He lifted his head and fixed his gaze on Carrick. "You, I will allow to come behind while I take her in front." He looked at Talyn. "You, I send to Calliope. I left her hot and wanting. Her passage is slick with need and she will welcome your cock within her. Later, you have my word I will make up the loss of Sienne to you in an adequate and fitting way."

"Thank you, my lord," Talyn answered.

Marken guided Sienne's hand to his member, which was rock-hard. Her gaze settled on Marken's blue eyes and she heard Talyn take his leave.

"I want her now," Marken said hoarsely to Carrick. "I watched her with you two, her responsiveness has left me needing to find my ease within her." Marken traced her lower lip with his thumb and her eyes fluttered shut at his touch. "Together, you and I will make her cry with pleasure and quench her thirst for sex with other men," he murmured, his voice laced with passionate heat.

Sienne opened her mouth to tell Marken she only desired him, but Carrick interrupted her.

"I will gladly aid you, my lord." Carrick let his trews slide to the floor.

But Sienne only had eyes for Marken. Her hands went to his tunic and drew it over his head, then her fingers went to the drawstrings of his trews, loosened them and sent them down. The short sword he always wore hit the floor with a heavy clank. She wrapped one hand around his hardened shaft and stroked him. Her lips closed around one of his nipples. She laved it and bit it, loving it with her mouth.

"Ah, Sienne," Marken murmured, brushing her heavy hair out of her face and over her shoulder. "How exquisite you are."

Carrick's body warmed her back. A wide cushion bumped the back of her heels. "Stand upon this to make yourself taller and spread your legs, my lady," Carrick said close to her ear, then kissed her neck. His voice was thick with desire.

She obliged him and felt his fingers at her anus, then the head of his thick cock.

Marken tipped her chin up with his index finger, lowered his mouth to hers, and kissed her long and deep. He set his cock to the entrance of her passage, and slowly pushed himself inside. He thrust once hard, until he was sheathed within her to the hilt and she was completely impaled upon his thick length.

Then Carrick entered her from behind. Inch by inch, he slid his cock within her until she was completely filled.

She closed her eyes and gasped. Her clit swelled and became sensitive. One brush against it and she knew she'd peak.

"Are you well?" Marken asked.

She let out a slow, careful breath and nodded.

Then they began to move in unison. Sienne set her hands to Marken's shoulders and let a low, primal moan rip from her throat. The sensations she experienced now were like nothing she'd ever had before. The hot, hard chests of the two men braced her. Their thick cocks surged in and out of both her openings relentlessly, driving her pleasure hard and high. With a cry her peak burst over her. Hot liquid trickled down her inner thigh.

Marken groaned and placed his hands to her hips. "Climb me, Sienne," he commanded softly in her ear.

With his aid, Sienne wrapped her legs around his waist and Marken held her at her hips. His biceps bulged as he supported her weight.

Carrick placed his hands to her waist and both men drove her up and down on their shafts, pounding into her. A second climax ripped through her body and pulled a long wail from between her lips. Could a person die from such pleasure?

Both men grunted and groaned. Sweat sheened their bodies. Marken found her mouth and slid his tongue in to play against hers as her third peak washed over her. He caught every passionate sound she made in his mouth.

Carrick cried out and she felt his hot seed flood into her. He withdrew his cock and Marken walked her over the wall. Bracing her against it, his hands gripping her tightly around the waist, he plunged into her over and over, the tip of his shaft massaging her pleasure point deep within.

On her fourth peak, Marken yelled out, pinning her hard against the wall and injecting his seed into her. She felt it bathe her ovaries and for a moment, Sienne hoped he gave her a child.

He held her tight in his arms, his cock still sheathed far within her. She opened her eyes to find him staring at her with a curious intensity on his face. She glanced over his shoulder and saw Carrick watching them, his cock erect again.

"Leave us," commanded Marken loudly. "Get out now!" The tone he used made even Sienne flinch.

Carrick gathered his clothing and obeyed.

Marken held her against him and found her lips with his. "Sienne," he murmured. "What is it about you that drives me so? Why is it the thought of another man taking your body is almost more than I can bear?" He kissed her hard. "I cannot share you with another again, little one. I hope you enjoyed that, for it will be the last time this winter."

Sienne buried her face in his hair and inhaled the scent of him—soap and spice. She smiled. She couldn't help it. He felt possessive of her. Did that mean she meant something to him? An absurd joy filled her. The idea that he might care about her made her lightheaded with happiness. Happiness was becoming a frequently experienced emotion for her, she realized with a start.

Then she remembered Cyrus and sorrow once again took over.

"My lord," she murmured. Tears pricked her eyes and she closed them lest he see. "I am yours to do with as you please." Her voice broke. "I am yours body and soul...for this season."

His arms tightened around her. "Mine," he whispered.

"Yours, my lord. I wish it to be so." Her heart swelled with the truth of those words.

He pulled her away from the wall, walked to the bed and lay down with her upon it. His cock slid from her passage, and he pulled a blanket over them and cuddled against her. She snuggled into the heat of his smoothly muscled chest and sighed.

Tomorrow she would think of Cyrus and the task she had in front of her. Tonight she would pretend she was free to give her love to this man.

For love it was coming to be.

Just for tonight she would dream of the possibility for happiness. Just for tonight.

The heavy hands of sleep beckoned and she was duly seduced.

Chapter Five

Sienne watched Marken as he slept spread-eagle on the bed. His hair fanned out like a raven's wing over the pillow.

She never thought she could find any positive attributes for one of the opposite sex. But here was this kind, passionate man before her and he was hers for the taking...at least for a little while.

Sienne realized she wished to give him the sexual gratification he'd given her. Not out of a sense of servitude, or obligation, but because she simply wanted to make him writhe with pleasure.

Sienne bit her lip in contemplation. But every time he touched her, she lost herself. When he caressed her body, she could not even consider using her sexual talents upon him. All she could do was hold on under the onslaught of pleasure he gave her. She had no presence of mind to use any of her skills.

She examined how he lay on the bed. The position he lay in now it was near perfect...

She slipped from under the blankets and searched the room for what she'd need. Returning with four long pieces of rope she'd found in a drawer by the fireplace, she saw that still he slept.

Gently, so as not to waken him, she tied the pieces to each of the bedposts. Then she looped them around

Marken's wrists and ankles. When he awoke and moved, they would tighten and he would be caught.

She slipped the blankets away and lay down between his legs. She laved his scrotum with her tongue, then drew one into her mouth and suckled it. His cock grew hard under her ministrations and she stroked it with one hand.

He moaned in his sleep and his eyes opened. She took the opportunity to sink his erection deep into her mouth.

He groaned. "Sienne." He moved his arms and the ropes tightened. He let out a surprised sound and fell back against the pillows. "What are you doing, little one?" His voice held a dangerous edge. The warrior lord was not happy to give up control.

He soon would be, however. Sienne would make sure of that.

She put the head of his shaft down her throat and used her tongue to rub at him. His head fell back against the pillows and he let out a tortured hiss of breath.

She drew him from her mouth and stroked him up and down with her hand. Her passage wept for him already. This feeling of having complete power over a man she was beginning to care for was an incredibly erotic thing.

He growled like a trapped jungle cat. "Why?" he asked.

She raised her gaze to find his dark blue one. "I wanted to pleasure you, my lord, but always you want to be in control." She climbed his body as she spoke and straddled him, pushing her slick core to his length and rubbing against him. Then she dropped her mouth to his nipples and gently bit one. He groaned. She raised her

71

head. "I tied you so you could not distract me from my tasks with your wickedly skillful hands."

She lowered her mouth to his nipples again, while rubbing her pussy against his phallus. Her clit pulsed and throbbed and she knew it would not be long before she found her peak.

"But it excites me to excite you, Sienne."

She rose up, straddling him, and rubbed her core along his length. She braced her hands on his chest. "I am excited, can you not see?" She reached up and cupped her own breasts, pinching her nipples and drawing her fingertips over the distended peaks. She moaned wantonly and ground herself against him. She closed her eyes and threw her head back.

"Sienne." He sounded desperate. He stabbed his pelvis up, pushing his hard length against her and straining against his bonds. "Loose me so I can touch you," he said hoarsely.

With her eyes still closed and her head tipped back, she shook her head. He moved again and brushed exactly the right spot. She cried out and came, her fluid coursing down over him. The pleasure ebbed and flowed over her, leaving her panting. She wanted to sheath herself around him, but it was too soon.

She opened her eyes and looked at him. "See, my lord. You can make me peak even with your hands tied."

He strained against his bonds again and the muscles of his arm muscles flexed enticingly. The bedposts creaked and Sienne realized with a start that he could break the posts or his bonds if he tried but a little harder.

She descended between his legs once more, making sure her skin slid along his and her breasts brushed his thighs as she went.

He pulled on his bonds again, and let out a roar.

Her hand closed around his phallus, her mouth poised at the head. "My lord, calm yourself. You will break the bed."

"I care not! I must have you! Release me at once."

She smiled and shook her head. "Nay, my lord. You are mine to do with as I please." She licked his rigid cock and he tensed. With one hand she massaged his scrotum, an oft-neglected part of a man, with her mouth she made love to his shaft.

She stroked deeper and faster down her throat until his breath came in pants and his hips raised off the bed. His body tensed to peak and she withdrew him from her mouth and placed her hand to base of his phallus. She tightened her grip until he stilled. He would not come so quickly. She wished to torture him as he'd tortured her.

He let out a roar. "Sienne!"

"Shhh, my lord. This is good for you," she said. Then she returned his cock to her mouth for another round of teasing.

* * * * *

Upon the third time she'd gripped the base of his cock hard to keep him from spurting, Marken had had enough. The little witch would drive him insane with her taunts. All he wanted driven was her sweet passage.

With one focused pull he broke the bonds that trapped his arms and ankles. Sienne gasped and backed away from him, until she hovered at the edge of the bed on all fours. Her breasts swayed as she moved. He let out a low growl, his attention focused on them, as well as the curve of her bare buttocks and hips.

Not bothering to free the bits of rope that were still bound to him, Marken went to his hands and knees and crossed the huge bed toward her.

Sienne watched his approach with trepidation clear in her eyes. Only dark, dangerous desire shone on his face, he knew. She'd soon realize just how far she'd pushed him. He grabbed her by the waist and threw her to the bed beneath him. She let out a little cry, and he stifled it with his mouth.

Inserting his knee between her knees, he parted her legs and settled himself between her thighs. In one long, hard thrust, he impaled her on his cock. He drove her straight into the mattress, so hard she hit the springs deep within. She came instantly, her muscles contracting around his length and the sounds of her pleasure filling the room.

A grunt of pure, animalistic satisfaction rumbled past his lips, mixing with Sienne's cries of pleasure. Six long, hard strokes made her come again and Marken spilled himself within her with a roar, unable to take any more.

Marken lay on top of her, completely spent. His mouth found one of her delicious ears. "Don't ever do that again, Sienne," he whispered as he nibbled. "I enjoyed it too much."

"Of course, my lord," she answered.

Marken heard the smile in her voice.

* * * * *

"But it's not natural!" Marken ground the heel of his hand into his eye and whirled on Haeffen who sat in a chair within his sitting room. "I have not the will to seek another. It has been two months and Sienne is the only woman I desire, the only woman I want to bring to my bed!"

Haeffen reached out a gnarled hand. "My lord, calm yourself and I will tell you a story. Sit." He motioned to a chair near his own and Marken sank onto it.

Haeffen twirled his long white beard between his thumb and forefinger, seemingly deep in thought. "There was a time when children were not so difficult to conceive, and men and women mated monogamously far more often than they do now. In fact each man and woman found another and aligned themselves, using a ceremony that told the world of their commitment."

"I have heard of this, Haeffen. It was a time so long ago our great-great grandsires, whoever they may be, were not even conceived yet. Women were treated as chattel to be traded in matings to secure political alliances, land, and power. The notion of paternity was important. A woman could only bed her husband and no other. If she did, she could be punished or put aside because the men feared another might sire one of their children and dilute their bloodline."

Haeffen grunted. "Aye, you've the right of it. Bloodlines were important back then. It was when Sudhra and Nordan were one nation."

Marken studied the ornate gold and green edged mantle above the hearth across the room. "The Goddess grew angry at having her chosen sex so mistreated and cursed the men, making their seed less potent. Soon, it would take root so rarely the population was much endangered. Mistrust grew. Anger at the Goddess for her curse abounded. Some renounced the Goddess and followed a new God who did not revere women as a life-giving force. Those people traveled south and war broke out between the followers of the God and those of the Goddess. It is because of this the original nation split and two were formed."

Haeffen nodded. "You know our history as well as I do." He leaned forward. "But I'd wager there is some you do not know, my lord. Have you any idea why a man and woman might choose to bind themselves as monogamous mates? Reasons other than political alliance, or land, money, or titles?"

Marken pushed a hand through his hair and let out a breath of frustration. "Those that mate for life claim love. They claim that one completes the other, satisfies completely on many levels, so that neither has a need to seek anyone else."

"Can you imagine how strong a bond they must have forged to renounce all others save each other, Lord Marken, in a place like Nordan where open sex play is considered normal and there is always someone ready to pleasure you?"

"I know. I have thought of this." He shook his head. "I confess I have never understood it."

"They are more than just mates of the body, my lord. They are mates of the mind and soul. Out of all the people of the world, they have found the one who fits them like a sheath to a blade, a glove to a hand."

Marken started, hearing his own words repeated back to him. Haeffen had been present at Annia's celebratory dinner two months past, but he'd been far across the room—too far to hear what he'd said to Ilyanna.

"Have you considered, my lord, that you, a high ranking lord of Nordan, may have found your soul mate in the form of a sex slave from Sudhra?" asked Haeffen.

Marken quoted Gol'an before he realized he was doing it. "Emotion knows no rank, no class."

"Aye, my lord. It's too true. Perhaps you have found yourself a bit of elusive love."

Marken shook his head. The notion of such a loss of control as love would bring caused fear to course through him. A man and woman joined in the sex act for the climax and to hopefully create a new life. Love... intimacy ...changed all that, made it complicated, messy. "Nay, it is not love." He made a dismissive gesture with his hand. "I am infatuated with Sienne. I will keep myself from her from now on. It's as simple as that."

Haeffen leaned back in his chair and smiled. His blue eyes twinkled. "You can try."

"I will not try! I will do!"

"We shall see. We shall see."

Marken ignored the smug look upon his face and decided to change the subject. "I think Sienne is spying for Cyrus." There was something the old man wouldn't know.

Haeffen stroked his beard. "Really? I thought Sudhra had no quarrels with Nordan."

"As did I. However, Sienne is far more interested in Nordanese politics and our military than any normal person should be. I do believe Cyrus planted her here in the hopes of seducing me into revealing information." Marken looked down, brooding. "I wonder what he's threatening her with."

"Have you revealed any information, my lord?"

Marken looked up sharply. "Of course not. I have fed her information of no consequence to carry back to Cyrus, so he'll have no quarrel with her, but also so he will not have an advantage over us in any way. By the time Cyrus realizes Sienne has given him worthless information, she will be too far from him to harm. I will make sure of that."

Haeffen stroked his chin. "Always Sudhra has reproached us our belief in the Goddess. They think we are weak to have a female deity. Aye, they may indeed be planning something, my lord. We have many spices and silks that are valuable to them. Our people would work well in their cambalt mines, our women forced into their beds. We have resources they would desire."

"Aye, Haeffen, these thoughts are not foreign to me. I may have to do some intelligence gathering of my own come the spring-tide melt."

Haeffen leaned forward. "What of the girl, my lord? What of her betrayal of you?"

He shrugged. "I hope she will eventually grow to trust me enough to confide her secrets." A part of Marken also hoped that Sienne did not feign her responses to him in order to gather information. He tried to tamp that thought down—tell himself it would not matter if indeed she did put up an act with him—but it rose up and pinched him with pain all the same.

* * * * *

Sienne closed the door to her chamber and walked down the corridor toward the gardens. An overhanging roof sheltered it from the worst of the snow, and sometimes Sienne went there to feel the outside chill air bite her cheeks.

Nearly everyday for the last two months, she had warmed Marken's bed. They had pleasured each other so many times she despaired he would tire of her and seek another. Indeed, she feared her worst nightmare had come true. Marken had not sought her attentions in five days.

He did not want her any longer.

Tears pricked her eyes and she blinked them away, furious with herself. She'd allowed herself to become emotionally attached to him! She knew a man could not be kept to one woman. She knew he'd eventually tire of her. Despite that knowledge, she'd allowed herself to care for him, to attach to him, to become infatuated with him.

One fat tear rolled down her cheek. Her pain was her own fault. She'd allowed Marken to kindle emotions within her that she'd never had. She'd allowed herself the fantasy of him while knowing well the reality.

And the whole time she'd been gathering information from him with the sole intention of betraying him and the country of Nordan to Cyrus. Marken had told her everything she'd wanted to know while they lay in bed, played boyant into the wee morning hours, and in between their discussions of artists and philosophers.

Another tear rolled down Sienne's cheek as she descended a flight of stone stairs and turned into the corridor leading to the gardens. She reached out a hand and idly ran her finger along the cool, bumpy stone wall as she walked. Tallow candles flickered over them from sconces inset in the corridor, casting long shadows along the floor.

As Marken had fed her bits of honey-coated pharing bird, he had told her of Nordan's military, how they guarded their borders. He'd told how they trained their soldiers and what countries with which they had the closest ties.

Marken suspected nothing. Why should he? Sudhra and Nordan had been friendly neighbors for years. How could Marken know of the growing Sudhraian faction calling for the domination of Goddess worshipping Nordan, so that they might make Sudhra and Nordan one nation again, under the Sudhraian God?

Sienne reached the door to the gardens and opened it. She shivered, but it had less to do with the wintry air that hit her and more to do with the thought of this culture being squashed, all the Nordanese women pressed into slavery…the bloodshed of their proud resistance. Sudhra's military was fierce and strong. For certain Nordan would not survive their onslaught.

Sienne stepped outside and pulled her long cloak around her. She knew that even though it would mean her own death and perhaps even that of her foster family, she could not provide Cyrus with the information she'd gleaned. As difficult as it would be, she knew her foster family would agree. Their sacrifice would save lives. Sienne would not be a party to war and bloodshed. She would not aid Cyrus.

She thought of Anna, her foster mother and how she used to weave her warm dresses in the winter, and Pentan, her foster father. Pentan had trained her mind, taught her to read and think for herself. He always told her that a sex slave had dire need of those abilities, so she would never lose all of herself to the dark reality of another. Kallian, her foster sister was two years younger than herself. Sienne wondered if she'd married yet.

Tears rolled freely down Sienne's cheeks and froze on her skin. In an effort to calm herself, she took deep draughts of the fresh air and let herself sob.

Something moved by the garden wall and Sienne let out a little scream of surprise. She had thought she was alone.

"Sienne," came Marken's deep voice. "Why do you cry?" He crossed the snow-covered ground, his boots crunching on the frozen layer.

Sienne wiped at her cheeks. She shrugged. "I am fine, my lord. I have but a speck of dust in my eye." She tried a smile.

He took her by the shoulders. "Look at me, Sienne," he commanded. "One does not sob from a bit of dust in one's eye. Tell me, why do you cry?"

She couldn't tell him the entire truth — that she'd just signed her own death papers and those of Pentan, Anna, and Kallian by deciding to disobey Cyrus. Nor could she lie to him. "I...I cry partly for the loss of you, my lord," she admitted softly as another tear rolled down her cheek. She looked away, embarrassed by her own honesty. He'd think her a fool.

He forced her face to his with a gloved hand and wiped the tear from her face. Sienne sucked in a sharp breath at the look in his eyes — like man denied food for a fortnight and then presented with a feast but was forced to abstain. His shoulders were hunched forward, his breathing ragged. His tenderness with her was forced, she could tell. He wanted no more than to tear her clothes off.

"Why did you stay away from me for so long?" she whispered.

"I did it to test myself. I tried to couple with other women, but that failed. So instead I tried to keep myself chaste. I had to hide here in the gardens at times to keep myself from coming to you." His eyes darkened. "Then you came to me."

She shook her head in confusion. "But that does not answer my question. Why did you stay away?"

He lowered his mouth to hers in response and kissed her hard and deep. His tongue branded hers with a fire that reached all the way into her womb. "Let me have you now, Sienne. Let me do what I will," he murmured into her mouth.

She nodded once slightly. He took her hand and led her into the castle. To the left of the door was a dark alcove. He brought her within, then fell upon her like a ravening animal.

Sienne could do little but hang on to the small table in the corner as Marken pulled her coat from her shoulders, then ripped her gown straight from her body. The sound of tearing fabric filled the small space. He growled low in his throat and rubbed his fingers over her erect nipples, then bent his head and licked them.

His breath was warm on her skin. She moved to touch him and he pinned her hands to her sides. Speaking a breath's space away from her nipple, so she could feel his lips move against it, he said, "Do not touch me. I will force myself within you and hurt you in my lust if your hands stray to my body. Let me play with you first, Sienne. Let me prepare you."

Liquid trickled from between her thighs at the sight of the feral look on his face in the half-light. She raised an eyebrow and smiled. "Believe me, my lord, I am more than ready."

He stood and looked down at her, pressing himself against her. "Trust me, Sienne. You are not nearly ready enough."

She could feel his hard cock against her lower stomach. She licked her lips. "I am yours to do with as you wish, my lord."

"Call me by my given name. Call me Marken."

Shock ripped through her. Even now, after spending so much time with him, she couldn't imagine... "I...I can't..."

"You can," he growled low in his throat. "Use my given name, Sienne."

"All right my...Marken."

Marken closed his eyes. "Better," he murmured. "It is music. I want my name on your lips as I make you come, little one. My name and no other."

"As you wish, my lord."

He growled dangerously, but said nothing about her slip. He put his mouth close to her ear and pressed his tunic covered muscled chest to her bare one. His erection ground into the tender flesh of her stomach. "I want you," he whispered into her ear, "like I've never wanted a woman before. Do you want me back?"

Her nipples responded by tightening painfully. She nodded, even though he couldn't see it and let out a long, slow breath.

He lowered his head and bit at her nipple with his teeth and it was all she could do to remain standing. He slipped a hand down, searching out her folds, and slipped a finger within. He growled in his throat and it reverberated through her body. "You're wet. Turn around. I want to take you from behind."

She turned, bracing herself against the table. He stroked her buttocks, making sounds of appreciation deep in his throat. "Push your beautiful buttocks into the air for me."

She complied. He ran a hand over her lower back. She felt the touch of cold steel against her skin and she started, twisting around to see what he was doing. In his hand he held a long, thick piece of metal, inset with jewels. It was the hilt of the short sword he wore always at his waist.

He reached around and rubbed it against one hardened nipple. "I'm going to use this on you until you cry for mercy," he promised.

She shivered with pleasure and began to turn toward him. He withdrew the hilt from her breast. "You don't have my permission to move, Sienne. Lift your buttocks, lower your head, and spread your legs for me. If you don't comply, I'll drag you back to my chamber and tie you down."

She did as he asked, pressing herself down against the table and turning her head so she could watch him.

His licked his fingers to lubricate them and rubbed her clit. She let out a soft moan and felt her clit grow large for him. She spread her legs farther.

"There's a good girl," he crooned.

He knelt and placed his tongue to her, soft and warm. She closed her eyes as he laved her, licking up all her juice. He found her clit and concentrated on it with the tip of his tongue, flicking it back and forth. He groaned deep in his throat and she answered in kind.

He moved his head away. "You taste delicious. I can't get enough of your sweetness. But I don't want you to come yet."

He placed the chilled tip of the jeweled hilt at her clit and moved it in a circular motion. She caught her breath. He brought it to her passage, pushed it into her, and began to thrust.

It wasn't as big as his phallus, but it still filled her. The jewels rubbed against the sides of her, giving her sensations she'd never experienced. He reached around and played with her clit, rubbing at it with his fingertips and the edges of his fingernails.

He moved it, letting the hilt slide in and out of her. Her impending peak built until finally she didn't think she could stand it anymore.

"Come for me, Sienne," Marken commanded softly near her ear while he stroked the hilt into her and his fingers played against her clit. She exploded, letting out a yell of release. She felt her muscles clench and spasm around the hilt and her juices drench it.

"Please, my lord," she whispered.

"What?" The word came harsh with his arousal.

"Please, fill me, my lord. Please," she panted. "I want to feel your flesh against mine."

"What did you call me? What did I say about using my name?"

She shook her head in frustration. She still couldn't bring herself to use his name. "Please."

He let his short sword fall to the floor with a loud clank. She could hear him scrabbling to undo his trews and braies, letting them fall to the floor with a soft whoosh of fabric. With no pretense, he pushed himself inside her to the hilt. She groaned and grabbed the opposite edge of the table with both hands. "Yes, my lord," she breathed.

With a low growl, he pounded himself into her. The sound of his flesh hitting hers alongside his growls of pleasure and her moans filled the alcove. He stopped for a moment and repositioned himself within her then began to move again. Now he rubbed against that spot way deep inside her. He ran himself over and over it. Sienne peaked again, her muscles spasming and he came with her, her orgasm milking him of his seed.

Still sheathed within her, Marken drew her up against him and held her, stroking her hair with one powerful hand. It was incredible how a man with his strength could also manage to be so tender.

"Why can you not say my name, little one?" he murmured to the top of her head.

She turned and he slipped outside of her. Shivering, she nestled into his body for warmth, winding her arms around his waist. He hadn't even taken his tunic off in his haste. "I will endeavor to do better, my lord...Marken."

He sighed heavily, almost sadly. "Do not try, Sienne. Call me what you will."

She buried her face in his chest. "Thank you." Calling him by his name aligned her too closely with him, and soon, after the melt, she'd be leaving him behind. Either Cyrus would kill her on the spot for her disobedience, or she'd be forced to accompany him back to Sudhra. No amount of money Marken could offer for her would deter Cyrus's wrath for her disobedience.

"I am sorry I destroyed your gown, little one."

"That's alright. I have gowns a plenty in my chambers."

He grunted. "Too bad you're not going back to your chamber." He scooped up her coat from the floor and placed it around her shoulders. "I'm not finished with you yet," he promised darkly. The candlelight from the corridor beyond the alcove licked over him.

She swallowed hard, hoping he told the truth. "We've the last five days to make up for."

His eyes glittered. "Aye, little one. You will not leave my bed anytime soon. I am finished abstaining."

Chapter Six

Sienne reined her horse around a tree and waited for Marken to catch up to her. His mount's hooves pounded hard on the path and he stopped beside her. "You're becoming a better rider than I," he exclaimed. His breath showed white in the chill spring air.

"Aye, and this is only the third time we've been riding together."

He lowered his voice seductively. "I'm not at all surprised you were a natural in the saddle. You always do well when mounted."

Sienne smiled, then dug her heels into her horse's sides and raced off down the path, knowing Marken would follow.

During the past month she and Marken had been nearly inseparable. The entire castle talked about them. Women shot her dirty, jealous looks and made snide comments when they passed her in the corridors. Sienne cared not. She was happier than she'd ever been in her entire life.

The wind caught the pin holding her hair up and her tresses tumbled down her back in a thick mass, obscuring her vision. She tossed her head, letting it stream behind her and pushed her mount to a faster speed. She raced over the ground feeling as though she flew. The cold wind numbed her cheeks, but Sienne cared not. She felt free.

Marken had given her that.

She came to the top of a high hill and reined her mount up hard. The smile fled her lips and her heart came up fast into her throat. All the joy she'd felt evaporated, leaving despair in its wake. Sorrow coalesced somewhere near her heart.

The sound of pounding hooves filled the air and Marken came up beside her. His gaze followed hers. "Already," he breathed.

"Already." Her voice held a note of finality. Snow still coated the frozen ground in places, and frost laced the trees, but still Cyrus came. In the valley below them marched a line of soldiers, the green and blue pennants of Cyrus's Sudhraian Lorddom proudly flying. Undoubtedly, he was eager to discover the secrets she'd gleaned from her lover.

Marken reached out and put a gloved hand to her forearm. She flinched. "Easy, Sienne. He will not take you. I will not allow it."

She laughed and it sounded short and bitter to her own ears. "You know not Cyrus, my lord. He takes what he wills when he wills it."

"I know men like Cyrus. He will not refuse the money I set down for your freedom."

"He will, my lord." She turned and looked at him. "I hold things dearer to him than coin." Not allowing Marken to ask any questions, she spurred her mount around and down the hill toward the castle.

The trees and bushes rushed past her, but she felt no joy in her flight this time, for this flight was back into the cage from which Marken had freed her. With every beat of her mount's hooves on the frozen earth, the noose around her throat tightened.

Sienne slid off the horse at the castle stables and threw the reins to a stable boy. Marken was right behind her and did the same.

He whirled her around to face him, his hands strong and warm on her shoulders. "Why do you run?" he demanded. "Do you not trust me enough to believe I'd protect you, Sienne?"

She looked down and away. "I trust you. I trust you with all my heart."

"Then do you think me cold enough to take you to my bed and keep you beside me nearly constantly for three months, then throw you to wolves?" He threw one arm wide in an angry gesture.

"I do not believe that, my lord." She shivered. "But you know not all that Cyrus desires of me, why he brought me to you."

Marken's hands tightened on her shoulders, then relaxed. He remained quiet for a long moment. "I think I do know, Sienne."

He turned and signaled to the stable boy. "Run to the portcullis and tell the guardsmen to admit the entourage flying Lord Cyrus's colors. Tell them I will be in my rooms and notify me when they've been ensconced in their chambers. Tell them to leave Cyrus and his thanes in the court and I will greet them presently."

"Right away, my lord." The stable boy bowed and ran off.

He crooked a finger at Sienne. "You. Come. Now."

Sienne followed Marken to his chambers. Her heart pounded in her chest. Would now be the moment she lost him? Could she not have one more night? One more afternoon? A moment? Anything?

But the time was over for subterfuge. She had to tell him of her treachery. How she'd gained his trust and gleaned his secrets. He'd never forgive her.

He said nothing until his door was closed behind them. "I could have you killed for what you tried to do this winter."

"My lord?"

Marken stalked to the fireplace and turned. "Did you think I wouldn't know what you were doing? Does Cyrus think me so feeble-brained?"

She stood stiff by the door, still wearing her riding coat. "You knew all along," she breathed.

"Of course I knew, Sienne. You are intelligent, so it took a little while to realize it was not merely out of eager minded curiosity that you asked me questions about Nordan's military. After all, there was no reason for me to suspect Cyrus would be foolish enough to plan an attack against Nordan."

She shook her head. "It's not only Cyrus, my lord. There is a whole contingent of lords in Sudhra who plan the destruction of your culture. They plan to invade and conquer Nordan in the name of the Sudhraian God."

Marken walked to her slowly. Every step reminded her of a Sudhraian jungle cat—beautiful, graceful and dangerous. He always brought that creature to mind. His long black hair was free and it shifted over his shoulders, obscuring his face. Sienne took two steps back before she realized she was on the retreat.

He stood in front of her and she felt his body heat radiate out and caress her, bleed through the fabric of her gown and brand her flesh. "And how do I know you tell the truth now, my pretty little spy?"

She looked up at him and she could not keep her lower lip from trembling. "I'm sorry I betrayed you, my lord. I did not want to do it."

"What does he hold over your head, Sienne? Your life?"

She laughed. "If it was only my life this would not be so difficult. Nay, he holds the lives of my foster family in his palm."

Marken closed his eyes. "Then I understand. I knew you would not do something like this out of love for Cyrus. I knew he threatened you with dire consequences for your failure."

"Why did you not tell me you knew before now, my lord?"

He opened his eyes. His smile was tinged with sadness. "I wanted you to tell me on your own. I wanted you to trust me enough to do that."

She ducked her head, ashamed.

"We will have to be careful in the moves we make with Cyrus," he continued. "I do not wish to start a war between our countries before Nordan is prepared. We will exhaust our ability to solve this problem with diplomacy. I would prevent innocent blood spilt if possible." His voice grew hard. "But…in the end, if it's a war Sudhra wants, it's a war Sudhra shall have."

Sienne shivered.

"I promise you, Sienne, that you and your foster family will be safe."

Sienne glanced down, betraying her doubt. "I know you will try, my lord. I will still care for you if you fail."

He gripped her shoulders and shook her gently. "Will you believe what I say? Would you believe that I...I love you, Sienne?"

She looked up in shock.

"It's true. That is why I've not desired another woman since you arrived. That is why I've wanted you beside me these last three months. The whole of the castle knows how I feel. Do you tell me you never expected it?"

She shook her head. "My lord...I..."

"Do you love me back, Sienne? Or were the last three months only about obtaining information from me to protect your foster family?" His voice held a note of uncertainty, vulnerability.

She squeezed her eyes shut and reveled in the sweet, unbelievable joy that coursed through her. She opened her mouth to tell him she loved him back sure as spring followed winter, but a knock sounded upon the door.

Marken closed his eyes and let a breath of pure frustration slip between his teeth. "Enter."

A guardsman peered within. "Cyrus and his thanes have arrived and await your pleasure in the court.

"Tell them I will be there shortly and tell Haeffen to attend."

"Aye, my lord." The door closed.

Marken brushed her cheek with the pad of his thumb. "Your answer matters a great deal to me, Sienne. But either way you answer, aye or nay, will not change the fact that I will protect you. We will speak of this later, when there is more time. Until then, you stay in my chambers. Stay away from the windows and do not venture outside for any reason. I will not have you near Cyrus or his men for the time he is here. He shall not speak to you or so much as lay eyes upon your form. Do you understand?"

"Yes, my lord."

Marken released her and strode to the door. "Use this time to think upon what I've said." He opened the door and turned to her before disappearing through it. "I meant it all."

He left and Sienne heard the lock in the door click.

Sienne turned and walked to the window. Cyrus's soldiers milled around the inner bailey. He'd brought many men into Marken's castle—a place just waking from a long, lazy season and not prepared for bloodshed. Indeed, it was undoubtedly what Cyrus intended.

The Sudhraian believed the Nordanese were weak. They thought that because they worshipped a female deity, treated their women well and spent so much time trying to make children that they'd be easy to conquer.

She remembered suddenly what Marken had said about staying away from the windows and went to stand at his bookshelves instead. Running her finger over the spines, she selected one containing poetry to read.

There was the sound of the lock being jigged and the door slammed open. Sienne jumped and whirled around. The book fell to the floor. In strode Ramdan, one of Cyrus's men. He stalked toward her. Sienne screamed and he slapped a hand hard over her mouth.

"Hush, girl. I've not come to harm you…yet," he threatened close to her ear in Sudhraian. "I saw you in the window. Your lord Cyrus is making nice with Marken now, but I came to make nasty with you."

She bit his hand. He yelped and pulled away. Sienne ran to the side of the bed where one of Marken's broadswords lay against the wall. She grunted trying to raise the heavy piece of metal and unsheathe it.

"Bitch," said Ramdan as he approached her. He grabbed the sword from her hands and easily unsheathed it, then laid the edge of it to her throat. "No whore dares lay a hand on a warrior of Sudhra." He twisted the blade and Sienne felt a drop of hot blood well and trickle down her throat.

"If you so much as swallow, this blade will kiss your flesh. I'm here to remind you of your duty, that's all."

"I won't, Ramdan!" she whispered, her head butted up against the wall, as far from the blade as she could manage. "I won't say a word of what I've learned to Cyrus. You can kill me if you want."

"Then your foster family dies, too."

She swallowed hard and the blade licked her skin again. She winced. "How can I trade the lives of the few for the many? For an entire culture, which the Sudhraian will lay to waste?"

"Perhaps I should simply kill you now and wait within Marken's chambers and torture him slowly."

Anger flared hot and hard. "Don't touch him," Sienne cried in spite of herself.

Ramdan raised a sand-colored brow. "Ah...so the little whore cares for her temporary keeper does she? Interesting..." Ramdan stroked his beard as he considered her.

Sienne closed her eyes in misery. She knew well she'd just given him leverage over her. The cold sword tip moved from her throat to just under her chin. Her eyes flew open.

"Meet Cyrus in his chambers at the stroke of midnight and tell him all you've discovered. If you do not, we will flay the skin from Marken's body while you watch. My threat is Cyrus's threat."

* * * * *

Marken sat in a chair on the dais in his court. Cyrus and his thanes stood before him in a line. "I will offer you five thousand gold Sudhraian flourentimes for the slave Sienne."

"It is a fortune you offer." Cyrus shrugged. "But she is my best, Lord Marken. She is not for sale."

Marken sat forward, his hands fisting. "Everything is for sale to a man like you." He bit his tongue and sat back. He needed to gain hold of his temper; Cyrus could suspect nothing was amiss. Marken was not good at dissembling. "You are correct about her being your best. She pleasures me like none other. I offer ten thousand."

Cyrus flinched. "Ten thousand? I could not make that sum from her if I worked her day and night for the rest of her life." He stroked his chin thoughtfully. "But, still…no."

"Thirteen thousand for her freedom, Cyrus."

The thanes gasped and murmured. One of them pulled Cyrus aside and spoke in his ear. Cyrus turned to Marken. "Fine, you can have my best slave for thirteen thousand, my lord."

Marken motioned to one of his accountants who stood near the door. "See to it," Marken commanded. "I want her papers now."

Cyrus laughed. "You are so eager, my lord. I should have sampled Sienne's wares more often to discover why she is worth so much."

Marken stood, anger infusing him from head to toe. "Now." From across the room, Talyn shot him a look of warning. Marken had taken both Talyn and Haeffen aside before meeting with Cyrus and discussed the current situation with them.

Cyrus stepped forward. "Upon our departure would be more—"

"Now!" roared Marken.

Haeffen climbed the stairs of the dais and laid a hand to his forearm. "My lord," his advisor said into his ear. "You are highly volatile. For Sienne's own safety, I bid you to desist."

Marken nodded once and tried to soften his facial features, which he knew had grown hard. "You are correct as usual, Haeffen."

Haeffen released his arm and went back to his place by the side of the dais, along with Marken's other advisors.

Marken sank back into his seat. "Forgive my show of temper, Cyrus. The winter has been long, and I'm afraid we suffer from a bit of spring-tide sickness here and are easily upset."

Cyrus bowed deep. "Totally understandable, my lord. Tonight at the evening meal, I will have Sienne's papers for you. Perhaps we might also talk of the trade routes we discussed in autumn-tide."

Marken forced a friendly smile. "Perhaps." He stood, ready to take his leave. "You and your soldiers and thanes are welcome in my castle until the day after the morrow. Until then you may engage in play here if the women so desire." Marken stabbed Cyrus with his hard gaze. "However, if I hear of any woman so much as sustaining a scratch from one of your men, I will take her pain out upon your flesh ten-fold with my blade. Do I make myself understood?"

"Completely, my lord. When in Nordan, do as the Nordanese."

"Now, if you will excuse me, I have things to attend to," said Marken in dismissal.

"My lord." Cyrus and his thanes all bowed as Marken left the court.

Marken took the steps to his chamber two at a time. He reached his door and flung it open. Sienne jumped up from her sitting position on the end of the bed and screamed. Tear stains tracked her cheeks.

"What's wrong?" Marken asked he approached her.

She shook her head and swiped at her cheeks. "Nothing. It's nothing. It is simply having Cyrus so near, I think."

He tipped her head back to take a closer look at the blood that stained the skin of her throat. "What is that?"

Sienne slapped her hand over the small cut. "Nothing. I tripped and fell against the fireplace mantle and nicked myself."

He glanced at the mantle. Indeed, it was at an equal level with her throat. He sat beside her and forced her hand from the gash. Gently, he used his sleeve to wipe the blood away. "Everything you suffer is nothing, isn't it, little one? You do not think of yourself even so highly as to allow yourself pain."

She said nothing, only stared straight ahead.

"I have purchased your freedom, Sienne. It took thirteen thousand Sudhraian flourentimes, but it's done."

That drew a reaction from her. She turned and stared at him. "But, that's a fortune!"

"Aye, and you're worth every coin. I will have your papers of slavery at the evening meal. I will burn them shortly after." He squeezed her hand. "We will do it together if you wish."

Sienne was rendered speechless. Marken helped her to stand.

"Now you will see the castle physician about your throat, then retreat to your rooms and do not leave them," Marken commanded.

"But, I must talk with you."

He kissed her quickly and moved her toward the door. "I know, and I wish to speak with you as well. However, I must meet with my captain and my advisors now to discuss this situation with Sudhra and Cyrus's presence here in Nordan. This night, after the evening meal, I will come to your chambers. We will talk then. Go now."

Sienne felt drained and stunned by the events unfolding around her. She could do little more than obey at this point. "Yes, my lord."

Chapter Seven

Marken took a deep drink of his wine, eyeing Cyrus who sat across the table from him. Cyrus had presented him with Sienne's papers at the beginning of the meal and Haeffen had borne them away to be stored safely until Marken could destroy them.

"We've always enjoyed a good relation, Sudhra to Nordan, haven't we, Marken?" Cyrus cracked the bone of a pharing bird between his teeth and spat a bit of tendon onto the table.

Marken took another long draught of wine. After viewing Cyrus's table manners, hunger had fled him in a rush.

"I would like to continue those good relations by opening more trade routes with our allies to the north," continued Cyrus around a mouthful. "We have a need of Nordanese textiles as you have a need of Sudhraian minerals." Cyrus tipped his wine goblet to Marken before taking a swig. "We could make many flourentimes, you and I."

Marken stared at him for a long moment before speaking. "Perhaps," he said at last. He dropped his head and examined a wine stain on the wooden table. And perhaps they'd be at war come the spring or summer-tide, too. Marken anticipated with relish meeting Cyrus on a battlefield.

The energy of the room shifted, then sighed. Marken could feel a change all around him even as Cyrus prattled on in his lies about good relations between their countries, while he planned nothing but war. A peace filled his mind and he raised his head to see Sienne enter the room from the opposite side.

She wore a long white gown that billowed behind her as she approached the dais. It shifted over her body and provided tantalizing glimpses when she moved right. It made her look like one of the Goddess's own celestial guardians.

Her gaze no longer downcast, she held her head high and surveyed the dining chamber like a queen. She'd come far in her confidence since the early winter. Pride swelled in Marken as he watched her cross the rush-strewn floor toward him.

Even though she'd disobeyed him.

* * * * *

Sienne approached the dais and climbed the stairs. Marken rose and went to her.

Speaking near her ear, he whispered angrily, "I told you I didn't want Cyrus's gaze upon you! I told you to stay in your chambers!"

"I will not allow Cyrus so much power over me, my lord," she replied sweetly. Also, she wanted to bask in Marken's love just for a short while longer. Before she met Cyrus at midnight and probably lost her life.

Marken made a low sound of frustration and pulled a chair from the table so she could sit.

Cyrus's poisoned gaze rested upon her. She met his brown eyes evenly. Beside her Marken looked as if he wanted to reach across the table and pull Cyrus's eyes from his head. But to make a move of violence toward Cyrus for no seeming provocation would cause all Cyrus's thanes and soldiers to draw arms. Sienne was sure Marken didn't want that...yet.

Cyrus pounded once on the table, causing Sienne to jump. "Where are the comely women to service me, Lord Marken?" He leered at Sienne. "Perhaps you could loan me yours for the evening." Cyrus reached across the table to touch her arm.

Marken drew the dagger from its sheath at his waist, and stabbed it into the table, right between two of Cyrus's fingers. "You will not touch her," he growled.

Cyrus snatched his hand back and the entire room went still. "Alright, my lord," said Cyrus, "I won't press your hospitality."

Marken pulled the blade from the table. "Good," he bit off and sat down. He left the blade on the table between them.

Sienne looked worriedly from Marken to Cyrus. It was clear Marken was not good at playing at diplomacy. She placed a hand to his upper thigh in an effort to calm him.

Ilyanna approached the table and put her hand to Cyrus's shoulder. "I will entertain you, Lord Cyrus," she said in a throaty voice, while staring at Marken.

"Ah, finally a wench worthy of my attentions!" He began to draw her down into his lap, but Ilyanna resisted.

"No, my lord. Let us go away. I believe my Lord Marken would prefer it," she purred.

Cyrus grunted and stood. Before following Ilyanna away from the table, he bowed deeply. "I will give Marken what he desires…for now."

Sienne watched Marken's jaw lock as Cyrus left the table. Undisguised animosity rolled off of him. "Why did you disobey me?" Marken asked without meeting her gaze. His took a long drink of his wine, his throat working.

Sienne rubbed his thigh again and found his length beneath his trews. Despite his anger, he hardened beneath her touch. "I am a free woman now, my lord. I wanted to be free in front of Cyrus at least once before you crush him and his thanes into dust."

She glanced around the dining hall at the men and women engaging in play. "Look around my lord, the castle is acting normally, giving no special heed to Cyrus and his men. I do not wish to allow them to alter my behavior either." She lowered her gaze and looked up at him through her lashes. "And I did not wish to be apart from you."

She tipped her face up, hoping he'd take the hint. He lowered his mouth to hers and kissed her. Under her fingers, his length grew harder.

"Take off your gown and come sit on my lap, Sienne." There was undeniable heat in his voice. "I can tell you are aroused. Your delicious nipples are poking through the material of your gown."

She smiled. "It is because of your kiss, my lord."

"Come to me and let me touch you. Show this room and Cyrus's men that you are mine and mine alone."

She glanced around at the men and women in the hall. There was a threesome two tables away. A man knelt between a woman's thighs, laving and sucking at her clit while another man suckled one of her erect nipples while stroking his own member.

She bit her lip. Never had she allowed Marken this, though he asked her repeatedly.

"Come to me, Sienne," Marken commanded again.

She hesitated, then relented, knowing this might be her last opportunity to join with him. She drew her gown over her head and shifted herself onto his lap. He was hard as a rock against her bare buttocks.

His fingers found her mound and stroked over it. He put his mouth to her ear and traced the whorls with the very tip of his tongue and sucked on her ear lobe. His voice when he spoke was a low, silken snare. "Let me pet you, Sienne. Let me play with you...in you."

She shuddered with pleasure.

"Let me work you with my fingers. I want to make you peak." He slid a finger between her wedded thighs and rubbed her clit. She thrust her head back, stabbing her breasts into the air.

She had no doubt he would.

"Good girl," he crooned. "It gladdens me that you allow this. I cannot tell you how much it excites me," he growled.

He cupped her breasts and pinched the nipples. They hardened instantly and he explored their ridges and valleys with his fingertips. Then he dropped his hand to part her legs, urging her to hook her feet around his calves to ensure her thighs were spread as far as they could go.

He drew one hand through her patch of fiery hair to the sweetness below. He slipped two fingers within and thrust. She threw her head back on a moan.

"You like that, little one? You want me to make you peak in front of all these people?" he whispered next to her ear.

His fingers delved deep, finding that place deep within her and stroking it over and over it without mercy. She arched her back, her swollen nipples begging for his touch. His fingers darted in and out of her, faster and faster. He didn't touch her clit. Sienne knew it was on purpose. He wanted to make her last longer before she released herself. She writhed on his lap, rubbing her buttocks against his erection and gripping the table in front of her.

With a growl, he stood, catching her in his arms and laying her onto the table so her legs dangled over the side. She moaned and spread her legs.

He undid his belt, dropped his trews, and sunk himself into her to the base of his phallus. He threw his head back and let a groan escape his lips. "Goddess, you are sweet," he said through gritted teeth. Grabbing her hips, he pulled her to the edge of the table and thrust in and out of her.

Sienne gripped the edge of the table and let him plunge into her. Always, he filled her completely, almost impossibly so. She would never tire of his cock. With every thrust, the exquisite friction sent waves of pleasure rippling up her spine. With a cry, she peaked.

Marken didn't even pause. He relentlessly thrust into her, drawing her beyond her first peak and straight into her second.

With a strangled cry he buried himself deep within her and released his seed. After a dazed moment, he lowered himself onto her and she wound her arms around him, holding on as if she never intended to let him go.

* * * * *

Sienne closed the door of her chamber while balancing a candleholder in one hand. A sheathed dagger rubbed the flesh of her hip, where she'd tucked it into the pair of trews she'd donned, and hidden it beneath one of Marken's tunics. The tunic smelled of him—soap and spice—and comforted her. Although it was far too big. It hung to her knees and the sleeves hung past her wrists.

Shivering against a draft that swept down the corridor, Sienne steadied herself and made her way toward Cyrus's chamber.

It had been difficult telling Marken she had not wanted to spend the night in his bed. In reality it was the only place she wanted to be—especially now, when the chill of the castle and of her impending meeting penetrated her skin and bit into her bones.

She'd even forgone the burning of her contract, telling Marken she felt ill and simply wanted to sleep. In truth, she had no wish to see the thing again, even if it was to burn it. Sienne trusted Marken to do that.

She turned a corner, padded silently down a flight of stairs, and all too soon found herself in front of Cyrus's door. She drew a breath and knocked once.

"Enter."

As the door opened, she saw Cyrus standing with his back to her, one hand braced against the mantle. Firelight licked up his body and cast long shadows on the stone floor.

"Come in, Sienne," came his low voice. "Close the door behind you."

She stepped into the room and set the candleholder on a nearby table. Her hand touched the dagger under her tunic, reminding her that it was there should she need it. Hope surged into her as she glanced around the room. The bastard was alone. Did he so underestimate her?

Perhaps she had an opportunity here after all.

"Sit," Cyrus ordered.

"I prefer to stand," she replied in a quivering voice. Movement caught the corner of her eye, startling her. Tied to the bed was a woman with long black hair, cowering into the pillows. Her long tangled hair hung in her face, giving her a feral look. She wore a scrap of a tan gown, only enough to hide her breasts and mound.

Cyrus turned and Sienne gave him her full attention. It would not do to become distracted now. She played with the edge of her tunic, ready to lift it and grab the dagger should she need it. Backlit by the fire, Cyrus's face was dark. Sienne's stomach knotted. Still, she didn't know what she would do. She knew only that she could not give Cyrus what he wanted.

"You may not be my possession any longer, but you will still obey me," he said.

She lifted her chin a degree and forced her lower lip to stop trembling. "I shall not. I am here because you bade me meet you and I decided to oblige you. Nothing more."

He walked toward her. Every step echoed through the room. Sienne resisted the urge to turn and flee. Every memory she had of this man rose up like bile within her. She nearly choked on the foul taste.

Out of the corner of her eye, the wild girl moved. Here was another innocent—another woman to be subjugated and forced into sexual servitude. Another woman whose life Cyrus would ruin. Sudden, hot hatred for Cyrus coursed through her, made her light-headed.

He stopped in front of her. She could smell stale bread and wine on his breath. "It was so simple to convince to you to come here and give up your knowledge." He reached out and ran a finger down the side of her face. "All I had to do was threaten the man you've fallen in love with. I always knew love could be a powerful weapon. I just didn't know how powerful. I'll have to remember that for the future." Cyrus rubbed her lower lip with the flat of his thumb.

Sienne bit him.

Cyrus ripped his hand away and yelled. He stalked toward her, and his fist arced as he tried to punch her in the stomach. Sienne jumped back, snaking her hand beneath her tunic and pulling her blade out in one smooth movement. She didn't analyze her action; hatred and fear were like a fine wine in her blood, making her drunk.

She held the dagger out in front of her. The firelight glinted along its edge. The girl on the bed screamed like a wild animal then fell silent.

Everything fell silent.

After a tense moment, Cyrus let out a harsh bark of laughter. "My," he said, "how you've changed. I do believe I like you better this way, Sienne. I wonder what you'd be like to bed now."

"You'll only be able to wonder, Cyrus, because if you ever bed me again they'll name you a lover of necrophilia."

Cyrus held out a hand, palm forward. "Sit, Sienne. Peace. I want what's in your head. That's all. Give it up to me freely and I'll let you live, your foster family live, and your lover live."

She had a bargaining chip here. Cyrus didn't know she'd come here with no intention of giving up her knowledge. "I do have information. I gleaned much. But I want one more thing, Cyrus."

"What?"

Sienne jerked her head toward the bed. "That girl's freedom."

Cyrus laughed again, but this time it was not in mirth, it was in anger and impatience. "She's my new favorite, Sienne. I'm calling her Raven. She's a special one, caught in the woods of Nordan, to the far north of here. She's a real wild child." He shook his head. "You can't have her."

Sienne turned and went toward the door. "Fine, then you don't get any of what I have."

His hand closed around her shoulder. The anger and fear coursing through her flared. Images of all he'd done to her in the past rose up, flashing through her mind in a moment of clear pain and clarity. Without thinking, Sienne pivoted on her heel, slashing out with her dagger. The tip of it sliced through tender flesh and warm blood spurted, ran over her hand.

In the glow of the firelight, Cyrus looked surprised. He gurgled, gripped his throat and fell backward.

Raven screamed again long and loud, sounding remarkably like her namesake. Sienne dropped the dagger and it clattered to the floor. Cyrus's blood felt sticky on her skin. Sienne ran to the side of the bed and promptly lost her dinner on the floor.

She held onto the bedpost and pressed her cheek against it, drawing shallow breaths until she thought she could stand on her own two feet unaided again.

The door burst open and Sienne whirled, afraid to find Cyrus's men drawn by Raven's screams. Instead, a portion of Marken's guard stood there, with swords unsheathed and raised. Talyn stepped forward.

He glanced at her and then at Cyrus. "Your handiwork, my lady?"

She nodded shakily and fisted the edge of Marken's tunic in her hand.

His eyes glittered in the firelight. "Lord Marken told us war would soon come to Nordan." His full lips curved. "I did not think it to come this night."

Sienne turned and dry heaved. Good God of Sudhra. With one swipe of her hand she'd ensured war and the death of thousands. They'd fight tonight—Cyrus's thanes and Marken's men. In the end, no matter who was the victor, word would travel back to Sudhra and troops would march forth. All chance of diplomacy was gone. She looked down at her bloodstained hand—all because of her.

Behind her, she could hear people entering the room and leaving, commotion, voices, yelling…battle beginning.

Talyn touched her and she straightened. "Are you all right?" he asked.

She nodded.

Talyn moved to the edge of the bed. Outside in the corridor, chaos was breaking loose. Raven whimpered and pressed herself into the pillows.

Talyn shushed her and broke her bonds with his sword tip. The half-naked woman scrambled across the bed to the closed window on the opposite side of the chamber. Clawing at it as though she had no idea how to open it, she finally freed the clasp. Cold air rushed into the room and Raven hoisted herself up onto the sill.

"No!" yelled Sienne and Talyn in unison. They were five flights of stairs from the ground. She would dash herself on the cobblestone below in her escape attempt.

Talyn rushed to the window and pulled the woman down. She clawed at his face and he restrained her by pinning her arms behind her back.

Sienne crossed the room and took a closer look at the woman. Gently, she smoothed her hair away from her face, revealing green eyes edged in gold. "Where do you come from?" Sienne asked first in Nordanese, then in Sudhraian. She received no response to either language.

"Is she simple of mind?" asked Talyn.

Sienne shook her head. "No, I don't think so. She is a child of the forests. She doesn't know our ways. She is an innocent." She shuddered. "All the worse Cyrus should have her."

"What should we do with her?"

"Keep her safe, Talyn. She'll hurt herself otherwise."

Sienne turned and walked toward the door. The sound of bloodshed was growing ever louder. God help her, but she had to be free of this place.

"Where are you going?" asked Talyn.

She stopped and half-turned toward him. "Away."

"What should I tell my lord? He will miss you."

Sienne swallowed the lump in her throat. "Tell him I'm sorry." She turned and walked out the door.

Chapter Eight

Marken battled his way down a staircase, sending Cyrus's thanes to the ground with every slash of his broadsword. Word had traveled through the castle like a tinder fire. Sienne had murdered Cyrus in his chamber at midnight while he'd been unarmed. It had provoked Cyrus's thanes to battle, though it was a battle they were quickly losing. The morning light would see every one of Cyrus's men that did not flee cut down. Indeed, most already lay dying.

The Sudhraian assumed the Nordanese weak. They were fast finding out how dangerous such misconceptions could be.

Cold fear ripped through Marken as he battled his way down the stairs, growing closer to Cyrus's chamber. Where was Sienne now? Was she injured? Dying? No one seemed to know.

He rounded a corner and met an oncoming Sudhraian soldier. Marken brought his sword up and thrust straight into the man's gut before he could land a blow. Another man came toward him, his face in shadow. Marken pulled his blade free of the first man, turned and raised his sword for yet another blow.

"My lord!" came a familiar voice.

Marken lowered his weapon. "Talyn."

"We've got these dogs on the run, do we not?"

"Aye, indeed we do. Have you seen Sienne?"

"Yes, my lord. She left the castle nigh an hour ago."

Fear rippled through him. There were escaping Sudhraian soldiers out there! She would be in the midst of them. "What?"

"She said to tell you she was sorry and she left."

"By the Goddess's eyes! Do you know which way she went?"

"I'm sorry, my lord. I do not."

"Do you know if she went on foot or by horse?"

"I apologize," replied Talyn.

Marken swore under his breath and pushed past him, heading for the stables. He mowed down every unlucky Sudhraian in his way without preamble.

He found a horse and mounted, digging his heels into the beast's sides as soon he was free of the building. The horse jolted forward and moved quickly from a gallop to a flat-out run. He was grateful for the full moon shining on mother Aran this early morning. The moon's light reflected on the remaining snow and created a glow bright enough to ride by.

He had no idea why she'd chosen to leave him. Perhaps now that she was free of Cyrus she'd decided to go. Apparently he did not rank very high on her list of people to whom to say goodbye. Marken's gut twisted. Had she feigned the last three months? Had she only acted as though she cared about him in order to get the information she needed from him? She'd never answered him when he'd asked her if she loved him back.

Marken compelled the horse to a faster pace with an angry yell as he led the beast onto a path through the forests. To the south lay Sudhra. Marken knew she would not have traveled in that direction. Even if it were her final destination, she would not have traveled directly into the country via that route. It was far too dangerous. To the west lay the wastes of Harmsdell and the wide, violent Nordan River. To the north lay the unending, unforgiving forests and colder weather.

Nay…there was only one direction for Sienne to travel in—east toward the tiny country of Laren'tar. It would have been the way Sienne would've traveled had she chosen to leave the day he set her free at the beginning of winter.

Marken pushed his horse to a faster speed. She had an hour's lead on him, but eventually he'd catch up to her.

Goddess help her when he did.

* * * * *

Sienne picked her way over a log and caught the edge of her cloak on a tree limb. The branch snapped and echoed through the dark, quiet forest. Somewhere an owl hooted and Sienne shivered. She would've liked to have left after the sun had risen, but she had not that luxury.

She'd brought war to Nordan. The angel of death could not linger until dawn. She must travel by darkness. Through her doings, her temper, many would die. She was not fit company for Marken, not worthy of his attention, his touch…certainly not his love. Nay…she was good only to banish herself and should death find her, then so be it.

She skirted a clump of elderberry bushes and finally found what she sought—the road to Laren'tar. A stable hand had told her the way to find it and had offered her a horse. Sienne had refused the beast. How could she steal one of Marken's horses after she'd condemned his people to war? He'd need every last steed to prevent the Sudhraian from dominating his people.

The stable hand had forced her to wait while he brought her good warm boots, a cloak, and other items to protect her from the cold, as well as a sack containing some dried meats, cheeses, and a bit of fruit. He'd also given her a small pan and tinderbox, telling her she could heat bits of leftover snow over a fire to drink.

The stable hand had shaken his head at her and sighed. He obviously thought her hideously stupid for venturing out into the Nordan wild lands so late and without much to protect her.

In shock over killing Cyrus, she'd simply wandered into the forest, searching for the road to Laren'tar. The cold was starting to bring Sienne out of her stunned state now, however. If it hadn't been for the stable hand, she would have gone with only the clothes on her back. If she'd done that, she'd probably be well on her way to dead already...not that it mattered.

Sienne tripped over a rock and sat straight down on her backside on the cold dirt road. She understood the futility of her journey. It was impossible she'd make it to Laren'tar — not on foot.

She struggled to her feet, leaving her satchel on the ground, and brushed the dirt from her clothing. Something rustled in the bushes beside her, distracting her for a moment. The sound of pounding hooves grew loud in her ears. She straightened and whirled.

A huge black warhorse bore down on her. Moonlight caught in Marken's loose black hair and reflected the hard, merciless edges of his face. He wore all black, his sword glinting silver at his side. Sienne could scarcely tell where the horse's flank ended and Marken's clothing began. They seemed one dark, dangerous beast.

Sienne darted into the forest at the side of the road. Behind her she heard Marken call for the horse to halt. The beast whinnied. After a moment, the sound of branches and leaves crunching underneath hooves filled the air as Marken urged the horse into the forest after her.

She didn't risk a look behind her. She simply ran. Branches caught at her clothing and ripped. They broke off in her hair, tangling it, and ripped at the exposed flesh of her cheek. A thorn caught the edge of her mouth and the warm, coppery taste of blood flavored her tongue.

Sienne found a path and took it, trying to avoid the vicious trees that seemed to be in league against her. She ran until her lungs felt nigh unto bursting. She tripped over a log and went sprawling. She lay stunned for a moment, trying to draw air into her starved air passageways.

The sounds of pounding hooves were upon her. She rose to her knees and tried to stand and fell back to her knees. Behind her, Marken halted the horse and simply watched.

Sienne did not look at him, though she could feel his gaze on her. At any moment he could reach down and catch her up. She knew it well. It was at his pleasure she was free now. She took a deep breath and stood, launching herself into another run.

All was silent behind her and for a moment Sienne thought he'd given up on her. Then the pounding hooves resumed. They grew louder and louder until he rode beside her. An arm made of steel and muscle snaked out and wrapped around her waist. Sienne let out an outraged yell.

Marken pulled her up easily so she lay stomach down in front of him on the saddle-less mount. "My lord —"

"Quiet!" Marken barked. "Slaves do not speak until spoken to. You will do as I say from now on." His hand strayed to her buttocks and caressed. His voice lowered. "Everything I say. Like the good little sex slave you are. Did you forget I held your papers? They have not been burned."

Sienne's eyes pricked with tears at the tone of his voice. Dark and cold, it reached into her body and touched her heart with hurt. He knew she'd killed Cyrus. He knew she'd brought war to his people…and he hated her for it.

He traveled back to the castle at a flat-out run. Once in the stables, he pulled her from the horse and forced her hands behind her back. There he wedded and held her wrists, gently but firmly in one large hand. The stable hand who'd gifted her with the provisions stared at her with dull eyes.

"Go find someone to fill the bathtub in my chambers and light a fire," he ordered the man.

"Yes, my lord," he replied and ran off.

He led her out of the stables and toward the castle without a word. In the inner bailey stood Talyn barking orders to his men. Sienne watched the captain do a double take when he saw them. "My lord," he called and walked to them.

"Talyn," replied Marken. "I am sorry I did not stay until the end of the battle. I had urgent business to attend to, and knew you could handle the problem of the Sudhraian thanes and soldiers without my aid."

Talyn wore a wary look on his face. His gaze flicked back and forth between herself and Marken. Her face was probably white with strain and Marken still held her wrists captive.

"My lord. It was easily done," Talyn answered. "Although some of them escaped. They will be traveling to Sudhra to tell of the happenings here, and we can expect war for certain."

Sienne let a sob escape her lips and Talyn looked at her sharply. "My lady, are you well?" he asked.

"She is fine, Talyn, and not allowed to speak."

Sienne dropped her gaze to Talyn's booted feet. Blood stained them, she noted dully. The moon illumed the dark patches spotting his clothing.

"Are you alright, my lord?" Unease threaded through Talyn's tone.

"I am fine," Marken replied tersely. "We are retiring to my chamber."

Talyn cleared his throat. "Very well, my lord. Then I should not worry about my lady?"

"I would never harm a woman, Talyn. Especially not one I love. Even if she has no love for me in return."

Sienne's head shot up at that and she found Marken's gaze. Didn't he know she loved him too? It was why she had to leave now and never see him again! She opened her mouth to say as much.

"Shush, Sienne," he ordered harshly. "I did not bid you speak."

She closed her mouth.

Marken pulled her past Talyn and into the castle. He did not utter a word as he dragged her up the stairs and down the corridor toward his chamber.

The door to his room stood open and servant boys went in and out, dragging buckets of water into the room. Marken forced her to sit in a chair by the roaring fire while the servants finished filling the bathtub.

When the last servant had gone, Marken turned to her. "Disrobe, but do not utter a word."

Sienne stood and layer-by-layer unwrapped herself until she stood only in her trews and tunic. The clothing was stained with Cyrus's blood.

Marken stood beside the bathtub. With every bit of clothing that dropped to the ground, his eyes grew darker. His face was a harsh mask. Sienne shivered. She did not know this man who stood before her. All of the Marken she knew and had grown to love had fled.

"Take off that clothing, take off your boots, and walk to me," he commanded. His eyes flashed dangerously.

The material felt soft against her skin as she pulled it over her head. Her hair fell to her waist in a heavy mass of glinting curls. She let the clothing drop to the floor and toed off the traveling boots. Completely naked, she crossed the floor toward him. His heated gaze took her in from head to foot.

"My lord," she began.

He held up a hand. "Do not speak."

"But—"

"No." Marken turned and went to a drawer by the side of his bed. From it he pulled long strips of material. Some he dropped on the mattress, one he brought to her and secured over her mouth as a gag. "I do not want to hear your lies any longer. I want you to listen and do I as command. Nothing more, nothing less. I want no explanations from you. I want nothing except your sweet body at my beck and call, wrapped around my shaft when I desire it. Do you understand?"

Tears sheened her eyes even as moisture flooded between her legs at his words. God, but nothing could make her stop wanting him. She nodded.

"Good. Now get into the bathtub and bathe while I watch you."

The water was warm against her flesh as she stepped into the water and sat. It lapped at her waist like a lover's embrace.

Chapter Nine

She glanced up at Marken. He'd positioned a chair in front of the tub and had one ankle resting on his opposite knee. He'd discarded his broadsword and short sword to the floor beside him, and appeared casual sitting there. But the look on his face and in his eyes betrayed him. Lust shown clearly there, blazing as bright as the fire across the room—mixed with his anger. It was a volatile combination.

But the lust...maybe she had some control here after all, she thought as she lowered her eyes. Cupping her hands she trickled water over her body, letting it stream between her breasts and down her stomach. She picked up the cake of soap and lathered it between her hands, then rubbed her arms slowly. She kept her eyes on him and noted every shift he made in his chair.

She put her hands to her breasts and began to rub. Marken uncrossed his legs and sat forward, his gaze intent. She palmed her breasts and cupped them, running her fingers over her erect nipples. Sienne closed her eyes and imagined Marken a week ago. She imagined his hands on her, finding all the sensitive hills and valleys of her body.

She pulled at her nipples, imagining his mouth at her breasts—his teeth nipping at her. Sienne tipped her head back and arched her back. Thus gagged, she could not voice her pleasure, but it was there in her body language.

She felt water trickle over her breasts and her eyes flew open. With cupped hands, Marken cleansed away the soap. He bathed the scratches on her face made from her run through the forest with gentleness at odds with his anger. He took her by the wrist and tugged, forcing her to stand.

Wrapping her in a towel, he dried her body thoroughly, his fingers slipping between her legs and finding her pussy and running over it with his fingertips. His thumbs found her sensitized nipples and rubbed. She closed her eyes and drew a sharp breath in through her nose.

He put his mouth next to her ear and murmured, "After tonight you will know to whom you belong Sienne—your body and your mind." Her eyes flew open. "After tonight you'll know just how displeased I was that you ran from me. Believe me, I'll make you pay for keeping up the pretense of caring about me for the last three months."

His words disconcerted her, even though his hands played upon her body like it was a musical instrument. He lifted her from the bathtub and set her to her feet on the plush carpeting. Then he led her to the bed.

"Take the towel from you and lay down," he commanded.

She dropped the towel and her flesh pebbled in the chill air. Her gaze holding his, she crawled onto the bed and lay down on her back.

He took the two of the remaining pieces of fabric and did what she expected him to do. He looped them around the bedposts and then around her wrists. It reminded her of the time she'd done this to him. She twisted her wrists and the fabric tightened. It was not painful, but she was caught, unable to free herself.

He placed another strip of fabric over her eyes and secured at the back of her head. Her breathing grew shallow with fear and she made a conscious effort to steady herself. She trusted him. She trusted him…didn't she? She hadn't trusted him enough to reveal her secrets, had she? The realization struck her hard.

All was quiet for several long moments. The gentle sound of clothing falling to the floor in a heap reached her ears.

A breeze swept over her skin and she shivered. She could feel him standing next to the bed even though she couldn't see him. His heat radiated out.

"Such a beautiful woman you are, Sienne," he said softly. "Too bad you're so treacherous." The pain in his voice made tears well in her eyes. She wanted to tell him why she'd left—why she could not stay here any longer with him.

His hand reached out and grazed the inside of her thigh. The mattress indented on her right side as he climbed onto the bed and centered himself between her legs.

His hand stroked her, starting at her thatch of hair and brushing down. She flinched. "Shhhh…Sienne, you know I won't hurt you."

Sienne knew why he was doing this. He needed to feel in control of her because he was not able to control his emotions.

He drew his hands over her shoulders feather-light, trailing them down over her breasts and stomach, down the length of her legs and then back up. His fingers grazed her sex, but did not linger there. Instead, he continued drawing his large, strong hands over her body, as if memorizing every hill and valley of her—as if he worshipped her very skin.

Every inch of her skin felt sensitized, and Sienne grew wet. She writhed in her bonds, wanting more of his hands on her. Wanting his hands on her breasts, between her legs. Still, he continued his gentle torment.

He dropped a hand to her pussy and ran his fingers over her. He made a sound of satisfaction deep in his throat. "Even my lightest touch elicits a sexual response from you," he said.

That was his point, she knew.

"You like this, don't you, Sienne?" he purred. "You enjoy being completely at my mercy. I can do anything I desire to your sweet body now, and you can do nothing to stop me."

He shifted and his warm breath brushed over her sex. Sienne had to stop herself from trying to thrust her hips forward toward his mouth. She wished it were not true! She wished he didn't affect her the way he did. Even his breath on her skin made her want him. Over the last three months he'd trained her to be responsive to his slightest movement.

Marken's tongue touched the skin just under her ear and she flinched at the sensation of the hot tip of it running over her collarbones and then lower, between her breasts, down her stomach. Sienne wiggled and emitted a muffled moan. He drew his tongue down her skin agonizingly slowly, dipping it into her bellybutton and continuing lower, over her pelvis and down to her inner thigh.

Marken kissed the crease where her leg and pelvis met, and Sienne's clit pulsed. He ran his tongue along her skin, leaving tiny, hot kisses along the way...headed straight for her core. He licked her pussy lips and let his tongue twirl around her clit before drawing his tongue back down to the opening of her passage.

He groaned low in his throat. "You taste so good, Sienne. You always have. I'll never grow tired of your flavor."

He returned to teasing her with his tongue. It slipped within her and she drew a sharp breath in through her nostrils. He thrust his tongue in and out of her, but did not touch her clit. She'd come to know Marken well enough that she knew he did not intend to bring her peak now. Oh, no. Slow torture would be the punishment for her transgression.

She writhed at the feel of his hot, slick tongue exploring her passage and delving out once in a while to lick her folds. If she hadn't been gagged, Sienne knew she would be moaning with abandon. Instead, she made muffled noises of pleasure.

Marken drew his tongue up to her clit and flicked at it with his tongue. He teased it with the tip and then stopped, then teased it again—keeping her on the edge of her peak. His touch was just enough to keep her unbelievably excited, but the pressure was not steady enough to push her over the edge.

"I don't want you to come yet. Do you understand? You'll only come when I say you can," he said.

Marken slipped a finger within and then a second while he laved her clit and Sienne thought she'd go insane. Gently, slowly...so very slowly, he massaged the inner walls of her passage with his fingers while he continued the torment with his tongue.

He added his teeth to the mix and lightly nibbled at her clit.

Sienne tensed to peak…and he was gone.

She made a sound of frustration in her throat and pulled at her bonds, her heels digging into the mattress. She remembered how easily Marken had broken his when she'd tied him with rope. She could not hope to rip even these flimsy fabric restraints.

She heard movement at the side of the bed. "Your lips are cherry red and engorged. Your clit is ready for my mouth again and I can tell all you want in the world is my cock inside you, to give you ease. Is it true, Sienne? Nod your head if it is."

Sienne nodded.

He leaned over her and whispered in her ear. "Know that this is how I felt when you left me. I loved you. I love you still. I never felt that way before I met you, just as your body never knew pleasure before you came to me. You left me wanting. You left me knowing that you were the only one who could fill me up. Just as I am the only who can fill you now."

Hot tears stung her eyes at his words. She'd made a mistake. She knew that now. She'd always professed to trust Marken, but still, she had not told him of her meeting with Cyrus. She had not told him of the threat Ramdan had made against him. She'd chosen to stand on her own…mostly because she'd always had to stand on her own. She'd had no other choice.

A cool breeze rushed over her and she knew he was gone. Tears soaked the blindfold she wore and trickled from the corners of her eyes. She heard Marken across the chamber laying more wood on the fire. The scent of fresh burning branches reached her nostrils. It reminded her of the first morning she'd been at the castle, waking up to find Marken standing across the room dressed in black from head to toe. He'd been there to teach her to have pleasure and she accidentally taught him to love in return.

As he'd also taught her to love and, finally, to trust.

A fresh sob ripped through her, muffled by the gag, and Marken was there on the bed between her legs. She'd not expected him to respond to her pain. His body heat radiated out and warmed her breasts. His mouth went to one of her breasts and his hard chest braced against hers. He took her hardened nipple into his warm mouth and sucked on it as if it was a hard sugar candy.

The tip of his shaft brushed her core and slid up to her clit. Idly, he circled it with its rigid tip and Sienne spread her legs as far as she was able. Tears streamed down her cheeks.

Marken lifted his head from her breast. "Don't cry, Sienne. Goddess, I can't stand it when you cry. Even now it tears at me."

He reached up untied her blindfold and her gag. She let out a sigh that racked her body and blinked against the firelight. Marken's concerned face came into focus.

A fat teardrop trailed down her cheek and Marken caught it on his fingertip. Then he kissed her cheeks, wiping her tears away with his lips. He moved his hips and the hard length of him ground against her.

"Untie me," she whispered.

Marken reached up and released her from her bonds. Sienne's arms came around his shoulders and she sighed happily at the feel of him. He shifted his hips again, deliberately teasing her. She knew as soon as he entered her, her peak would come like an arrow hitting its target.

She caught his gaze and almost smiled at the worried expression on his face. "Make love to me," she murmured.

Marken pushed himself into her slowly, inch by tantalizing inch. Sienne let out a hiss of breath and threw her head back into the pillows, arching her back as best she could with his body against her.

He rocked his hips back and forth, thrusting into her with agonizing deliberateness. Bracing one hand on the bed beside her head, he reached his hand down between their bodies and took some of her moisture on his finger to use as lubrication as he circled her clit. Sienne instantly peaked.

He didn't stop the pressure. He thrust into her leisurely and kept up the play at her clit. Sweat broke on his brow and Sienne could see the slow pace cost him.

Her peak built again under his ministrations. Before she came again, he removed his hand and covered her body with his own. The hard muscle just above the base of his cock kept up the delicious friction against her clit and the position rubbed him deep inside her in just the right place.

She moaned and he caught the sound in his mouth. He kissed her, taking his time and exploring the inside of her mouth thoroughly. He pulled away. "You've made sex into something more for me, Sienne." Pain threaded his voice. "You complicated it...but made it better somehow at the same time."

"I do care about you, Marken," she whispered against his lips.

His thrusts faltered. "What did you call me?" The question held a note of amazement. He stiffened. "More lies," he whispered harshly in her ear. "You think to save yourself by using my name."

"No!" She reached up and threaded her fingers through the hair at the nape of his neck, angling his head toward hers for a kiss. Still, he kept up the gentle thrusting in and out of her passage. It connected them. Made them one. She kissed him and he pulled away. He rose up, sliding her so the back of her thighs braced on the front of his. At this angle his thrusts grew deeper and harder.

She sucked in a breath and grabbed at the blankets on either side of her. "Marken," she said, finding his gaze. "I was wrong not to trust you. I...I thought I wasn't worthy of you...so I left."

Marken rotated his hips and increased the speed of his thrusts. He appeared not to hear her. He grabbed her hips and held her as his pace grew in intensity.

Sienne tossed her head back and forth as another peak built, pleasure cresting within her to an incredible degree.

"You...might care...about me," Marken finally said through gritted teeth. "But...you admit...you never loved me." He shifted, driving into her with long hard strokes.

Her peak broke over her in a blinding wave, robbing her of all thought save one. "Marken, I love you!" she cried as she came. Her muscles contracted around him.

He let out a bellow and his hot seed spurted. He came down on top of her, bracing himself on the bed so he did not crush her.

Sienne placed her mouth to his ear. "I love you, Marken. I love you so very much, and I'm sorry I ran from you. I should have trusted you," she repeated.

Marken was still for a long moment, his exerted breathing harsh. Sienne held her breath and waited. She ran her hands down his sweat-slicked sides. Still, she held him within her and she didn't want to let go.

After what seemed like an eternity, he raised his gaze to hers. "Why did you run from me?" he asked.

She averted her eyes in her shame. "I killed Cyrus. I brought war to Nordan. Because of me a diplomatic solution will not be found and many Nordanese will die."

Marken smiled. "Do you truly believe you caused all that, little one?"

"One of Sudhra's most powerful thanes was murdered unarmed within your walls. That started a battle between your men and Cyrus's men." She nodded. "Aye, I did indeed start a war, Marken."

He sighed. "Goddess, but my name sounds sweet coming from your lips." His dark blue gaze held hers. "War was destined to arrive anyway, Sienne. I feel certain the problems between our nations could not have been solved by diplomacy. I know now how long Sudhra has been planning an invasion. They wish to take our religion from us. It's a highly charged reason to wage a war. It's a highly emotional one. Diplomacy would have been tried, it's true, but it would not have worked."

Sienne closed her eyes as the images of Cyrus slumping to the ground filled her mind. The feel of his hot blood coursing over her hand asserted itself in her recollection. "I killed a man," she said softly.

Marken kissed her cheek and with one hand, smoothed the hair from her face. "I am sorry for that, little one. I would have spared you the pain and killed him for you had I realized what was going on. Why did you go to Cyrus's chambers in the first place?"

"He threatened you."

He rolled to the side and she nearly wept for the loss of him within her. He pushed a hand through his hair in a gesture that screamed frustration. "So...let me understand this correctly. He threatened me and you put yourself in danger?"

She nodded.

He drew her into his arms so her back was braced against his warm chest, and he feathered the side of her face with kisses. "You did not lie when you said you loved me just now, did you?"

She let out a sigh and snuggled against his chest. "No."

His arms tightened around her. "Never...ever do anything like that again. Do you understand me? I can take of myself—especially against such badly trained men as Sudhra produces. Sudhra will soon know the might of Nordan." His voice had a cold hard edge to it. "How did you kill Cyrus, Sienne?" he asked.

"It was because of the woman tied to his bed, his new slave. After so many of months of life by your side, of knowing how sweet freedom could be, the sight of her drove me to a rage I'd never know I'd had."

"I am sure Cyrus never expected you to act out against him."

She laid a kiss to his forearm, which was nestled between her breasts. "He underestimated me, my love."

"It was a mistake. You are not a woman to be taken for granted. I am sorry I treated you as a slave just now. I am ashamed of myself. I allowed myself to be blinded by my emotions."

Marken gave a sigh and released her. She rolled to her back and watched him slide on a pair of trews, then walk across the room toward the fireplace. She caught the edge of the blanket and pulled it back, then slid down under the covers, reveling in the soft warmth that surrounded her.

The rustling of papers drew her attention back to Marken. In his hand he held a sheaf of them, which he dropped into the fire. The flames flared up, consuming them, curling the pages and turning them to ash.

Sienne knew what they were and sweet pleasure suffused her. She was completely and utterly free now. Even were she to return to Sudhra, she could walk around as a freed citizen.

Marken turned from the fire, his long hair brushing over his back and falling loose over his shoulders. He walked toward her on bare feet. She studied the way he moved, the muscles of his chest and stomach rippling.

He reached the edge of the bed and knelt. Dark blue eyes met hers. "You are free now. You can leave here if you wish it. I will give you as much money as you desire, horses, and men to accompany you to Laren'tar, or even to your foster family's home in Sudhra. I'm giving you a choice, now, Sienne."

She sat up, clutching the blanket to her chest. "That is one choice. What is the other?"

"That you stay here in Nordan with me and become my monogamous mate, forsaking all others. Together we will rule and if you do not produce a child, we will choose one to foster and make our heir."

She bit her lip. He looked so serious, as though he truly thought she would choose the former. She reached out and ran her hand down his face. His stubbled chin scraped her palm. "I wish to stay here with you, Marken."

He sat on the edge of the bed and the lines of his face grew harsh in the firelight. Half his face was in darkness, half in light. "And you promise never to leave me again in such stealth and break my heart? You promise to always trust me with your secrets and never endanger yourself so foolishly again?"

She leaned forward and kissed the hardness of his lips until they softened and captured hers. "I promise to stay by your side and trust you always, Marken," she said against his lips. "I promise to give you my love for the rest of my life." She smiled. "I can do no other anyway."

His perfect lips curved in a smile. "Good. We have that in common."

Chapter Ten

Talyn stepped into the corridor outside his chamber. Fresh canne-blossom rushes crushed under sending up a sweet, slightly spicy fragrance. Draped along the sconces inset in the stone walls, were boughs of fresh spring flowers interspersed with holly twigs.

Marken had resurrected an old tradition and had held a monogamous mating ceremony last night. The castle remained adorned still this morning...well, early afternoon, really. It had been a late night.

He shook his head. Marken had done a fine job letting himself become ensnared by one woman. Why ever would a man tie himself to just one woman, when he had all the women in the castle to choose from? True, as lord of the castle, Marken was expected to take a mate. But he didn't have to make the women his monogamous mate. Marken could take her to mate and still have a different flavor every single night without fear of repercussion, as could Sienne.

Realization hit him with a dull thud. Goddess...Marken would start a trend! All the women in the castle would begin desiring monogamous mate status and ceremonies to go with it!

Talyn turned and headed down the corridor toward the court. His cock would never be so dominated by a single woman. He had no fear of that. No...he'd continue to have his pick. As captain of the castle guard, he was highly sought after and known widely as a generous lover.

He had to admit that Marken had never looked so happy as he had last night with Sienne standing beside him. She'd been radiant and smiling. It was the first time Talyn had ever seen her smile.

After the ceremony, there had been a large celebration and a feast the likes of which had never seen by the castle. Wine and ale had flowed freely and everyone had laughed and danced into the wee hours of the morning.

Talyn had attracted two lusty beauties who'd accompanied him back to his room—a blond, busty woman, and a tall, slender one with long dark hair. A pair matched for contrasts. Their hair had looked so pretty tangled together across his pillows. One had ridden his cock while the other straddled his face. All three of them had come together, their cries filling the chamber.

Even now the two women slept sated, tucked under the blankets on his bed and the both of them filled near to bursting with his seed.

Aye…Marken didn't know what he'd be missing.

"Hold her down!" Sienne's slightly accented voice reached him from around the corner.

"I'm trying, my lady," called Carrick, sounding winded. "She's impossible to keep still!"

He wondered why Sienne was not still in her joining bed and picked up his pace.

Talyn rounded the corner. Sienne stood just inside the doorway of the chamber of the wild woman, Raven. It was a windowless room. He'd thought that a better place to keep her since the woman had shown a fondness for heights. "Can I aid you, my lady?" he asked.

Sienne turned to him and instantly relaxed. "Oh, I'm glad you're here." She moved to the side to allow him access into the room.

Carrick, not a weak man by any stretch of the imagination struggled to hold Raven in his arms as Ryn, the castle physician, tried to brace and hold her legs still.

The woman's hair was tangled and fell over her face. Green-and-gold eyes glowed angrily at him through the tangled mess. She wore a white dress that was ripped in places, no doubt from her current struggles. It was too large for her thin frame and the neckline had slipped down, showing one milky smooth shoulder.

The physician raised the hem of her gown, revealing a shapely leg, which sported a long gash crusted with dried blood.

Sienne came to stand beside him. "She escaped last night and was captured by one of the men as she attempted to climb out one of the tower windows. He pulled her down and restrained her, but she sustained that wound in the process. We have been trying to hold her still to cleanse it. We don't wish for her to contract an infection."

Talyn rubbed his chin and realized he'd forgotten to shave when stubble abraded his calloused hand. "The woman is simple of mind, I'm sure," he mused aloud.

The woman stopped struggling and focused her gaze on him. She spat with exuberance, and Talyn moved just in time to avoid being spattered. "Not...s...simple," she seethed.

Talyn raised an eyebrow. So she spoke Nordanese after all.

She began to fight again in earnest when Ryn took the opportunity to place a soapy cloth to her thigh. Carrick swore under his breath, his muscles flexing as he fought to control her.

Sienne sighed. "On the contrary, Talyn. It appears she did not speak Nordanese at all when she first arrived. She is teaching herself our tongue slowly—without any outside aid. That means she's actually incredibly agile of mind."

Talyn took a step toward her and murmured to himself, "She is a mystery, isn't she?"

"Even now Haeffen researches in the archives for some hint of where she may have come from," replied Sienne.

He took another step near her and held out his hand as though trying to tame a wild animal. "Shhhh…I won't hurt you. No one here will hurt you."

She stilled. Her eyes glowed green and gold and incredibly wary through her tangled hair. Ryn set the cloth to her thigh and she kicked out at him with one slender bare foot.

Talyn came closer and set his hand to her shoulder. She made an angry grunting noise at the contact. He caught Carrick's eyes. "On the count of three, release her and I'll take her."

"Be my guest," muttered Carrick.

Talyn counted to three and Carrick moved away from her while Talyn spun toward her. He caught her around the waist, pinning her hands to her side. As soon as they made contact, a light vibrational pulse coursed through his body. It stunned him for a moment, but there was no time to wonder at it for the wild woman began to struggle against his grip.

"No!" she cried. Her back arched and her feet lifted from the floor, kicking at him. Her heels connected with his shins.

Talyn merely held on and let her wear herself out. "Shush," Talyn said, close to her ear. "Shush now. Calm...calm," he crooned.

He grabbed her wrists and pulled them together behind her back and held them with one hand. The woman made an enraged noise and twisted, but found she couldn't free herself.

Talyn pressed her against him and stroked her hair with his free hand, all the while crooning to her, telling her it would alright and that no one meant her harm. He buried his nose in her hair and inhaled. She smelled of the forest, of green trees and blue, blue skies.

She stilled and leaned back against him.

Sienne laughed softly. "You have a way with her, Talyn. Her eyes are closed."

From across the room, Carrick chuckled. "Amazing isn't it? Women enjoy his touch, it's true. His hands and voice can even tame the savage beast."

Talyn shot him a sharp look. The woman was not a savage beast—merely misunderstood. He'd been that way himself once...long ago.

Ryn placed the cloth to her thigh and cleansed her wound. The woman did not make a sound or a movement.

Ryn finished and looked up at him. "Thank you for your help, captain. I despaired of helping the woman. I don't know what to do with her. We cannot set her free or she'll kill herself for certain."

Her body went heavy as she slumped against Talyn. He released her wrists and lifted her. Walking across the chamber, he laid her on the bed and pulled the covers over her. Her breathing had the cadence of sleep.

He gazed down at her. She looked so innocent and pure. He would not guess her to be such a troublesome hellion while she rested in the realm of dreams.

He turned to find Sienne staring at him speculatively. "What?" he asked her.

"Nothing." She turned and Talyn noticed for the first time she wore a cream-colored nightdress made of flax-cloth. Her nipples poked lush pink from under the fabric and her buttocks were just the right size for his hands. He raised an eyebrow and his mouth went dry.

But Sienne was forever off limits to him now. Unless he wanted to feel the sharp edge of Marken's broadsword, that was.

All four them walked toward the door. Ryn opened it and they filed out. Ryn and Carrick walked down the corridor together, commiserating about their recent ordeal.

Talyn tried not to look at Sienne's luscious body under her gown and met her eyes instead. "Why are you not in bed with Lord Marken?"

"He wanted to come himself, but I thought it best I attend to the girl. I didn't want such a bear of a man to scare her." She winked. "It's my first act as mistress of the castle. I am headed back to bed now, however." She walked past him. "Have a lovely day, Talyn," she called back and laughed. The joyous sound of it warmed him. "I know I will."

Talyn watched her retreating form and swallowed hard. Goddess, he hoped she stopped wearing flax-cloth.

He walked over to stand at a window and gaze beyond the pane of glass at the rolling hills of Nordan. Nearly all the snow had melted and spring had asserted itself over the land. The trees were even beginning to bud and early flowers poked their heads up from Aran's soil.

It was a time of renewal and new beginnings.

His gaze shifted to the north and he lapsed into memories of his younger years. He shook his head. Nay…it was not a place to go on such a fine day. Seeing the wild woman had triggered them, but they were best left to history.

Instead he looked to the south. War would be coming to Nordan…and soon. Spring-tide would possibly bring death as well as beauty.

Clouds gathered in the southern sky, darkening the day. Foreboding gathered around his heart for the future.

Chapter Eleven

Marken pulled Sienne into his arms as soon as she closed the door to their chamber and peppered her face with kisses. He caught her mouth with his and sucked on her lower lip before pulling away and resting his forehead against hers.

"You must stop wearing flax-cloth around the men, my love. You are like a piece of candy they can never enjoy," he said. "It's cruel."

"There are many women in the castle for them to select from, Marken. I highly doubt they'll bemoan the loss of me."

He slapped her buttocks lightly. "You have no idea just how desirable you are."

He scooped her up in his arms and she squealed. He crossed the room and threw her down on the bed, then climbed on after her. With a sexy growl deep in his throat, he attacked her throat with his mouth, licking and sucking and biting.

Sienne's eyes fluttered shut under the onslaught and she moaned. Gods, she would never tire of him. Her hands found the tunic he'd had the audacity to don and began pulling it over his head.

He pulled away from her and affected a look of shock on his face. His black hair swung around his face, brushing the skin of her upper arms and her nipples through the fabric of her nightdress. "Again?" he asked in feigned surprise.

She wrapped her legs around his waist and pulled him toward her for a kiss. "Always," she murmured against his mouth.

His hands fumbled for the edge of her nightdress and he ripped it in his efforts to pull it over her head.

There went another perfectly good item of clothing—a victim of their passion. Sienne let the gown float to floor, thankful it no longer came between them. He pressed his warm, hard chest to hers and she rubbed against him, reveling in the friction against her sensitive nipples. Marken settled himself between her thighs.

"I think I know a way to remove the constant melancholy from Talyn," she whispered to Marken as he eased himself into her.

"Wh...what?" Marken raised his gaze from her breasts to her face. His eyes narrowed. "Why are you thinking about Talyn?"

She laughed. "I saw it in his eyes—just a little, just for a fleeting moment—as he stared down at the wild girl."

"Saw what?"

She smiled. "Love, Marken. It takes one in it to recognize it in others. Even if it's just a whisper...a shadow of a possibility for the future."

Marken laughed and shook his head. "No. Talyn would never align himself to a woman the way I've done with you. Never. You don't know him like I do. It's ridiculous to even consider."

"I don't know. I know what I saw...oh!" Marken's thrusts picked up in pace and he rotated his hips, driving all sensible thought from her. She lapsed into moans, her hips arching to meet her mate's thrusts.

She'd think about Talyn later.

SPRING PLEASURES:
THE TRANSFORMATION

Chapter One

Raven reached up and knotted the thick quilt she lay on in both hands and twisted her hips, dragging her legs across the mattress of the four-poster bed and enjoying the brush of the soft material against her bare skin. Candlelight flickered over the walls of the opulent chamber, drawing long shadows on the rush-covered cobblestone floor. Her gown bunched around her hips as she shifted to stare at each tapestry-hung wall in turn. The chamber they'd locked her in had no window for her to use as an exit to freedom.

She closed her eyes and imagined the wind on her face, enveloping her body as she plummeted toward the ground. There was always that moment of release and acceptance when she thought maybe this time...*maybe this time*...she'd connect with the stretch of unforgiving ground beneath her—fold herself into Aran's earthy embrace forevermore. But then the telltale crisp snap and brief lightning-fast bolt of pain would signal feather ripping through flesh, always quickly followed by the sound of muscle, bone, and tendon exploding, melding, and reaching out for flight as her half-life wings unfurled to the gentle winds.

Raven twisted on the bed and arched her back, gritting her teeth and tightening her grip on the blanket. She tossed her head and her long hair spread like a curtain over her face as she imagined the ecstasy of flight...of freedom. In her mind, her long, strong wings bore her body up on the edge of a gust, high above this castle and the people within it who were not like her, who would never understand her or what she was.

She released the blankets and brought her knees into her chest, wrapping her arms around her shins and burying her face between her kneecaps as the tears came. Three weeks ago, she'd been content, living in the northern Nordan forests with her grandmother. Theirs had been a quiet life, at least until the foreign men had come.

Raven hadn't known there was such a thing as these creatures who'd intruded on their peace. She'd never seen a man. She'd never seen anyone other than her grandmother before, so she hadn't known to be afraid. Not then.

She knew now.

Two weeks ago, in the furthest northern reaches of Nordan, when the golden man had appeared to her from around a tree and smiled, she'd been entranced. Always she'd dreamed of seeing a man. Her grandmother had told her of them and they'd fueled her fantasies as she grew to womanhood.

She'd gone to the man and touched his brightly colored clothing, his golden hair, his face and lips. The stubble on his chin had tickled the palm of her hand.

She'd been naïve, allowing him to touch her in return—tracing the edge of her chin, limning the curve of her bared shoulder with his fingertips. She'd closed her eyes and enjoyed it because she'd longed for that her whole life—for a male to touch her, cherish her. In the strange man standing before her, she'd thought all her hopes and dreams had come true.

Then his touching had changed, grown more demanding, and far more threatening. Memories of him flooded her mind; his hot groping hands taking what she didn't want to give, his foul breath tainting the air between their too close mouths, fingers clenching around her breasts, her nipples. She'd twisted out of his reach and ran, falling through the remaining patches of snow and dodging brush and tree limbs.

Desperately, she'd sought the steep incline she knew lay ahead of her and jumped off it. But the man had been ready. Right after the violent sprout of wings from her shoulder blades he'd thrown a looped rope around her throat and pulled so it tightened around her esophagus.

Nails scrabbling at the noose as it choked her, she'd tried to fly away from him. But inch by agonizing inch, he'd pulled her down to the ground, into his arms, and to the wicked edge of the blade he wielded.

He'd hit her so she lost consciousness and when she'd awoken, she'd been in a wooden cage along with Grandmother.

They'd known what she and Grandmother were all along. They'd tracked them and hunted them down. She'd found that out from Grandmother on the way south through the woods, as they left all they'd known behind them. In the gentle cooing language of their people, Grandmother had told Raven many things. She'd told her stories of strangers imprisoning their ancestors, hunting them down and cutting off their wings as trophies to mount on their walls. As Grandmother had grown sicker and sicker from the loss of her freedom and the harsh traveling conditions, she'd told her of heartbreak and hatred, of bloodshed and fear.

And Raven's naiveté had forever been extinguished.

The first time after her capture that the golden man had touched Raven, she'd blackened his eye and got one in return. He'd shackled her to him after that, so she never left his side. Every time he'd touched her she'd fought him tooth and nail, frustrating his every attempt, but she'd paid for her successes in her own blood and tears. He could've restrained her, beat her into submission, but he'd never done that. It had seemed he'd enjoyed her struggles and was merely biding his time until she finally broke.

The golden man would have eventually won. Little by little he'd been destroying her, eating away at her will. When Grandmother had died one cold morning, Raven had nearly given in to him in her sorrow. But then they'd buried Grandmother in the ground. *In Aran!* Not wrapped and hung in a tree with her possessions and symbols of her life in the way of her people. It had been a sacrilege—defamation. Rage had overtaken her sorrow, and that rage hadn't disappeared.

Hot tears fell onto Raven's cheeks at the memories, and she pulled herself into a tighter ball in the center of the bed.

"Shush." A hand brushed her hair and Raven unfurled her body and scrambled over the edge of the bed to the floor on the opposite side. She hadn't even heard the door open. Her heart beating hard in her chest, she peered up over the edge of the bed.

The one they called Talyn peered back at her. Of all of them, he disturbed her the most. Every time the man came near, he sent a wave of deep comfort through her. He was not safe, that one. He held the ability to calm her, make her do what he wished. She didn't like that loss of control. Not one little bit.

Not only that, but his touch made her long for what she'd wanted from the golden man before he'd revealed his ruthlessness—she wanted Talyn's hands on her body. Places she never knew could ache, wept with desire at the mere thought of this man's hands exploring her.

"Easy, Raven," he said. "I came with servants to fill your bathing tub. You have not had a bath since you've arrived and you have caked blood on your skin and in your hair." He held out one strong hand.

She narrowed her eyes. For a long time she hadn't understood their speech, but she'd known the key to her survival depended upon learning it. Eventually sounds and syllables had coalesced, then separated, and finally had become understandable. She guessed it was a quirk of her race, a survival mechanism. But now that Grandmother was dead, there was no one to ask. She was the very last of her kind.

She studied Talyn through the tangled mess of her hair. His eyes were the color of the deepest forests, a rich green, and were shaped like almonds. Long, dark lashes fringed them, nearly as long as her own. Those eyes glittered with intelligence and secrets from a face that was all hard angles and edges. It was a handsome face with a strong chin and full lips. His hair fell to his shoulders when it was unbound, but most of the time he kept the glossy mass secured at the nape of his neck with a thin leather thong. It was the color of the earth when you dug deep into her—a brown so dark it was nearly black.

Muscles rippled under his tunic and jerkin when he moved. It was clear from his body, which was honed by physical action, that this was no idle man. The servant women talked about him oftentimes and called him

'Captain Talyn.' Was he captain of the castle guard? Raven suspected so.

The door opened and servants entered, each carrying buckets of steaming water they dumped into the bathing tub in the corner of the room. Raven skittered back at the noise and hit her head on the bedside table.

Talyn rounded the bed and knelt beside her. He put a hand to her crown, seemingly to soothe her pain, and she forced herself not to shrink from him. "Do you understand a word I say to you?" he murmured, stroking her head like she was a wild animal in need of taming. He inhaled. "Goddess, but you smell good. You smell of the forests and of the sky, even filthy as you are, you still smell of freedom."

As always, his touch did something to her she couldn't explain. She fought the urge to close her eyes and purr at the sensation of his strong fingers trailing over her scalp and catching in her long hair. She let a shuddering sigh escape her.

She'd been aware of this man from the first time she'd seen him. Something about him thrummed through her bloodstream...like a low-level vibration. He was different from the others, but why she knew not.

"Sienne says you're learning our language on your own." He shook his head and smiled. Raven let herself become fascinated with the dimple that popped out on his left cheek. She'd never seen him smile before. "I don't know about that," he continued.

It took all the strength she had to reach up and still the motion of his hand, when really all she wanted was for him to continue stroking her. She took his wrist and pushed it to his chest while meeting his eyes steadily. The symbolism was clear. *Hands off.*

He laughed. "Aye, but you're not simple. I can see intelligence glimmering in the depths of those eyes." He squinted. "Green edged in gold. Most beautiful eyes I've ever seen."

Raven didn't understand why those words pleased her so very much.

He stood. "Come, Raven. Lady Sienne and Lord Marken have put you into my care. Don't ask me why. I never asked for this duty."

She picked up a hank of her hair and inspected it. It was a dull gray when normally it was a black so dark it shined with shades of purple and blue. She hadn't had a bath since the golden man had taken her. That had been almost an entire moon cycle ago. She dropped the tendril and stood. "Fine. I'll…take a…bath." Her mouth wrapped around the strange words carefully and with a noticeable accent—but she was understandable. She had a talent for imitating the sounds others made.

Talyn's jaw dropped and his eyebrows rose.

"Your language is not so" --she frowned searching for the word—"difficult. My native tongue is much harder to learn for one not born to it." The words were coming easier now that her tongue was catching up to her mind. She stepped past him.

The servants had filled the bathing tub and set more candles around the room, brightening it considerably. She walked to the edge of the tub and dipped her finger into the water. She could already imagine the warmth enveloping her, washing away the touch and stench of the golden man.

Grasping her tattered gown at the waist, she shrugged it over her head and let it fall to the floor. The cool air pebbled her skin.

Talyn let out a long, low whistle behind her.

She turned to look at him and frowned. "Your women here often go nearly unclothed. I have seen this and thought it your culture. Have I made an error in undressing before you?"

"Undress in front of me whenever you wish, Raven. Believe me, the pleasure is all mine."

She stood for a moment, feeling his gaze take in her body. Her nipples hardened and a shiver of pleasure ran down her spine. Her body needed this man in ways she didn't understand. She turned back to the bathing tub and stepped in. "My name is not Raven...ahhhh," she finished on a sigh as she sank gratefully into the water. "That is merely what the golden man called me."

"Golden man? Ah. You mean Cyrus." Boots sounded on the floor as he walked to her. "Then what is your name?"

She dribbled water over her shoulders and shrugged. "I have none. There was Grandmother and Granddaughter. We were the only two. No need to call each other anything else." She looked up at him to see if he understood.

"Since I cannot call you Granddaughter" --his eyes flicked down the length of her body— "and nor would I want to. I'd like to call you Raven."

She shrugged and picked up the soap that sat in a little dish on the side of the bathing tub.

He put a finger to her shoulder blade and ran it down one of the long, mottled scars that tracked down each side of her back. "What are these from?" he asked.

Fear rippled through her. He could not know what those scars were from. "How...how did you see those in this nearly darkened room and from so far away?"

"I have excellent vision and can see without much light. Now tell me. What caused these? They look fresh; no less than a month old and it looks like they've been cut open repeatedly. Who did this to you...Cyrus?" He sounded angry.

She glanced at him and then concentrated on lathering the soap between her palms. "They're nothing. You're wrong. They're not fresh...they're very old scars from when I was a child."

"You've got an awful lot of secrets, Raven."

She looked up at him and narrowed her eyes. "Are you going to stay here and watch me bathe?"

He leaned over her and picked up a razor. "I won't leave, not while this is here, nor the water. My lord and lady told me not to let you kill yourself. And since you've got such a penchant for windows, we all know that's what you want to do."

She looked down at the soap she was busy lathering into her hands. "You misunderstand." But she couldn't reveal the real reason she'd twice tried to jump out the castle windows. What if these people were like the others and wanted her because she was the last of her kind? She couldn't take the chance. "You can take the razor. I have no hair to shave. The females of my people grow no hair below the neck, except for...." Her eyes flicked down.

"I noticed that, actually," Talyn bit off. He set the razor down and braced his hand on the opposite side of the tub. The action brought his face near hers. She could smell mint on his breath and the scent of his body. He used some kind of soap that smelled like the woods. She couldn't help it. She inhaled and memories filled her mind. It was almost like going home.

His aura, his energy, whatever it was—the vibration he gave off made her dizzy. Having him so near her was like having him touch her. It made her go passive, made her want to wrap herself in his arms. At the same time she wanted to pull away. Would his hands on her be like Cyrus's hands on her?

"What do you mean we misunderstand?" he asked. "Who are your people?"

Her eyes flew open. She shook her head in place of an answer and began soaping her body. She had to find a way to escape this place before they found out what she was.

His gaze, heated now, followed the path her hands took, leaving a burning trail behind and making her body tighten. "Why were you trying to jump out the windows, then?"

She said nothing, merely scrubbed the soap through her hair, running her fingers over her scalp and massaging away the grit of the last sennight plus a week. She ducked under the water to rinse. When she broke the surface, he was standing.

* * * * *

"You will answer those questions one day, Raven," Talyn threatened softly.

He let his gaze travel slowly over her body as she rinsed herself free of soap and stood. Her breasts were small and pert, with beautiful hard nipples perfect for flicking with his tongue. Her hair, now clean, was a fall of black silk with purple highlights slicked back from a face with high cheekbones, a full pouty mouth, and a sharp chin. He'd been rock hard since she'd shucked her gown off onto the floor.

He grabbed a towel, wound it around her body and rubbed her dry. Every time he touched her she went still. It wasn't a scared kind of still. It was quite obviously from the look of rapture on her face, an *I-want-you-to-touch-me-more* kind of still.

Goddess, and did he want to touch her more.

Lord Marken and Lady Sienne had given Raven into his sole care. He didn't understand why. Nordan was in the beginning stages of the preparation for a war. Sudhra to the south threatened them over religious reasons and in greed over Nordan's plentiful spices and silks. He'd told Marken and Sienne that as captain of the castle guard, he had no time to worry over the care and feeding of a wild woman — much less her taming. Marken and Sienne would have none of his arguments. Raven was his project, and no one else's.

They'd told him that if she were amicable to his touch, he should soothe her with his body within hers. It was said a man's seed could calm an out-of-control woman. Although, now, docile and sweet as she was in his arms, she hardly seemed out-of-control...and she definitely seemed amicable to his touch.

He let his hands massage her breasts through the towel, feeling the hard peaks of her nipples against his fingers. She let out a small sigh and her eyelids fluttered shut—small signs that she enjoyed his touch as much as he enjoyed touching her. He let his hands trail down her stomach, around her waist and over her buttocks.

There seemed to be some kind of energy between them when they touched. A gentle vibration thrummed deep in his blood whenever his bare skin met hers.

He pulled the towel away and he cupped her chin. Her eyes came open. "There's something about touching you, Raven. What is it? Why do you feel different than other women?"

"I...don't know. You feel different to me as well." She bit her bottom lip and he focused on her small white teeth and the bit of succulent looking pink flesh caught between them. All he wanted was to throw her down and slide his rigid cock between her slick folds and ease his painfully hard length within her. It would not be right, however. She was a captive, helpless. He'd be taking advantage of her. Goddess, she seemed innocent. Perhaps she was even a virgin.

"I'll get the fresh gown I brought you," he murmured, releasing her and turning away.

Water splashed and something whooshed past him. He knew without turning what had happened. He ran to the door and slammed a palm against it, pushing it closed just as she'd managed to open it. The front of his body pressed up against the full length of the back of her naked one. He dropped his head, placing his mouth to the delicate shell of her ear. "Going somewhere?"

Her breath came in short little gasps, probably from fear. The vibration they shared heightened considerably when so much of their bodies made contact. It thrummed through him, tightening his cock, priming him for her, tensing his muscles through his arms, shoulders, and chest.

She turned and he let her. It broke their contact and the vibration lessened, but did not fade. He kept his hand palm-flat against the door to prevent her from trying to escape. Having her but a breath's space away from him, looking up at him with those luminous, vulnerable, and beautiful eyes, it was all too easy to imagine her under him on a bed, wrapping those long legs around him, her fingers digging into his shoulders as he eased himself in and out of her tight, wet slit.

"I am captain of the castle guard for a reason. Did you think you'd escape me that easily?" he asked.

She wet her lips, her small, pink tongue darting out momentarily and leaving him with the luscious fantasy of catching it between his own lips. "I had hoped," she murmured.

He slid his hand to her bare waist, immediately feeling the light hum of their connection, merely as a way to gauge her reaction to his touch. She tipped her head back and released a sigh. He leaned down and found her ear. With the tip of his tongue, he traced the whorls down to her lobe and sucked it. "Desperation becomes you," he whispered. "Especially when it puts you naked and in my arms."

She relaxed against him, her fingers finding the hair at the nape of his neck and tangling in it. He breathed her in, smelling the soft lavender-scented cleanliness of her skin and enjoying the constant hum of their contact. He released his hold on the door and wound his other arm around her waist. The other, more secret parts of her body beckoned and he wanted so much to let his hands explore, but she was not ready for such contact.

Like an untried youth, he gritted his teeth against the temptation. For some unfathomable reason this woman gave him a carnal hunger like he'd never experienced. It was as though he didn't have his pick of women in the castle to choose from and Raven was the only one.

Allowing his lips to skim over the still damp skin of her chin and cheek, he sought her mouth. His lips brushed hers gently, and then sought a hungrier contact. Her hand slipped between their bodies and pushed, and her knee came up and connected with his solar plexus in the same smooth movement. The air whooshed out of him and sharp pain blossomed. He doubled over, holding his stomach and thanking the Goddess she hadn't aimed lower.

She went for the door and, still doubled over, he reached out and caught her wrist. "I don't think so," he ground out.

She tried to wrench her wrist from his grasp, attempting to open the door with her other hand. A desperate keening sound issued from her throat. Talyn straightened and yanked her back away from the door with one movement and into his arms—like some strange dance step.

"You try my patience, Raven," he said. But with a helpless sounding whimper, she had gone passive against him. Her struggles ceased, and she merely tucked her head in the crook between his shoulder and chin and remained still, her breath hot and harsh against his neck. He almost forgave her for the knee to the stomach.

A night wrap lay over a chair near him. He reached out and caught it up, then pulled it over her shoulders. With a couple murmured words of encouragement, he guided her toward the chair by the fire. He spotted a comb on the way, and moved to pick it up, intending to untangle her wet hair. As soon his body separated from hers, she whirled on him, catching the short sword sheathed at his side. With a ringing hiss it came free of its scabbard.

She angled the blade out in front of her, both hands on the grip. "Don't touch me," she snarled. "Get out and leave me alone."

Talyn raised his hands in a gesture of surrender. She made an entrancing picture, wet, naked, and wielding a blade. He raised an eyebrow. "Fine, I'll leave...for now. But you can forget about me not touching you. Touching you is all I want to do."

She took a step closer, making a slicing motion through the air with the blade. "Do it at your own risk." Her voice quavered. "I'm not here to be your personal toy. Cyrus tried to use me that way too."

Talyn shook his head, "I'm not Cyrus." He stepped forward until the blade touched his throat. "And you don't fool me, Raven. You couldn't cut me. It isn't in your nature."

She pressed and a drop of hot blood welled and traveled down his throat. "Assumptions can be deadly."

Talyn spoke the truth from his heart. "Then do it, Raven. I don't care. Cut my throat and you'll have your freedom. There's no one to stop you on the other side of that door, and I don't have anything to lose by dying."

Her gaze darkened and darted from his face to the door and back again. She stared into his eyes and he watched her gaze harden. For a moment he really thought she would slash his throat. With a strangled cry, she dropped the blade to the floor and turned away from him.

Talyn reached down and sheathed his sword. He stood for a moment watching her delicate shoulders shake as she cried. He took a step toward her, but decided the last thing she wanted was comfort from her captor and left the room, locking the door from the outside. Until he knew more about this woman, and knew she would not hurt herself if set free, there would be no way he'd let her go.

* * * * *

Rue finished rubbing his horse down and, after one last check of the hunting equipment secured in a bundle at the base of a nearby tree, turned toward the fire in the center of his campsite. Flames licked the black air and sent sparks up into the star-strewn sky. A breeze blew through the treetops, making them creak and sway and causing the rustling sounds of leaves to join with the crack and snap of the fire. Rue closed his eyes and inhaled the scents of pine, earth, and fresh, fresh air.

His traveling companion, Gavin, rested against a fallen log, one long leg outstretched, the other bent at an angle. They'd met each other where the borders of Kappan and Sinha Priestdoms touched, both traveling the dusty road south from Sudhra into Nordan to the north. They'd decided to travel together to share the spoils of their hunting and for a bit of company.

Rue walked over to the campfire, his boots crunching on the rock and gravel-strewn area, and picked up a joint of rabbit that had been cooking over the fire. He sat down and bit into it, savoring the salty, sweet meat that filled his mouth.

"So you never said exactly why you're heading up to Marken's Lorddom," Gavin said by way of inquiry.

Rue swallowed his mouthful and met Gavin's clear brown gaze. Gavin had seemingly honest eyes, but Rue didn't trust anyone...*ever*. "There might be something there I need to have," he answered simply. He wasn't about to divulge his secrets and plans to this man. "Why are you headed up there?" he asked so Gavin didn't probe any more into his own affairs.

Gavin heaved a sigh and looked up to the treetops. "When I heard about Lord Cyrus being killed in Marken's Lorddom and how his men battled with Cyrus's thanes, I knew then that Sudhra would wage war against Nordan. "

Rue took a bite of rabbit and spoke around it. "So, what? You're fleeing?" He didn't bother to keep the derision from his voice. He tossed the rabbit haunch, now gleaned of all its meat, into the fire where it popped and snapped.

The other man turned his head and gazed at him coolly. For the first time, Rue saw a hint of the icy steel that lay beyond the other man's seemingly amiable exterior. "I'm not fleeing," he answered evenly. "I don't fear battle. I just decided I was on the wrong side, that's all. I'm going to Nordan to fight. If you have a problem with that, we can part ways now."

Rue held up his hands. "All right. I'm sorry I misjudged you. I'm offering Lord Marken my services as well." He shrugged. "I'll fight for Sudhra, Nordan, for whatever nobleman will pay the most for my skills."

Rue looked into the fire and went silent. Like Gavin, he, too, had decided to travel to Nordan after hearing of Lord Cyrus's untimely demise. Rue knew that Cyrus had been in the northern reaches of Nordan looking for something, a thing Rue also coveted. Had Cyrus found it?

Was it still in the northern forests? Could it be residing in Marken's Lorddom even now? Rue didn't know.

The hilt of his hunting knife jabbed into his waist and Rue pulled it free. The wickedly sharp edge of it glinted in the firelight. He laid it on the ground in front of him.

All he knew was that he'd find it, master it, and possess it. No matter the cost.

* * * * *

Talyn knocked on Raven's door. Over his arm hung a gown he'd had made for her. During the past week Raven had been subdued and uncommunicative — as determined as ever to keep her secrets. Haeffen, Lord Marken's chief adviser, had been scouring the old texts for some hint of her origins, but had found nothing thus far. Talyn had decided it was time to lay to rest the negativity that existed between them and had brought a peace offering.

Raven called out and he entered. He walked into the room and stopped short, memories of long ago, when he'd been a captive here, flooding through him. She sat on the bed, propped up with pillows and her long legs tucked beneath her. Her skin had been growing paler with every passing day over the last week. A vacant expression oftentimes shone in her eyes. Now she stared at the fire and did not even note his entrance.

He knew how she felt, what she was thinking. When it had been himself locked away in this castle as a child, he'd wanted nothing more than to feel the sun on his face, the wind in his hair. He'd known that longing to the center of his bones. Talyn felt a strange kind of attraction to her that had less to do with sex and more to do with the commonality of their pasts. Talyn had been thinking more about his shadowed, mysterious past than ever in his life since Raven had arrived. She'd inadvertently brought all the ghosts out from the shadows to wreak their havoc.

He cleared his throat and she turned to look at him listlessly, a blank expression on her face.

Jerking his head to the side, he indicated her untouched breakfast. "Why do you not eat?"

She shrugged. "I haven't been hungry."

Goddess, she looked like she'd lost weight and with such a slender body, that was not a healthy thing. Talyn knew what she needed to the center of his being. He hesitated for a moment, and then walked toward her. "Come with me."

Her brows furrowed in bewilderment. "Where?"

"Let's take a walk, just you and me. It's beautiful outside today. Spring is here and all the snow has melted. Flowers are poking their head through Aran's soil, and you could use a little wind blowing through that fall of hair of yours."

Hope blossomed on her face, but was quickly supplanted by suspicion. "Aren't you afraid I'll escape?"

"Oh, you might try, but you won't succeed. Not with me by your side." He extended his hand.

For a few moments, she regarded his hand as though it were a snake, then unfurled her legs from beneath her and climbed off the bed. "Fine. Just don't touch me."

He offered the gown. "I've brought you a present."

She eyed the clothing. "Why did you do such a thing? Lady Sienne has presented me with many gowns."

"I wanted you to have something I'd given you."

"Thank you," she said quietly. A trace of a smile touched her lips. She reached out to touch the soft material, then snatched her hand back. She gazed up at him warily. "Lay it on the bed."

He did so, and she pulled her gown over her head, letting it settle to the floor at her feet. Firelight licked at her luscious round breasts and dark nipples, and cast long shadows on her stomach, hips, and buttocks.

Talyn swallowed. Goddess but he wanted her. She was like some forbidden piece of fruit he could never taste. He wanted to tumble her down on the bed right now, spread her legs and lick her clit until she shuddered in release beneath him.

She caught the gown off the bed with a smooth movement and slipped it over her head. The green flax-cloth was nearly transparent, showing the dark shadow of her areolas and revealing the hills and valleys of her body. The hem and the edges of the sleeves were edged in gold.

"It matches your eyes," he pointed out.

"It's beautiful, but what do I do with these?" She flapped her arms, indicating the sleeves that had an extra length of material attached to the back of the cuff, which were so long they touched the floor.

He picked them up and brought them around to her back. "It's a fashion for ladies here in Marken's Lorddom. They're called angel wings." He fastened the material to small buttons at the small of her back, completing the effect.

"W...wings?"

"Aye. See how your hands and arms are free to move, but at the same time your sleeves are attached to the back of the dress?"

"Yes."

"Wings."

"Oh." Raven flapped her arms. "Not as good as the real thing."

Talyn laughed. "Probably not. Doubt we'll ever know. Now, shall we show your gown off to the rest of the castle?" Unthinkingly, he took her by the elbow. The vibrational response always present when they touched sang lightly through his blood.

She gasped and pulled free of him. "Don't touch me."

"All right. I'm sorry. I won't touch you, as long you don't try anything while we're on our walk. Agreed?"

She eyed him warily. "Agreed."

He walked to the door. "Then let's go."

He ushered her out the room and Raven squinted at the bright light of early afternoon. He led her down the corridors that would take them out of the castle and into the inner bailey. As they walked, their feet crushed the haffberry rushes, sending up a sweet scent. The sunlight lit the gray stone walls and the unlit tapers in their scones. Talyn showed her different parts of the castle, and explained what life in Nordan was like.

Men, Talyn noticed uneasily, watched Raven wherever they went. Some emotion close to anger rose up in him every time a man looked at her with a covetous expression on his face. When he examined that unfamiliar emotion closer and discovered it was jealousy, he was not happy.

Why should he feel jealous over this woman? She was not his to feel thus about. Why should he even want her when he had more than enough access to women as it was? Talyn pushed a hand through his hair in frustration.

The open double doors leading to the inner bailey came into view. "Oh, sweet Aran," Raven breathed beside him. He looked over at her and saw that she'd stopped in the middle of the corridor and closed her eyes. Her arms stretched out on either side of her, she took deep breaths of the sweet spring air that gusted through the doors into her lungs. The breeze molded her gown to her body, showing it in beautiful detail.

Talyn took several steps toward her before he'd realized he'd done it. When he was a breath's space from her, her eyes popped open. She took a step back and then another until she was against the stone wall behind her. He put his hands on either side of her head. His chest almost brushed her nipples and he watched, fascinated, as they hardened at the near contact. He bent his head and brought his lips close to hers. She exhaled and he caught her breath against his lips.

"You said you wouldn't touch me," she said shakily.

"I'm not touching you, Raven. I'm only thinking about touching you and wondering what your sweet clit and passage taste like." His eyes flicked down. "Not to mention your nipples."

She exhaled again. This time there was a catch in her throat. Her eyes darkened with something Talyn knew well — desire. His cock grew harder at the sight.

He pushed away from the wall and dragged a ragged breath into his lungs. "Come on."

Tentatively, she picked her way around him and walked toward the door.

* * * * *

The fresh air bathed her flushed face and calmed her blood. Still, Raven's hands trembled from her close contact with Talyn. Every night since they'd nearly kissed she'd

168

dreamt of him. In those dreams he worked her body like it was a musical instrument, drawing sounds of passion from her throat. She'd awoken drenched in perspiration, her core throbbing with need, her nipples so hard they hurt. Every time he touched her, she wanted more from him. But she would not present her body like a gift to the man who kept her imprisoned.

Her eyes darted around the place he'd called the inner bailey. Always she searched for a hill, an incline, a window, anywhere steep enough that she could launch herself into the air and let her wings unfurl. Only tall stone walls met her gaze everywhere she looked. A well stood in the center of the sand strewn ground and men led horses from the gates leading to the outer bailey to the stables.

Talyn came to stand next to her.

"Grass? Flowers? Are any near here?" She hated the desperation in her voice.

"This way."

She followed him around the corner of the castle and a garden met her searching gaze. It stretched the entire southern side of the castle. She knelt in the thick grass and brushed her fingertips over the new spring blooms that shivered delicately in the air.

He knelt beside her. "You greet the flowers cordially."

She shot him a sharp look. "I am used to being close to nature and do not deal well with captivity. Especially when I have done nothing wrong. Nothing except be abducted, abused, and forced to watch my only living relative die."

"I am sorry about your grandmother."

Raven picked at the grass and blinked back tears.

"You are only being held so that you will not hurt yourself. I need to know where you come from, Raven, so that we may help you get back to your people. You must admit you have treated us more as enemies than as friends. Believe me, we are friends."

Friends. Her people, the Aviat, had no friends. They only had hunters. Her entire race had been hunted to extinction. With herself, the Aviat died, according to Grandmother. "You know not what you say," she replied bitterly.

"I do. I, too, was a captive here once, much like you. I was young. I had only about six years behind me. But I remember being locked here vividly. I also sought any method of escape, and fought those who would have prevented me from endangering myself."

She looked at him. "Where did you come from and how did you come to be here?"

Talyn shrugged. "I don't know. Lord Marken's foster father Lord Fallon found me while he was hunting in the forest. It was late fall. I was locked in a cage and half-starved. My captors lay dead about half a mile away, slaughtered by a band of thieves. Lord Fallon brought me back here and Haeffen, Marken's advisor, took care of me like I am taking care of you."

"You don't remember your family? Your people?"

"No."

"And you stayed here?"

"I had nowhere else to go, Raven. I did not speak Nordanese, though I do not know what I spoke. I was so traumatized by what my abductors had done that I lost both my memory and my language. I suspect those men killed my family, though."

She looked down at the grass. "Then you and I have some things in common," she said softly.

"Hold your palm up, Raven."

She looked up him. "Why?"

"I won't touch you. Just hold it up."

She complied and he placed his palm as close as he could to hers without touching it. She noted how small her hand looked compared to his. The vibration crackled and danced between their hands, massaging her skin with restrained energy.

He caught and held her gaze. "Aye, I'd say we've got some things in common."

Chapter Two

Don't leave." Saria, one of Talyn's favorites caught his arm as he walked toward the exit of the common hall. Her blond ringleted hair cascaded over her shoulders. A shimmering and transparent gold flax-cloth dress sheathed her, revealing her tempting body for all to see.

"I cannot talk now. I must take my leave, Saria. I've things to attend to."

Saria sniffed. "Is one of those things the wild woman?" Undisguised jealousy flavored her tone. "You've been spending a lot of time with that one. I've heard she's completely dumb, can only grunt, will not eat, and throws things at the servants. I've heard her hair is always tangled and she's—"

"Enough! Saria, do you truly put stock in that gossip? I thought you more intelligent than that." Her lower lip protruded slightly at the rebuke, and he immediately felt guilty for snapping at her. "How is Alia?" he asked.

"She's fine. She is with the nannies in the children's wing." Her expression brightened. "She turns three on the morrow."

"I will come by later to see her, and I will bring a trinket for her birthday," said Talyn.

"She will like that. You are one of her favorite visitors." She walked to him and traced the line of his shoulder with a finger. "As you are one of mine. I think you are Alia's father."

"I would be proud if I were." Saria said that often, but in reality, there was no way to know. Since it was so hard to conceive children, women mated with many different men. There was no way to know the fathers of any of the children, and it simply did not matter. All the children were raised communally, with many "fathers" and "mothers."

She jerked her head at the room where some had fallen to the erotic activity of sampling each other's bodies. Open sex play was a part of Nordanese culture. Across the room a man had a woman in a chair. Her legs were spread and he was busy thrusting his cock into her.

"It's been over a week since you've lain with me," Saria pouted. "Ever since the wild woman came, you've not come to me."

Saria walked over and sat on the bench flanking the table and spread her own legs, her hand dipping down to caress the blond hair of her mound through her gown. She crooked a finger at him.

Talyn took a step toward her, his body responding automatically. Images of Raven flooded his mind. He'd wanted to rut like a stag in mating season ever since his near kiss with Raven. She had heated his blood, infected it with herself. Her scent teased his nostrils at all hours of the day, even when she was absent. The feel of her soft skin was constantly on his mind. She even plagued him at night in his dreams. In those, he could kiss her and touch her as much as he wished and she allowed him that, sighing under his hands and spreading her legs for his hard cock.

He could not have her in his waking days since the woman would not even let him touch her, and he would never force her. So, for the last week, he'd tried to fill his longing with other women. But every time he kissed another woman, his mind filled with Raven's face and he could go no further. She was the cure to his obsession, but he could not have her.

Instead of going to Saria, he sank onto the bench beside her and cradled his head in his hands. He was doomed.

The shift of flax-cloth signaled that Saria had straightened. She touched his back. "What is wrong with you, Talyn? I have not seen you take another woman in over a week. Has your blade lost its edge?"

He looked up sharply at that. "Is what they're saying?"

Saria shrugged. "You have been as a monk these past days. What else is there to think? You of all the men in the castle, except for perhaps Lord Marken himself, have the hardest, most eager cock. Aye, people are wondering."

It was not that he didn't want to take a woman. It wasn't that his cock had grown soft. Nay, nothing at all like that. It was simply that he couldn't take another woman when the only one that would satisfy him was Raven.

Goddess be damned! He'd always prided himself on his ability to select from the finest women in the castle and pleasure many in a night!

It was time to put an end to this! He wanted Raven out of his blood so he could go back to things as they had been before her arrival. He already knew that Raven wanted him as much he wanted her, but she had erected barriers against him. He was through being nice. It was time to wage a war and pull those barriers down.

He didn't bother to knock before he unlocked the door and entered. She'd been sitting by the fire and now she sprang from the chair. He didn't break stride, but simply closed the distance between them with a look on his face that must've said doom.

She stumbled over the chair. The skirt of her long, pale rose-colored gown bunched between her legs, impeding her movement. He stalked her like she was wounded prey. She finally backed herself up against the wall and held one hand in front of her. "Don't come any closer!"

He pretended he hadn't heard her and didn't stop his relentless stride. He took both her wrists in his hands and pressed them against the wall behind her. His mouth hovered close to hers. "I'm at my wit's end, my lady." He pressed his hips into her stomach so she could feel his erection press into her warm, soft skin. He groaned. "I can't go a day without thinking of all the ways I want to make you scream with pleasure, all the positions I want to put you in to best facilitate the slide of my cock into your slick pussy. I can't sleep at night without thinking about it. I can't even take another woman for the want of you. What am I supposed to do about that?"

Raven's eyelids fluttered, then her gaze steadied. Her tongue slipped out to wet her lips and he watched it with a hungry gaze. "I don't know...find a sheep?" Her beautiful mouth curved into a smile.

He pressed his body against hers so she couldn't knee him and rubbed his chest against her breasts, making sure he gave her nipples a proper amount of friction. His lips skimmed her cheek and came to rest a breath's space from her mouth. Her smile faded and her breath caught. "You want me even if you act like you don't. Your body betrays you."

She glanced away, visibly steeled herself, and then found his eyes. "You don't know what you're talking about. All I want is for you not to touch me. Every time you do, I...."

"What?"

"I...."

"What, woman?"

"I...want you to touch me more," she admitted softly.

Her words heated his blood to boiling. "How do you want me to touch you, Raven? Tell me. I'll touch you any way you want me to."

She pressed her mouth into a thin line as though forcing herself not to speak. He kissed her taut lips, and she made a surprised sound in her throat. He flicked at her lower lip until she softened them, and then he went in for the kill. Her body remained tense, but as he slipped his tongue between her lips and stroked it up against hers, she went limp with a shudder and sighed into his mouth.

* * * * *

Raven was aware of Talyn releasing her wrists, but not of much more save his mouth on hers. His lips worked in tandem with hers like some erotic piece of music. He angled his head for deeper access to her mouth, his hands going to either side of her cheeks to cup her face and a shiver of pleasure ran up her spine.

She wanted this man more than she'd ever wanted anything. Raven frowned. She just wasn't sure *how* she wanted him. She knew it had something to do with the long, hard length of him, the thing he called a cock, and her own weeping passage...but beyond that, she wasn't sure. All she knew was that she wanted more.

Damn him for making her want more! He was her captor, and she his captive—not his personal plaything. Indignation rose within her every bit as hard and hot as her passion and the two feelings warred within her.

Her breasts ached for his hands and her nipples stood at attention. He dropped a hand to her breast and rubbed his thumb over one of her aching nipples. Her lips stilled against his as she absorbed the exquisite feel of his hand on her.

Then memories of Cyrus flooded her mind, made her suck in a surprised breath. For a moment it was Cyrus's hands that pinched and grabbed, not Talyn's masterful strokes over her nipple. It was Cyrus's breath that soured the air, not Talyn's mint-scented exhalations bathing her lips.

Raven pushed Talyn away and closed her arms over her breasts in a protective gesture. She sank to the floor.

Talyn went to his knees beside her. "What's wrong? Your face has gone pale." He reached out to touch her arm and she recoiled.

She shook her head. "Don't touch me." She drew a shuddering sigh. "It's true that I want your hands on me, but just now when you touched me I saw Cyrus's face—felt his hands on my body." She shuddered.

He withdrew his hand and fisted it. "That bastard. I can only imagine what he did to you."

Raven struggled to stand. She pressed a hand to her temple. "*Please*," she implored.

"I am not Cyrus, and I would never force you, Raven. In Nordan it is against the Goddess's law to force a woman. In Sudhra, the country we are nearly at war with, it is condoned. Cyrus took you to become a sex slave, Raven. You were to be used by men in Sudhra for their pleasure. Here, in Nordan, things are different. It would be beautiful between us. I can help you find completion and joy."

Completion... that's what she wanted from him. But not while images of Cyrus flashed through her mind when he touched her.

A knock at the door startled them both. Raven peered around Talyn to see a soldier's head peek in the room. "Captain," he queried uncertainly.

Talyn muttered a heartfelt oath under his breath and turned. "Yes?"

"Lord Marken bade me find you. You're wanted in the receiving chamber."

"Thank you," replied Talyn. The guardsman left and shut the door behind him.

He turned back to her. "I must--"

"Please, just go," she cut him off.

"We're not through with this discussion, Raven."
"*Go!*"

His boots clicking on the stone floor signaled his compliance with her request. The lock on the door slid home.

And emptiness rose up to swallow her.

* * * * *

Talyn adjusted his crotch as he strode down the corridor leading out to the receiving chamber. Goddess!

He'd been so close to tumbling her down onto the bed and easing this ache of her out of him.

He slammed the door of the receiving chamber open and strode within. Lord Marken and Lady Sienne sat in two chairs upon the dais. Two strangers, both with short hair in the way of Sudhra stood before them. Guardsmen lined the sides of the chamber. He raised an eyebrow. Something interesting was underway.

Talyn's gaze went to Lady Sienne. He had wanted her so badly before Marken had claimed her as his monogamous mate. Her dark red hair cascaded over her slim shoulders and her pale green eyes regarded him as he stalked toward Marken.

She'd come at the beginning of the winter as a sex slave from Sudhra. Never having experienced pleasure at a man's hands, Marken had vowed to train her to enjoy sex. He'd succeeded, and in turn Sienne had taught Marken to love her so much he'd forsaken all other women.

Talyn thought Marken's brain had simply turned to mush.

His eyes flicked down to his mistress's full breasts peeking through a gown made partially of silver flax-cloth. His mind wandered to Raven and he thought how nice she would look in such a gown. Talyn pushed a hand through his hair. "Goddess!" The exclamation flew from his lips before he even knew he'd uttered it. Was she to be constantly on his mind?

Lord Marken stood, his loose long black hair shifting over his broad shoulders. "Are you all right, Captain Talyn?"

Talyn came to halt in front of the dais, his gaze flicking quickly to the two strangers standing not far away. He bowed. "All is fine, my lord. Please forgive my outburst."

Marken's eyebrows knit. Talyn had known Marken since childhood. Even though Marken was his lord, he was also his friend and undoubtedly knew that all was *not* fine.

"We were sorry to disturb you," said Sienne in her cool, melodious voice. "We knew you were probably occupied with our mysterious guest from the north, Raven."

Talyn bowed deeply to her before speaking. "I was indeed, my lady."

All went silent as Marken regarded him. Talyn shifted uncomfortably from one foot to the other. "And all is well?" asked Marken again.

"Completely," he responded.

"Very well. I would like you to meet two guests from the south," Marken motioned to the two strangers. "This is Rue of Kappan Priestdom of Sudhra." He indicated the blond man. "And this is Gavin of Sinha Priestdom, also of Sudhra." He extended a hand toward the tall, black-haired man.

Talyn gave them both a quick once over. Rue was a tall, broad-shouldered man, obviously a warrior. His skin was deeply tanned and his blond hair was short and slightly spiky on the top. Rue's cool, intelligent light blue eyes regarded him from a face he was sure would make many of the castle's women swoon.

Gavin was tall with thick, coal-black hair that barely brushed the collar of the brown tunic he wore. He sported a broad chest, strong arms, and eyes so dark a brown they were nearly black. He was also obviously cut from a warrior's cloth.

Marken sat back down. "Rue, Gavin, this is Talyn, the captain of my guard."

"Thank you, Captain Talyn," they said in unison, bowing.

"Rue and Gavin say they have left Sudhra and would like to join in our ranks in the coming war," said Marken. He glanced at Talyn. "They will be housed in the castle for the time being and will report for duty in the guard on the morrow. All will be done according to *proper protocol,* Captain Talyn."

Talyn knew what that meant. These two would be watched carefully and research would be done on their stories. No trust would be given until they'd proved themselves. "Very well, my lord."

Talyn turned to regard the two men, suspicion coursing through him. "And why have you taken such a drastic step?"

Gavin cleared his throat and stepped forward. "Captain, my father was Nordanese, my mother Sudhraian. I was raised in the tradition of the Goddess and never pledged my allegiance to Sudhra, though I was born and raised there. With this coming war...with my homeland pledging to stamp out the Goddess and erect their own God, planning to enslave the Nordanese men in the spice mines and the woman to sex, I find I cannot spill blood for them." He shook his head. "I cannot fight for that and I...I" --he put his fisted hand to his chest— "am a warrior. Since I cannot pledge my sword to Sudhra, I will instead pledge my sword to Nordan."

Talyn studied the man through narrowed eyes. His expression and voice seemed earnest, but that was not enough to compel Talyn to trust him.

Rue stepped forward and spoke in a bored tone, one hand resting idly on the hilt of the short sword sheathed at his waist. "I am not here for any high-minded principles, captain." He cast a glance at Gavin. "I am here simply because my sword can be hired for a price to the highest bidder. I am a blooded warrior with special combat skills. The stories are told everywhere the amount of money Lord Marken paid Cyrus for his monogamous mate, the Lady Sienne. I feel sure he will pay for the precious information I have to impart, and for the skill with which I can dispatch your enemies."

"What of your religion, Rue? Do you not follow the Sudhraian God? Religion is in large part what this war will be fought over," said Marken.

"Religion is a lie told in the fog. It's untrue, but you cannot see it." He shook his head once. "I have no religion."

"Why should we trust you?" asked Talyn. "You could be here selling disinformation and be gathering our information to sell back your Master Priest in Sudhra for all we know."

Rue sighed. "Fine. I'll be blunt. I am hunting something, Captain Talyn. You have something in your northern forests I want—a very rare creature. Lord Cyrus was looking for it when he so suddenly met his demise." Rue looked at Sienne and she paled. "I thank you for cleansing Aran of that scum, my lady." Rue turned his attention to Marken. "I request permission to hunt your northern forests for this game I seek. In return, I will furnish you with information."

"What kind of game is it?" Talyn asked.

Rue flashed a feral smile. "A very rare bird, captain. A very valuable one, at least to me."

"What is the bird called," asked Sienne.

"I fear I do not wish to speak too much of them, my lady," answered Rue. "I fear describing the unique and beautiful creatures would give me too much competition in my hunt. "

"You must if we are to give you permission to hunt it, Lord Rue," Sienne's voice had gone steely and Talyn noted then how much she'd grown in such a short amount time from the timid sex slave she'd been. Amazing how love could transform a person.

Rue opened his mouth and hesitated before speaking. "I seek a creature called an Aviat, my lady."

Chapter Three

Talyn fingered the stem of his wine-filled goblet and fought the melancholy that had threatened to overcome him since shortly after Raven had arrived. His past was mostly a blur to him, but he could remember being in a cage, dirty, confused and uncomprehending of the Nordanese his captors spoke. He remembered feeling alone and frightened. Much like Raven undoubtedly now felt.

For the past week, Raven had fended off every overture of friendship he'd made toward her. Every day, he would visit her and she would keep herself far from him, not allowing him to come close to her, or touch her. All attempts to find out more about her, to determine what she meant to do once she had the freedom she so desperately sought, had failed.

He raised the goblet to his lips and drank deep. He was becoming frustrated.

"What's the matter, Talyn?" asked Lord Marken as he sat down at the table beside him. A servant instantly found and filled a goblet for him. "Is it the war...or the woman?"

Talyn rose from the table and bowed before sitting back down. "My lord," he acknowledged. "The woman. How did you know?"

He shrugged and took a drink of wine. "Women have the capacity to make even the strongest warrior fall to their knees in grief, betimes. Tell me what is wrong."

"Beyond the fact that the woman will not cooperate, there is something about her that calls to me of my past." He fisted his hands. "There is something special about this woman, but I cannot discover what it is. She plagues me. During the day I think of her, and she haunts my dreams even at night."

"The woman is beautiful, mysterious and unattainable. You, of all the men in the castle, have had no trouble finding women to fill your bed. Now there is one who has resisted your advances. That resistance must make her all the more desirable to you, no?"

"It's more than that." He toyed with his goblet. "Has Haeffen been able to discover anything about her?"

Marken shook his head. "He still searches through the old records. We know little of the few peoples who live far to the north. They are secretive and tribal. Many of them are now extinct because of starvation, war, and other disasters. Many times they wouldn't record any history of themselves."

"So it falls to her to tell us. Did you tell him of her strange ability to quickly learn languages?"

"I did, Talyn. We await the results of his reading."

Talyn downed the rest of his wine and fell silent.

"You must earn her trust," said Marken. "I remember when they first brought you in. You were the same age as I—both about six summers."

"I remember, but they are not happy memories."

"I remember how long your hair was, how matted. And I remember how dirty you were and caked with blood from beatings at the hands of your captors. Your arm was broken and the castle physician had to break it again simply to reset it. It took Haeffen weeks and weeks to earn your trust enough so that a servant could so much as touch you."

Talyn remembered all too well and wondered why Marken was making him recall such painful memories. He opened his mouth to change the subject, but Marken spoke first.

"Do you remember how Haeffen earned your trust?" Marken asked.

Talyn shut his mouth. In his mind, he went back all those years ago. He was cold and frightened and he lived for one thing only—to escape and feel the wind on his face. Haeffen had stayed with him day and night. He'd even slept in the same room with him, rolled up on a pallet near the fireplace while Talyn had slept comfortably in the bed. When nightmares had woken Talyn from his sleep, which had been a frequent occurrence, Haeffen had been there to soothe him. Little by little Talyn had come to understand that Haeffen and the others in the castle were not like the ones who'd kept him before. He'd finally understood that they meant him well, not ill. Finally, Haeffen had set him free. *That* had been the thing that had finally won him over.

"He did it by spending time with me, by caring about me," Talyn answered finally.

"Perhaps that is what you need to do with this woman. Do not leave her side. Let her become accustomed to your presence."

Talyn gripped his goblet. Marken didn't understand how this woman affected him. He'd be happier away from her altogether when she initiated such a wide and painful array of emotions within him. "Do you not need me to help the men prepare for the war with Sudhra, my lord? Already I split my time between the guard and the woman. If I do what you are suggesting, I will have no time but for the female."

Marken leaned forward. "Sudhra has made no advance in our direction yet. Right now our two countries lay like coiled snakes, waiting to see who will attack first. You know this already, Talyn. I have sent men to gather intelligence and soon we will know more. For the time being, I can spare you from the guard. I think dealing with this woman is a good thing for you. Sienne believes so as well. She says you fight demons within yourself and the woman might help you defeat them. Sienne believes dealing with those demons will make you a better captain."

Talyn raised an eyebrow. "Does she now?"

"I promised once long ago to make up the loss of Sienne to you. This is my gift. Seduce Raven, Talyn. Show her pleasure at your hands. Get her to trust you and maybe soon we can set her free knowing she will not injure herself. Slake the need you so obviously have for her. Then, if you are able, you can forget about her and go back to your duties with the guard."

Talyn stood and bowed. "The sooner this is over, the better. You are wise, my lord."

He took his leave and headed straight for Raven's chamber. Marken was right, as always. He could slake his need of Raven and at the same time, he could get her to trust him if he showed her pleasure at his hands.

He slipped into her room, which was lighted throughout with candles. A merry fire burned in the hearth, chasing away early spring's chill. Creeping up to her bedside, he saw that she slept deeply. One hand rested over her abdomen and her chest rose with the cadence of a deep foray into the realm of dream.

A smile touched his lips. How innocent and peaceful she looked in sleep. She lay on her back and her small, slender feet were bare. The nightdress she wore was not of transparent flax-cloth, but made of cream-colored opaque linen. Buttons ran down the front of it. His fingers strayed out to play with the top one. It would be so easy to slip them open and free those luscious breasts he'd seen when she bathed.

* * * * *

Strong hands massaged her breasts. Fingertips raked over her distended nipples and teased and pinched gently. Raven sighed and settled back into the pillows to enjoy. In her dream, Talyn filled his hands with her breasts, telling her in his low, sexy voice how beautiful she was. A low, thrumming ache began between her legs. She tossed her head back and forth and moaned deep in her throat. She wanted more. She wanted him to slip his hand down and massage away the ache at the juncture of her thighs. She wanted some unnamable, unknowable thing.

She slid her own hand down when he continued rubbing her nipples with his calloused thumb pads. Her hand traveled past her stomach before Talyn stopped her, pressing her wrists onto the bed. Then his palm planed her lower abdomen and dipped lower, and lower…until…*yes…right there*. She moaned and gripped the blankets on either side of her, spreading her legs for this welcome invasion of her sex.

His finger stroked her folds through the material of her nightdress. He found the exact source of her ache and circled it around and around until she bucked, her toes curling at the delicious sensations just one of his fingers could give her.

He stroked and massaged her clit until pleasure spiraled up and up, then exploded. It blossomed and spread out, consuming her. She'd already been wet, but now moisture bathed her sex anew. Exquisite contractions and spasms rocked her core. She arched her back and cried out, coming fully awake. When her eyes opened, it was to a real, waking life Talyn as he watched her with hungry eyes set in his lean face. She came to the swift realization that it hadn't been a dream.

She gasped and backed away from him on her hands and feet, retreating back against the pillows of the bed. Her hand flew to the bodice of her gown where he'd undone many buttons. "What did you do to me?"

"I gave you pleasure, Raven. I brought you to peak."

Her brow furrowed. She'd never known such a sensation. She'd craved contact with a male for many years, but she'd never expected it to be anything like that. In her sudden curiosity, she forgot to be angry. "Did...you just mate with me?"

"You really are an innocent aren't you, Raven? When I mate with you, there won't be any question in your mind."

"If that was not mating, what was it?"

"A simple act. My gift to you. Although I will not say I didn't also think it a gift to myself. Watching you, and especially touching you, was quite...nice. I gave you pleasure, but we did not mate."

Surprise finally melted into swiftly rising anger. She grasped the nearest thing to her and threw it at him. "Good! Because if we mate, I want to be conscious."

The pillow bounced off his chest and landed on the floor. He laughed and it made her brows draw together and her jaw set. "Did you not enjoy it?" he asked.

Raven glowered at him. Of course she'd enjoyed it. She'd never felt anything more glorious in her life. It made her want other things. *What* other things she wasn't sure of, specifically. She narrowed her eyes at him. "You already know the answer to that question."

He took a step toward her and, without removing her eyes from him, her fingers sought out and gripped another pillow. "I could show you more ways a man can give pleasure to a woman, and vice versa," he said.

"Don't touch me again," she spat, but her words quivered with the slightest bit of uncertainty.

"Are you sure, Raven?" He took another careful step forward. "You don't sound sure." He was close enough to touch her now — far too close for her comfort. "I can banish all your thoughts of Cyrus and replace them with much more pleasant ones. Let me."

She hurled the pillow at him in response and scrambled over the bed, seeking to put the huge piece of furniture safely between them. A strong hand clamped over her ankle. Laying face down, she let out a cry of rage and grasped the bedcovers as that hand pulled her belly-down and inexorably over the bed toward him.

His hard body came down on top of hers gently. The low, sweet hum of their connection coursed through her blood. Talyn groaned and let out a string of curses under his breath. He pinned her wrists to the bed on either side of her and put his mouth close to her ear. Speaking in a low, velvet rasp he said, "There is no shame in admitting you want me, Raven." He thrust his hips and she gasped at the hard erection pushing between her buttocks. "I can admit I want you. There is no shame in the coming together of a man and a woman. We would share ourselves in pleasure."

He released his grip on her wrists, but she didn't move. She hated the fact that he knew she wouldn't fight him. Shifting to his side, he massaged the muscles of her back, running his fingers over her shoulder blades in circles and then making wide sweeps lower, petting her, calming her. He brushed her thick hair to one side and laid his lips to the nape of her neck while his hand stroked her buttocks, his fingers delving between her legs and brushing her sex.

Raven's breathing, which had been short and shallow, evened out. She closed her eyes and allowed herself the enjoyment of another person's hands on her, the intimacy of their contact—but fought the heartfelt sigh she felt rising from the depths of her.

"Turn over," Talyn whispered.

She turned in his arms and he wound one arm around her waist. He lowered his mouth toward hers, and she turned her face away. His lips, feather light, brushed her cheek, her chin.

"You don't trust me, do you, Raven?" he asked.

She looked back at him wordlessly, but she knew he could see the answer well enough in her eyes. *Of course not*, they said.

Before she could turn her head, his lips brushed hers. The feel of his mouth on hers in that teasing swipe sent a jolt of reaction up her spine and left her wanting more. She sucked in a surprised breath.

His hand massaged her side and the heat his body gave off as it pressed against hers bled through the fabric of her dress and penetrated her skin. He brushed his lips against hers again and her hands came up, seeking out and finding his shoulders.

His lips hovered just above hers. "Tell me you want me to kiss you, Raven. Tell me you know I'm not Cyrus and will not do you any harm. Tell me you know that if you ask me to stop, I will."

She did know these things, and she did want him to kiss her! She wanted more from him than simply a kiss. Resistance was not an option anymore. She wanted to fill this empty ache she had inside her and something told her that Talyn was the only man able to do that. It was time to surrender to him.

Her fingers traced the line of his shoulders and found his mass of silky hair. She freed it from the thong that held it and it fell loose around his face. "I know you are not Cyrus, and I want you to kiss me."

He needed no other encouragement. His mouth found hers and sipped from her lips gently, rubbing back and forth and pulling her bottom lip between his.

Raven threaded her fingers through his hair and pressed her body against his. Not knowing how to kiss, she tried her best to capture his lips with hers. She whimpered low in her throat and pressed her breasts to his chest. With a growl, Talyn parted her lips and slid his tongue between them. Pleasure jolted up her spine at the intimate touch of his tongue against hers. With devastating thoroughness, he worshiped her mouth. His free hand, the one not propping himself up on the bed, did not stray from her waist, though it tightened as if he wished to let it roam.

She closed her eyes and concentrated on his warm, delicious mouth moving on hers, the foresty scent of him in her nostrils, and the long, hard length of him pressed against her body. It was ecstasy—better than the "peak" he'd brought her to earlier. A low throb began between her legs. Her nipples tightened and she became very aware of her breasts all of a sudden. She wanted nothing more than for him to drop his hand and massage her into the glorious explosion of pleasure she'd had before. She wanted that, and she wanted a more intimate contact with him.

She dropped one hand to his chest and felt the expanse of hard muscle that lay beneath the fabric of his vest and tunic. The top of the tunic was laced with a leather thong, but it did not go all the way down the front, instead stopping a short ways from the collar. Wanting to feel his bare skin, she found the edge of his tunic and pushed her hand under it. Tentatively, she explored the warm, hard ridges of his chest muscles and drifted upward. He had scars of his own, she felt. They marred the perfection of his skin in mottled lengths over his sides and stomach. Her fingers found a smattering of coarse hair on his chest and brushed over his nipples. She touched them as he'd touched hers, rubbing over them in exploration.

He pulled away from her mouth and looked down at her with a heated gaze. They looked at each other for a long moment, sharing each other's air. "You play with fire, my lady."

She smiled, shifted beneath him, so she was pressed even closer against him, and laid her palm flat on his warm chest. "I know," she murmured. "I think I like fire."

Talyn's face went slack as though surprised. "You smiled."

The smile left her face at his comment, and the realization of what she was doing slammed into her. She was allowing her captor, whom she could not trust, to seduce her!

He lowered his head and kissed her. He spoke as if reading her mind — or maybe her face. "You can trust me, Raven. I wish you would. I won't let anything harm you. I want only to protect you and keep you from hurting yourself. That is why you are locked in this room. We seek to discover who your people are so we can help you return to them, that is all.

"I saw you try to jump from a window with my own eyes. I stopped you the first time, do you remember?"

She licked her lips and carefully chose the words that would comprise her lie. His gaze followed her tongue. "Yes...but I promise not to do that anymore. I am no longer panicked, after all. I know your language now. I...I know you now."

Talyn cursed under his breath, and then fell silent for a long moment before finally speaking. "If I allow you to leave this room, do you swear you will not hurt yourself?"

Her hope soared as high as she would as soon as she was free of this place. She'd swear anything to get out of this room and feel the sweet wind on her wings once more. She fought the note of desperation she knew would be in her answer and forced calmness instead. "I do, Talyn. I do. I need to feel the sun on my face and the wind in my...hair. Please."

A knock sounded at the door and it opened. Servants entered, carrying trays of food. "Her afternoon meal, Captain Talyn," said one as they spread the table by the hearth with the food. The door closed behind them.

The smell of the food wafted on the air to her. Roast lamb with sauce, various vegetables, sweet capa fruit. Her sense of smell had always been exceptional, able to select specific scents from many. Her stomach growled. With freedom nearly promised her, her appetite had returned.

He traced the line of her cheek. "You will eat, my lady." He rose and took her hand, pulling her up with him and over to the food. She sank into the chair he pulled out for her. "You will eat and then you will be free to roam the castle at will." He took her by the shoulders and forced her gaze to his. "But if you leave here without our aid, I will track you down. I'm exceptionally good at tracking. I have senses unequal to any in the guard."

"Why do you care so much what happens to me?"

His grip loosened. "I care because...because in many ways you remind me of myself long ago."

Raven reached up and touched his cheek at his words. The note of emotion in his voice resonated within her. "I am alone in this world, Talyn. I have nowhere to which to flee." The truth of those words impacted her hard. Tears pricked her eyes as she thought of Grandmother. Truly, she was the last of her kind.

Talyn smiled sadly. "We have much in common then, my lady." He picked up a fork and speared some meat, then set it to her lips. She swallowed gratefully and took up the utensil herself and began to eat.

Talyn knelt in front of her and set his index finger to the first button that remained fastened on her gown—right between her breasts. Raven swallowed a bit of capa fruit with an audible gulp. With fingers long accustomed to undoing the buttons on a lady's gown, he undid it, then slowly undid the next and the one after that.

"I am not Cyrus, Raven," he repeated. "I will not take what you do not offer freely. Do you understand? I want you to see my face when I caress your breasts. I want you to know it is me that touches you and no other."

Mute and staring into his eyes, she nodded.

His finger undid another button, then another. The back of his finger stole in to brush against the bare edge of her breast.

With a clatter, her fork hit the plate. She was hungry, yes, but her body demanded a more carnal desire be satisfied. The food could wait. She craved the touch of another, especially of a man, after so many years spent in isolation.

The only sounds in the room was of the fire crackling, the gentle slide of Talyn's finger over the material of her gown, and their mingled breathing. The sides of her gown parted and fire- and candle-warmed air bathed the bare flesh of her breasts.

"Why do you not eat?" he asked.

She licked her lips. "I'm a little distracted from the food at the moment."

A smile touched his mouth and she fought the urge to kiss it. Then he drove all thoughts from her mind as he parted her gown, causing it to slip over her shoulders and pool at her waist. He leaned forward and caught one nipple between his lips, laving over it with his tongue. Raven arched her back and gripped the edges of her chair. A tortured hiss of air escaped her.

He wound his arm around her waist, placed his hand to the small of her back and pulled her to the edge of the chair in order to better accommodate his lips around her nipple. He palmed the breast not being attended to by his mouth, running his finger over the nipple and lightly pinching it. An ache began between her legs again.

She reached out, ran her hands over his shoulders, and down his back. "Let me touch you," she murmured.

He stood and helped her to stand. When she did, her gown slipped past her hips and fell with a whoosh to a pile at their feet. She stepped out of it, and at the same time, her hands went to the edges of his tunic. She drew it up, revealing inch after tantalizing inch of his chest. She pulled it over his head and it joined her gown. Seeing that hard, glorious expanse of man in front of her is when Raven first realized what a joy undressing could be.

He drew her into his arms and she felt the soft hardness of his chest against her bare breasts for the first time. His hair rubbed against her sensitive nipples and she sighed. His fingers stroked over the scars running down her shoulder blades. To prevent him from asking any more questions, she pulled away from him and placed her hands to the waistband of his trews. "Let me see all of you."

He walked her back a few steps and tumbled her onto the bed. "Oh, you'll get to see all of me, Raven. You'll get to feel all of me too." His teeth flashed white and feral in the half-light. "Have patience."

He climbed onto the bed between her parted legs and ran one finger from the inside of her knee, up to her pussy. "You don't know how long I've wanted you. I'm going to savor every moment of this." He kissed her bellybutton and ran his tongue down over her skin to her mound.

Raven closed her eyes as her blood raced through her veins and her heart beat faster. She didn't want him to stop. He kissed the inside of her thigh and her hands tightened on the blankets. She squeezed her eyes shut, hoping no images of Cyrus rose up to haunt her.

"Open your eyes," Talyn purred at her from between her legs. "I want you to see that it is me and no one else that makes love to you."

Raven opened her eyes and looked down the length of her body at him. He held her gaze as he lowered his mouth to her clit. Holding his gaze while his tongue explored her was incredibly intimate and erotic. His tongue flicked her clit and retreated, then came back and bathed it. Raven arched her spine and let out a hiss of breath.

His hands found her breasts and his thumbs stroked over her nipples while he buried his face in her pussy. His tongue slipped inside her passage and she rose up, bucking her hips and pressing herself against his mouth. She tossed her head back and forth against the pillow, moaning out her pleasure.

He drew her pussy lips into his mouth and sucked them, then thrust his tongue into her passage. He took her clit, that most sensitive tender bit of flesh in his mouth and twirled his tongue around it, sucking at it relentlessly, and brushing at it with edges of his teeth. At the same time, he slipped one finger into her pussy, followed by a second. In and out he stroked her, finding the place of intense sensitivity deep inside.

Her peak hit like a lightening strike. Tremors racked her body and intense pleasure pushed all thoughts from her mind. A long, low keen of pleasure escaped her throat.

Talyn lapped up all the moisture that flowed from her like a cat with a bowl of cream.

Her body still thrumming from her climax, Raven struggled to sit up. Her peak had made her want more from him. She had to have his trews off *now*.

Her hands went for the tie on his trews, fumbling to undo it. His breathing harsh, he gently pushed her hands away and stood. He undid the laces of his trews and braies and let them fall to the floor, revealing every blessed hard inch of him.

Raven sucked in a breath. And there were a lot of inches.

Having never seen such a thing, she climbed off the bed and went to her knees in front of him. "It's magnificent," she breathed.

Talyn chuckled. "I'm glad you approve." He drew a fingertip down her cheek to her mouth. She kissed it. "If you don't touch it, my darling Raven, I am going to explode."

Tentatively, she reached out and stroked it. He tipped his head back and let out a careful breath. She wrapped her hand around it and eased the foreskin down and then back up. Talyn's hands went to her shoulders and squeezed.

In that moment, Raven realized the secret power a woman wielded over a man. One stroke of her hand and he reacted. She wondered what he'd do if she.... She licked to find out.

"Sweet Goddess," Talyn breathed around a groan.

She slipped the head of his cock into her mouth and stroked over him, using the flat of her tongue to rub down the length of him. Licking and sucking, she used her tongue and lips to draw more sounds from him. His hands fisted in her hair.

She could not bring his entire length into her mouth, but he seemed not to mind. He tipped his head back so his Adam's apple bobbed every time he let out a low moan, and Raven knew she was giving him pleasure.

And herself pleasure. Liquid trickled out of her passage and her clit pulsed at just the thought of his hands and tongue on her once more. His muscled thighs brushed her nipples and she moaned around his cock.

Before she knew what had happened, he'd pulled away from her. From the look that burned in his eyes, Raven knew what he wanted. She went down on her hands and knees and turned so her ass was up in the air and facing him.

Behind her, he let out a savage groan. His hand caressed her buttocks and his fingers slipped down to massage her pussy lips. In response, she wiggled her ass.

"Sweet Goddess, Raven. You're killing me. Not that I don't love it, but what are you doing?"

She turned to look at him. "This is how I've seen the animals in the forest do it. Is this not how you'll take me?" He slipped a finger into her drenched pussy and thrust. She sucked in a breath and let it out in a moan.

He swooped her up and sat her on the edge of the nearby table, standing between her spread legs. He kissed her and then set his forehead to hers. "I will take you that way, Raven. There is no doubt about that. But not the first time."

He positioned her so her bottom was at just at the edge of the table and her legs dangled over the side. Her passage brushed his cock, and she moaned and wiggled her hips, trying to get some friction going. He grabbed her waist and stilled her movement. "Don't," he said through gritted teeth. "I've never felt this close to losing control with a woman before, Raven, and you are a virgin, aren't you?" It was less a question than a statement.

She nodded.

"Brace your hands behind you on the table, so you have some support and your lovely breasts are bared for me."

She complied, feeling completely vulnerable to him now, with both her legs spread and her breasts exposed thus.

His hand went to her pussy, and he slipped his fingers over and around her slick labial folds, using her moisture to bathe her clit. His finger slipped around her clit and it grew under his ministrations, the blood coursing into it. She whimpered from the pleasure and let her head fall back.

Then his finger slipped down and slid into her passage. A feral sounding moan ripped from her throat and her back arched with the incredible feeling of her passage stretching around his finger. Further and further it slid within.

"You have no maidenhead," he stated.

She tipped her head up to look at him. She knew she looked confused. What was a maidenhead?

"Shh, Raven. I didn't mean to distract you." He pulled his finger out and thrust it in again.

"Oh, sweet Aran," she breathed, closing her eyes. "I had no idea anything could feel so good."

"It will get better. I promise," he said in a strained voice. He rotated his finger as though searching for something within her. When he found it, he thrust in and out of her, brushing over it. "Your pleasure point is deep within, sweet Raven," he purred.

Raven bucked and moaned under the influence of his finger working her. His thumb went to her clit and circled it around and around until she peaked again and called out his name.

He removed his hand and set his cock to her entrance. "Goddess, my name sounds sweet on your lips."

She pushed her hips forward so the very tip of him barely entered her and she rocked her hips. "Please, Talyn. More," she whispered hoarsely.

He slid within a little more. Raven noted that his muscles were strained, his jaw locked. He was obviously proceeding slowly for her benefit.

Inch by glorious inch he entered her, stretching her, filling her until she thought she could take no more and then there was more to take. Finally, he was sheathed within her to the base of his cock. He fit her perfectly, the head of him just brushing her womb.

"You have the tightest, silkiest sheath I've ever felt," he said with a shudder. Lowering his mouth to her breast with a growl, he took a nipple into his mouth and laved it with his tongue...and thrust in and out of her hot pussy.

Raven's world shattered. The vibratory connection they shared intensified for a blessed moment and another peak hit her fast and hard. Her vaginal muscles held onto him and convulsed around his cock. Talyn groaned.

He pumped into her relentlessly harder and faster until Raven was keening. He pushed her to yet another peak, and Talyn came with a bellow, bathing her womb deep inside with his seed.

He wrapped his arms around her and, still buried deep within her, laid his lips to her throat. The connection they shared was only a background buzz now, a special sensation Raven enjoyed. She wrapped her arms around him, enjoying the ecstasy of their connection.

What was it that made it so? Why should she feel that way? Her mind rolled over possibilities until she came to one that gave her pause.

Could it be that Talyn was Aviat? He couldn't remember his past. He'd been trapped and caged like she. He could see in the dark, he'd said, had excellent vision…could track like none other. Depending on the kind of Aviat he might be, those traits might fit, just as her ability to mimic language was a trait of her kind. His name was Talyn…*like talon.*

She sucked in a breath at the realization that it could be true. "How did you come by your name?" she asked.

He lifted his face and caught her gaze. "I don't know. My parents, I suspect. Talyn is what I called myself when I arrived here."

Her hands moved to his back, stroking over his skin and tracing in circles to his shoulder blades as she discreetly felt for ridges in his flesh. No scars. But if he'd been taken before the age of eight, it was possible he'd not spread his wings yet. Perhaps he'd never spread his wings. She shook her head. No, it was impossible. She was merely being fanciful.

There was one way to find out for certain if he was Aviat. She could speak her native tongue to him and see if he understood. An Aviat's blood always remembered the language if they heard it spoken by another, according to Grandmother. But if Raven were wrong she'd be giving her secret away. It was too large a risk.

"What's wrong?" he asked. "You look deep in thought."

She smiled and kissed him. "I'm happy for the first time in a long while." She said the words automatically, realizing the truth of them belatedly.

He began to pull his cock out of her, but she stopped him. "No, please. Stay within me for a bit." She moved her hips. "I enjoy the feel of you." He hardened inside her. There was no mistaking the flex and swell of her vaginal muscles around him.

"You affect me like no other woman has before," he said. "I'm ready to take you again."

Sliding his hands beneath her buttocks, he lifted her, and she wrapped her arms around his neck. He lay on the bed with her beneath him and gently began to move inside her again, leisurely thrusting his cock in and out.

Raven spread her legs as far as she could, wanting him to have complete access to her. "Yes," she breathed, throwing her head back into the pillows and arching her spine. Sweet Aran, he felt good inside her, as though she'd found a part of herself she'd lost long ago. Closing her eyes as he worked the thick length of his cock within her pussy, she pretended he really was Aviat.

* * * * *

Raven walked down the corridor, eyeing the open floor-to-ceiling windows she passed at regular intervals. Dropping her hand to her thigh as she walked, she fingered her gown—the one Talyn had given her—between shaky fingers.

The air called to her and the scents of spring sang through her blood. She longed to launch herself from the sill of one of the windows and let her wings unfurl. But she couldn't without letting the entire castle know what she truly was.

Then the hunt would begin.

She turned her attention to her progression down the corridor and away from those thoughts. Smiling and nodding at those she passed, she made her way to the chamber where Talyn had requested she meet him. When she arrived, she pushed in the heavy wooden door and stepped inside.

Candlelight filled the small room and flickered over the walls intimately. So many tapered candles lit the chamber that she could clearly see the table in the center of the room. A delicious looking array of foods—cheeses, meats, fish, and sugared confections sat alongside a carafe of wine and two glasses. Along one side of the room stretched a wall of mirrors that gave the chamber an illusory depth, and at the far end was a pool of water.

Warm arms encircled her and pulled her against a strong chest. Talyn's hot breath smelled sweet against her cheek. "Are you hungry?"

Her stomach growled as if in response and, blushing, she nodded.

He ushered her over to the table, filled the glasses with wine, and handed one to her. She sat down and let the sweet and slightly bitter liquid run down her throat as she watched Talyn. His trews molded to his powerful thighs nicely and his shirt was unlaced halfway down his chest, revealing his solid, muscled chest. His dark brown hair was loose and brushed the collar of his shirt, and his eyes, green with brown flecks around the irises, regarded her with something she recognized as anticipation.

Talyn filled her plate and then his own and they ate quickly, both knowing what was planned for dessert. After Raven finally pushed her plate away, Talyn held a hand out toward her. "Come with me," he said.

Raven stood, placed her hand in his and followed him to the pool at the far end of the chamber. A small trickle of water cascaded from the wall. She knelt and dipped her hand in the water. "It's warm!"

"Aye. Warm water is funneled here from the baths," Talyn said while pulling his shirt over his head.

Raven's mouth went dry as she watched his chest come into view. His biceps flexed as he removed his trews and braies and finally his boots. His thick cock stood at attention and Raven felt herself get damp between her legs and her nipples harden at the thought of his cock sliding in and out of her passage.

He walked to her, drew her gown over her head, and let it settle to the floor beside them. Together, they walked down the steps into the warm pool. She turned into him and let her wet flesh rub against his chest.

Talyn scooped up handfuls of water and poured it over her shoulders. The warm water trickled down between her breasts, and Raven sighed happily. He picked up a chunk of soap and began to wash her. His wide, calloused hands slipped over her narrow shoulders and around her breasts.

Lowering his head to her neck, he nibbled and sucked on her collarbones, then worked his way up to the tender, sensitive flesh just behind her earlobe. He brushed his thumbs back and forth over her nipples, exploring every ridge and valley thoroughly. A jolt of desire went straight from her breasts to her pussy. She moaned and sighed and shifted as he worked her breasts. Raising her hands from the water, she ran them over his broad shoulders, down his back to his tight buttocks and around front to stroke his hard cock.

His body tightened in the way she was starting to know meant he was very aroused. "Spread your legs," he ordered in a low voice.

She complied and he slipped his soaped fingers between her thighs, running them over her pussy lips and anus. Her clit engorged and became sensitive, and Talyn zeroed in on it. His wet, soapy finger slipped around it massaging it with perfect pressure. The play of his finger against her clit combined with his teeth grazing her throat made her body tense as sweet sensations flowed over her. She closed her eyes.

"Not yet, Raven." He rinsed her, braced his hands around her waist, and lifted her. She felt herself slide into a comfortable, smooth seat on the edge of the pool. Talyn guided her heels into little footholds on either side, so that her legs were spread. Straps secured her ankles.

"Talyn…" she began uncertainly.

He looked up at her, his eyes dark with desire. "Raven, do you trust me?"

She regarded him in silence and chewed her lower lip. Finally, she nodded. She did trust him.

Even though she was wet, she wasn't cold. The candles warmed the small chamber nicely and Talyn's skillful hands, combined with the knowledge that her body was his to play with, warmed her blood.

He climbed out of the pool and came around behind her. "Look," he said.

She looked straight ahead and saw herself in the mirror opposite her. Her eyes grew wide as she saw herself wantonly displayed. Her breasts hung heavy and swollen with desire, the dusky tips standing erect. Her pussy was spread wide-open, cherry red and engorged.

Talyn cupped her breasts, drawing his fingertips up and over her nipples. The sight of herself, nude and completely open to him, was arousing. But the sight of his tanned flesh against her pale skin was electrifying. He teased her breasts and nipples until she was moaning and sighing and on the verge of begging him to slide his cock into her. Her clit throbbed, begging to be touched or, even better, licked.

He reached behind himself and came back with a cylinder-shaped object in his hand. He rubbed the cool metal over her nipples, ran it down between her breasts and over her stomach to rub through the coarse curls covering her mound.

"What—" she started.

"Shh…watch," he crooned in her ear.

He worked the tip of the cylinder over her clit, making her suck in a breath and writhe in the seat at the unfamiliar sensation of the object moving over her excited flesh. Back and forth, he rubbed it and the beginning of a climax sparked and caught fire, drawing moans from her throat.

He lifted the cylinder away from her clit and dropped it down. With one hand he spread her pussy lips apart, so she could see herself completely, then slipped the cylinder into her passage. At the same time, he let his other hand play with her clit. Talyn thrust the object in and out of her.

Seeing the cylinder disappear into her pussy while Talyn's hand worked it sent her over the edge and she came with a cry of pleasure. The muscles of her passage contracted and pulsed around the metal and she felt her hot juices run out and dribble down her thighs.

* * * * *

Talyn nearly spurted all over Raven's back as he made her come using the cylinder. Watching her in the mirror was almost more than he could take. Her sweet, lusty cries kindled desire in him like no other woman's. While Raven was recovering from her climax, he placed the cylinder to the side and lowered himself into the water. He had to taste her succulent juices.

He positioned himself between her thighs and licked from her inner kneecap to the crease where her thigh met her torso. Then he lowered his mouth to her pussy. It was ripe for his tongue, begging to be licked and worshiped with his mouth. With his thumbs, he spread her pussy lips apart and licked from her anus to her clit. She let out a sigh of pleasure and her back arched. Her fingers tangled in his hair and when he glanced up from his work, he saw that she was watching everything in the mirror.

He licked around her folds, drawing them into his mouth and sucking at them. From time to time, he'd delve down and slip his tongue into her passage, wringing moans of pleasure from Raven. Then he settled on her clit, drawing it into his mouth, laving it with his tongue and sucking on it relentlessly. Her body tensed and Talyn knew she was ready to peak again. He slipped two fingers into her passage and found her pleasure point. He rubbed his fingers against it and that was enough to push her over the edge. She came against his mouth and her juices coursed over his fingers.

He didn't stop there, though. He kept up the massage of her pleasure point, drawing his fingers in and out of her tight, wet pussy and sucking and laving her clit without mercy. She tossed her head back and forth, begging him to come within her, but he wouldn't—not until he felt her come against his tongue.

With a cry of pleasure that made his cock so hard he thought it might break, she came. Quickly, he replaced his fingers with his tongue, so he could feel her muscles pulse and contract around it. He groaned happily at the intimate sensation that filled his mouth.

"Talyn, please," she implored.

Without delay, he walked up the couple of steps built into the side of the pool just for this, bringing his eager cock level with her pussy. With one long, hard thrust that sent her buttocks hard into the chair she was sitting in, he impaled her on his cock. Her soft, warm heat surrounded him.

He pounded into her, his flesh slapping against hers making an audible sound. He let free an animalistic grunt of pure pleasure.

"Yes," she moaned into his ear.

He kissed her hard, his tongue slipping in and mating with hers. Then he braced his hands on her waist, dedicating himself to the serious task of fucking her. Her eyes were large and dark as she watched the mirror behind him. He could imagine what she saw. Her legs were spread wide and her ankles secured to the footholds. He was thrusting into her with abandon, the muscles of his buttocks flexing and releasing with every deep stroke.

She tipped her head back and keened her peak. He came with her, releasing a groan of satisfaction as pleasure rippled out from his groin and overwhelmed him. He thrust into her to the hilt and let his hot seed fill her.

He remained sheathed inside her and held her, enjoying the tremors from their shared climax.

Chapter Four

Raven stared out one of the windows lining the corridor and watched the treetops just outside the castle's battlements sway in the fresh breeze. The skies called to her, heated her blood, and made her itch to unfurl her wings.

But she could not leave Talyn behind. Yes, she admitted to herself, leaving him would bother her greatly. For now she would stay. In any case she had a very practical reason for wanting Talyn's company.

She placed her hand to her abdomen. Every night for the last two weeks Talyn had made love to her. She hoped his seed had taken root in her belly. Even an Aviat halfling would be better than none at all.

She turned away from the window and walked down the corridor, passing a shadowed alcove with a couple within it. A woman knelt, greedily taking a man's cock into her mouth while his hands fisted in her long blond hair. He groaned and grasped her shoulders, pulling her up. He took her by the waist and lifted her, pressing her back against the wall and impaling her hard with his cock in one smooth movement. The woman's surprised squeals quickly changed to moans of pleasure as he began to work his cock in and out of her, his buttocks clenching with every thrust.

Raven had grown accustomed to seeing such acts openly displayed. She understood that it was difficult for the Nordanese women to conceive and so they took many men within them, copulated many times. The fact that some did so openly was a quirk of their culture. When she'd asked Talyn about it, he'd shrugged and said, "Why hide the beauty of the act behind closed doors? It is not the Nordanese way to be ashamed of physical pleasures."

She brushed her stomach again. As far as she knew, Aviat women were not afflicted with such problems of infertility. They were only afflicted by the lack of Aviat men—the lack of any Aviats at all.

She paused at a window that overlooked the training yard and did a double take. Talyn was below, engaged in training. Sweat sheened his shirtless chest and back as he wielded his sword, parrying back and forth with an opponent. Gathered around him were a number of guardsmen. On the defensive, the soldier Talyn fought took several steps back under his captain's masterful attack and went to one knee. Talyn brought the sword to the soldier's throat, symbolizing his death had it been a real battle.

Talyn glanced around at his men and took on a new opponent. She watched, enraptured as his well-honed muscles flexed and his sounds of exertion, not unlike the sounds he made when he made love to her, reached her ears.

Heat unfurled low in her belly and reached down, bringing her clit to sudden sensitivity. It was always so when she saw him. Always, she wanted him within her.

A tall blond man came to stand beside her. Raven glanced at him as his eyes focused briefly on the training yard before turning to her. "Beautiful day, my lady."

His deep, melodious voice had her staring into a face carved by the Goddess herself. Deep blue eyes met hers. "Your name is Raven, is it not?" he asked.

He was handsome, that was for sure. He'd set any woman's heart to pounding. In her mind, he couldn't hold a candle to Talyn.

"Yes," she answered.

"A very interesting name you have." He bowed in the traditional Sudhraian way of greeting. "My name is Rue. It is so nice to finally meet you after hearing so many stories about you. "

She smiled. "My arrival and subsequent restraint caused quite a stir around here. Many make up stories when they do not understand things."

"Indeed. I, myself, come from a land strange to the Nordanese. The castle's inhabitants also wonder about me." He smiled, but it did not reach his eyes. Those deep blue orbs were busy raking over her body hungrily.

Many men here had viewed Raven in lust, but none before this one had caused her to want to cover herself. This man clearly had a lustful hunger that neared dangerous. It was as though he was contemplating stripping her gown from her and plunging his cock into her right there at the window.

"But, amid all the untrue gossip, isn't it true you arrived with Lord Cyrus of Sudhra one moon's cycle ago?" he asked. His ice blue eyes glittered. "I ask because the swine was an acquaintance of mine, you see."

Raven licked her lips and thought of a response. It was common knowledge. Why did she feel a need to lie to this man? She decided to modify her answer instead. For some reason, he left her with a strange feeling in her stomach. Grandmother taught her to listen to those feelings. "Yes, I arrived with Cyrus and his men. They kidnapped me from my village in the north and desired to make me into a whore for them."

He raised his hand as if to touch her face and Raven backed away. "If you will excuse me. I must go now," she said quickly. She stepped around him and he blocked her way. She took several steps back so she was further than an arm span from him.

"There aren't many villages in the north, my lady. Just one more question, if I may?" he asked, looking at her with that same lustful, hungry look on his handsome, lean face.

"I'm sorry. I must leave." She tried to walk away and he closed the distance between them with amazing speed and grabbed her wrist.

"Rue, this is not Sudhra. They don't manhandle women in Nordan."

A deep, powerful voice had her looking away from Rue and into a set of kind, dark brown eyes. "Are you all right, my lady?" the man asked.

Rue released her wrist. "Gavin, I'm not manhandling her. I simply wanted to ask her if it's true she tried to jump out two windows. "

Raven shook her head and tried a smile. She didn't want this dangerous man to have any knowledge of her. "How silly. Of course I didn't. Why ever would I do that? I have no death wish. It's a bit of gossip only. Now, really, I must take my leave."

She walked away, but Rue's next comment made her steps falter.

"Then why did they lock you away so you would not injure yourself, my lady?"

She picked up her pace and rounded a corner.

The dark-haired man called Gavin caught up to her. "Not all Sudhraians are despicable, my lady. Only most of them."

Looking up at his short brown hair, which was the style for Sudhraian males according to Talyn, she noted, "But aren't you one?

"Well, yes, half."

She halted and looked up at him. "So then, you are half despicable."

He smiled and it warmed her, put her at ease. When he smiled he was as handsome as Rue...but nothing close to Talyn. "Some would say completely, my lady."

She couldn't help but smile back. "Well, I don't think you're despicable."

"I'm glad for that. I wouldn't want such a beautiful and mysterious woman to dislike me. She might not agree to accompany me to the dining hall where we could speak more comfortably than in this drafty corridor. Anyway, in the dining hall I hear they have wine."

She hesitated for a moment and then hooked her arm through his offered one. She had so few friends here. Another would be nice. "All right."

* * * * *

Raven laughed. "So you're happy to be here in Nordan then?" In the last hour, Gavin had told her what life in Sudhra was like. He'd not painted a pretty picture, but he'd told stories of his life there with humor.

"I am." He lifted his goblet of wine and studied her over the rim. His gaze grew intent and dark. "Especially now."

Raven shifted in her chair and glanced away, suddenly uncomfortable. She enjoyed Gavin's humor and his easy familiarity with her. She felt at ease with him. At the same time, she recognized his attraction for her. It was something she could not reciprocate. Talyn was the only man for whom she felt desire.

She raised her gaze and it met Talyn's across the room. A smile spread over her mouth. She watched him spot her and then spot Gavin. He walked toward them with all the muscular presence of a mountain cat stalking its prey.

Saria, a beautiful woman she often saw Talyn talking with, stepped into his path. Gavin spoke to her, but Raven was not paying attention to him. Instead, she watched Saria throw her arms around Talyn and do her best to brush up against him with her full breasts and shapely hips. Talyn embraced her, and then excused himself, telling her he'd see her later, and walked on.

He'd see her later?

Raven tried to suppress the mix of negative emotions suddenly swirling within her. She had no right to claim Talyn as her own exclusively, she reminded herself.

When Talyn reached their table, he nodded at Gavin without breaking a smile. "I see you're making yourself at home."

Gavin set his goblet down. "As Lord Marken requested."

Talyn only grimaced back at him in response. He touched Raven's arm. "Can I talk with you?" He threw a glance at Gavin. "Alone?"

She stood. "Of course. Gavin, thank you for the conversation. I will see you again soon, no doubt."

Gavin stood and bowed, flashing a grin at Talyn. "I hope so."

She smiled at Gavin, completely enraptured. Talyn pulled at her elbow. "Come, my lady."

Raven let him lead her into one of the shadowed alcoves that graced so many areas of the castle. He turned to her with an expression on his face that neared anger. "I would prefer it if you did not spend too much time with either of the men from Sudhra."

"Why not? I have seen you many times talking with that woman, Saria, among others."

A grin tugged at his lips. "Are you jealous, my little one?"

She lifted her chin. She hadn't realized until she'd said the words, that indeed, she was jealous. She wanted Talyn for herself, no matter if it was against his nature and against Nordanese culture. "Aren't you jealous?"

He walked her back until she was pressed against the far wall. His hard chest rubbed her nipples into stiff peaks. "This has nothing to do with jealousy." Possessively, his hand hiked her dress up and he grazed her clit with his fingertips. "And everything to do with your safety."

He fingered her clit and she spread her legs for him, allowing his fingers to slip within her.

As he stroked her, it was becoming increasingly difficult to think. "Why would it not be safe to talk with Gavin?" she managed to push out right before he slipped another finger within to join the first and began thrusting slowly, tortuously.

"Because, my lady, they are Sudhraian and we have not determined if they are telling the truth about why they are here. They are being watched carefully right now. The man called Rue has given us information we deem accurate about Sudhra's war plans, but we have nothing yet from Gavin indicating his worthiness."

She tipped her head back and closed her eyes, focusing on the pleasure climbing higher and higher between her thighs. His finger rubbed her clit and she moaned.

He put his mouth close to her ear. His deep, silky voice caressed her. "Do you like that?"

She nodded.

His voice took on the rasping, mesmerizing quality it always did when he was aroused. "You feel so good around my fingers, Raven. Your passage is so warm, so tight. I'm imagining spreading your legs right now and sheathing myself inside you to the hilt."

She shuddered in pleasure. Around and around went his thumb, caressing her clit. In and out stroked his fingers until she was tossing her head back and forth and panting. She mumbled something unintelligible.

His mouth nuzzled her ear again and she stilled. His tongue flicked out to trace the whorls. "Come for me, Raven. Come hard."

She obeyed. With a cry, she came. The muscles of her core spasmed, and he caught her moans in his mouth as it covered hers.

"Every time I see you, I want you, Raven. After having you in my bed every night, do you think I have time for other women?" he asked. "Do you think I even want them? Let me show you how you affect me."

He turned her around, pressed her head down to her knees and lifted her skirt. She heard his trews slide down and with one smooth movement he surged into her. Raven let out a gasp of both pleasure and surprise. His thick length thrust in and out of her faster and faster and harder and harder, until she could hear the slap of his skin against hers. She splayed her hands against the wall in front of her to brace herself and closed her eyes in ecstasy. His abrupt actions nearly undid her. Her clit swelled and throbbed. One brush against it and she'd be over the edge once again.

Every time he surged into her, he brushed against her pleasure point deep inside and it sent racking spasms of ecstasy through her. He brushed her womb with every thrust and the slightest bit of pain magnified the pleasure.

He slipped a hand around the front of her, between her legs, and rubbed her clit.

With a climax so hard she momentarily lost control of her pelvic muscles, she cried out his name and felt her juices soak him and run down her inner thighs.

With a muffled yell, he released himself into her.

He stayed sheathed within her. Their breathing sounded harsh in the enclosed space. Then he pulled her up and turned her to face him, enclosing her in an embrace.

She nuzzled his neck with her eyes closed, feeling wonderfully sated and languorous—how she always felt after being loved by Talyn—and breathed in the scent of him. When she opened her eyes it was to find Rue standing outside the alcove staring at them. He'd undoubtedly been watching the entire time. The idea at once repulsed and excited her.

Rue turned and walked away as Talyn drew her mouth to his for a kiss.

* * * * *

Talyn balanced his armful of books, trying to prevent the very top volume from slipping off and crashing to the floor. It was so old, its spine was decaying and such a fall would probably destroy it. He'd found them stashed in the bowels of the castle while he'd been looking for some shields that had been stored in one of the armament chambers by mistake. Perhaps the books would aid Haeffen in his search for clues to Raven's past.

He cursed under his breath as he fumbled at the doorknob to Haeffen's outer chamber. Someone he couldn't see because of the pile of books in his arms turned the knob for him.

"Doing a little reading, Talyn? I didn't think you were the type."

Rue's voice. Talyn peered around the stack and regarded him with unmasked hostility. "Out of the way, Rue. I don't have time to waste with you. I've got business with Haeffen."

"Raven is all alone, then?" Rue said nearly to himself with a thoughtful expression on his face.

The books hit the floor with an ear-pounding thump. Talyn advanced on Rue, but the Sudhraian didn't back away. "I want you and your friend, Gavin, to stay away from her."

Rue raised an eyebrow. "Last time I checked I was in Nordan, not Sudhra. And you're not even her monogamous mate. Do you have a say in the company Raven keeps?"

"Why are you so interested in her?"

Rue smiled coldly. "She's beautiful, has the body of an angel, and makes the most arousing sounds when she's being fucked. What man wouldn't be?"

Talyn took a couple threatening steps toward him, but Haeffen blocked his progression with one gnarled hand to his chest.

"What is going on out here?" asked Haeffen, squinting up at Talyn. "I am trying to read in my room, which is difficult enough for eyes as old as mine without having enough noise out in the corridor to rouse the fires of inner Aran." He crooked a knobby finger and shook his head. "The two of you come in and leave some of your testosterone at the door."

Talyn eyed Rue until the other man turned and walked through the doorway behind Haeffen. Talyn gathered up the books and followed.

The room smelled of lavender and Talyn spotted a vase full of it on Haeffen's desk. He deposited the books beside it and went to sit beside Rue in one of the padded wooden chairs beside the fireplace. Thick tapestries lined the walls of Haeffen's outer chamber and two tall spears were set into the wall flanking the door leading into his inner bedchamber.

Haeffen busied himself at a table in the corner of the room and came back to them carrying two clay cups filled with lavender tea. Talyn took his and sipped at it. Maybe Haeffen thought to ease the tensions that still ran high between himself and Rue.

Talyn would keep Raven safe. The mere thought of harm befalling her was enough to cause cold fear to course through his bloodstream, and he didn't trust either Rue or Gavin.

Haeffen settled himself on the edge of his paper-strewn desk and set one hand flat on top of the stack of books. "What is it you bring me, Talyn?"

"I found them in the lower chambers of the castle. They appear to be records from long ago and I thought they might aid in your discovery of Raven's past."

Haeffen picked up a book, opened its cover, and blew dust from its pages. With an expression of interest, he read a bit of it. "Very good, Talyn. These may indeed contain exactly what I've been looking for. I'll begin reading through them immediately." He snapped the book closed, causing a cloud of dust to surround his face. He sneezed.

Rue took a sip of his tea, made a face and set the cup on the table near him. "What are you trying to discover about Raven?" he asked. His voice sounded casual, but Talyn sensed great interest behind his question.

"You have no right to ask," came Talyn's swift answer.

Rue bristled. "I—"

"*Hold,*" Haeffen commanded in a low voice. "Rue, would you mind leaving Talyn and I alone so that we might talk."

Rue simply sat and stared at Talyn with ice in his light blue gaze.

"Rue," said Haeffen once, softly.

Rue stood and left the room.

Haeffen stood and walked over to the fire. Talyn took another sip of his tea while Haeffen fed some bits of wood to the flames. "What lies between you and the woman?" he asked.

"I…I don't know exactly, Haeffen. She affects me strangely."

Haeffen turned from the hearth. "So I see. I have never known you to become possessive over a woman before."

Talyn pushed a hand through his hair. "There is something special between she and I. Some kind of strange bond. Like—"

"Marken and Sienne?" Haeffen suggested.

Talyn went silent. He hadn't been about to say that. Goddess, he hadn't even thought about it. Was it true? Did he share a relationship with Raven that went as deep as that?

Perhaps.

But Marken and Sienne were monogamous mates. Talyn shook his head as if to clear it. No…he could never limit himself to only one woman. True, he'd not taken another woman since Raven had arrived, but that was temporary. Soon he'd sate himself on her and that would be that. He would return to bedding other women and she…well…she would take other men.

Talyn felt his jaw lock. The thought of Raven taking another man to her bed stopped him cold. Goddess…he *was* jealous. The thought of another man touching her hair, her skin, sliding his cock into her sweet passage was too much to bear!

Talyn knew then that he might be doomed.

"Monogamy does seem to be catching around this castle lately. Have you thought of taking her as your monogamous mate?" asked Haeffen.

Talyn looked up, trying to clear his mind of the sudden tangle of thought that choked it. He shook his head vigorously. "No. I could never take any woman to that status."

Haeffen raised an eyebrow, but said nothing.

Talyn fisted his hands, unable to verbally express his feelings. "With Raven, I feel as though I have regained a missing part of myself. I always felt so alone before... and now, I don't. But monogamous mate...I'm just not ready for that."

Haeffen stroked his beard. "Have you told Raven how you feel about her?"

"No. Not in so many words. But she must know. I haven't taken another woman since she arrived." He put a closed fist to his chest. "I, Talyn, have lain with but one woman for an entire moon cycle and one half."

"Quite impressive, Captain Talyn. What do you think it means?"

"I don't know." But he did know that he needed to tell Raven how much she meant to him. Even if he could not make her his monogamous mate, she had a right to know just how important she was to him. Talyn hesitated for a moment, then stood and strode to the door. "I have to find Raven and tell her all of this," he explained before heading out the door.

Talyn crossed the inner bailey with purposeful strides. Raven would probably be in the ladies' solar now. He didn't understand his sudden urge...no...need to tell Raven how he felt. He only knew that he had to hold her in his arms and tell her.... Tell her what? That he loved her? His steps faltered.

Could it be true?

* * * * *

Raven stuck her needle though her piece of fabric and stabbed her finger. She dropped the material to her lap and brought her finger to her mouth. The coppery taste of her blood flavored her tongue. Lady Sienne had been patient enough to show her how to embroider, but judging from the unruly and inartistic slashes of colored thread crisscrossing the fabric, it was not one of her talents.

"Having trouble, Raven?" asked Saria from across the room. "Perhaps your nightly exertions with Talyn are fatiguing you?" Her daughter, Alia, a brown-haired, blue-eyed babe of three played at her feet.

Raven didn't miss the bitterness in the other woman's voice. She knew well that Saria believed Raven had taken Saria's place as Talyn's favorite. The entire castle was abuzz with the rumor that perhaps Talyn had fallen under the same strange spell Lord Marken had succumbed to a season ago.

Raven smiled at the child and the girl smiled back and giggled. "I'm fine," Raven said in response. "You have a lovely child, Saria."

"Thank you." Most of the women lucky enough to conceive and give birth to a child preened over the fact. Saria was no exception. "I think she's Talyn's," she finished smugly.

With a sigh, Raven looked out one of the nearby windows. The only thing she truly wanted to do was spread her wings. The last month had passed quickly, nearly every day spent with Talyn, but even he could not quell her need to find the air beneath her wings.

The door to the sitting room opened and all the women looked toward it. Gavin walked in, his eyes going to each of the ladies with a slight nod. A collective sigh went through the room. Gavin and Rue both had been very popular males with the Nordanese women.

Gavin often tried to talk with Raven, but she always put him off, remembering Talyn's request that she not spend time with either of the Sudhraians. Gavin walked over, stood in front of her, and bowed.

"My lady," he said to her. "It is a fine day for riding. The air is warm and heavy with the scent of flowers. We could push our horses so swiftly it would feel as though we were flying."

She glanced toward the window. A ride sounded nice, and Talyn was busy with the guard right now. *So swiftly, it would feel as though we were flying....*

She looked up at him. "You definitely know what to say to seduce me," she murmured.

He knelt and covered her hands with his own. "That's what I am trying to do, my lady...seduce you. Rue and myself both desire you. And you take no one but Talyn to your bed while Talyn gives himself free rein with all the other women," he said softly.

Her heart squeezed painfully at his words. "What do you mean?"

"Oh. I'm sorry. Did you not know?" Gavin swore softly under his breath. "I didn't know he was playing such a game with you. Well...he told me...." He trailed off and looked away.

"He told you what?" Did her voice sound as tight as her throat felt?

"He...he...." Gavin swore softly again. "No, I can't tell you."

"Tell me," she whispered. "I have a right to know!"

"You're right." He drew a deep breath. "He told me he cannot stand the idea that another man might make love to you. That he is the only one he wants within your passage, but he cannot give you the same respect. His own sexual appetite is too great and he must go to other women to slake it. Apparently, he hides this from you so you will only welcome him into your body and no other."

Raven pulled her suddenly cold hands away from Gavin. "I don't believe you." At the same time images of him embracing Saria ran through her mind. Images of times she'd seen Talyn talking and laughing privately with the blond paraded through her mind's eye....

"Whether you believe me or not does not change the truth of it," answered Gavin.

"It's true," asserted Saria. "He comes to my bed on a regular basis."

Dread rose up and choked Raven. She had no right to feel possessive of Talyn, or hurt by his actions. He was not her monogamous mate. But she felt possessive and hurt all the same.

"I am very sorry to have to tell you this, but I don't want you to be hurt any further than you already have been," said Gavin. "Come riding with me, Raven. You and I could be so beautiful together."

She stood, pushing the embroidery from her lap onto the rush-strewn floor. "No. I must see to something else," she managed to push out from a constricted throat.

Already hot tears were falling. She walked swiftly to the door.

"*I'll* go riding with you, Gavin," purred Saria. "I'll make you forget all about her."

Raven pulled the door shut on Gavin's response.

She ran blindly down the corridor and up the stairs at the end that led to a tower. She needed time to be alone to sort out her jumbled thoughts. She sought the highest window she could find. It was time to leave. Time to go home. Even the word made her blood course faster in her veins...*home*. She would find Grandmother's grave and consecrate her body in the way of the Aviat. Then she would return to the northern forests. If she was seen flying away from the castle this afternoon, if she was hunted, then so be it. She would learn to hide, learn to hunt the hunters, and kill.

And she'd learn to be alone. Her eyes filled with tears as her feet pounded on the stairs and her skirts swirled around her legs. But she wouldn't think of that now. She would concentrate on getting out of this castle.

She reached the top of the steep flight of stairs and pushed the door of the uppermost chamber open with the flat of her palm. The plain wooden door swung wide and hit the stone wall with a resounding thump.

She inventoried the room's contents quickly. A supply of weaponry stood in one corner, and an old spinning wheel in the other. A long table dominated the center.

Movement by one of windows startled her. Sunlight glinted off blond hair and burnished already tanned skin. He sat on the sill, one long leg propped up, while the other was braced on the cobblestone floor. Her heart dropped. "Rue."

"Raven."

"What are you doing up here all by yourself?"

He turned his head to the open window, closed his eyes, and inhaled deeply. "The air is fresh and clean and I am alone. I like to be alone." He opened his eyes and caught her gaze. "And you can see forever from this vantage point. I enjoy heights." He motioned to her. "Come and see."

She walked to him and looked out the window at the sun hanging low in the sky and the courtyard far below. One little hop onto the windowsill and a leap....

"And now I return the question. What are you doing here? And with a tear-stained face and such a wild look in your eye?" He picked up a tendril of her long, loose hair and rubbed it between two strong fingers, then brought it to his nose and inhaled.

She took a step back, but he didn't loose her hair. A twinge of unease flickered through her. "I...I also needed a place where I could be alone."

He raised a light-colored brow. "Ah. And the fact that this is the highest place in the castle that contains a window did not figure into your decision at all?"

She went silent and merely stared at him, noting dully the look of barely contained lust in his blue eyes. Why should he be so interested in her penchant for windows?

"Come here, Raven," he commanded softly. "Let me touch you."

A part of her wanted Rue to touch her. She wanted another man to take her simply because Talyn did not want that to happen. She let her gaze slide over his muscular torso, his handsome features, but she did not move. It would be no hardship to let Rue touch her, after all.

Rue stood, still holding her hair, and walked toward her. She stepped backward until the backs of her thighs met the worktable in the center of the room. His body pressed against her. He reached up and cupped the back of her neck. She let out a gasp as the same low-key vibration she shared with Talyn also sang through her blood at Rue's touch.

Rue closed his eyes, tipped his back and sighed. "Oh, aye, I was right," he murmured. "Thank the Gods and Goddesses both. You're an Aviat."

Horror coursed through her, chilling her blood. Was Rue a hunter? She positioned her knee properly to provide her easy access to his groin. She wouldn't go with him easily. She would fight until she was dead....

"Hush, Raven. I see your fear. Relax. I know you are an Aviat, because I am of your kind."

Her jaw dropped. "You? You're...?" she trailed off.

"I could never get close enough to touch the back of your neck. Talyn or someone else was always near, always guarding you from me."

"But...but," she stammered.

"I knew Lord Cyrus had traveled to the Nordan northlands searching for the Aviat it was believed still remained there. I thought they'd all fled that region long ago." He touched her cheek. "But two were left. I didn't find out until it was too late. Right after the news of Cyrus's death reached Sudhra. I came here not knowing if he'd captured you and brought you here, or if you still remained in the northern forests. I was sorry to hear of the death of your grandmother."

She was not alone in the world after all. With trembling fingers, she touched his face, feeling the hard stubble that always stood on his chin and cheeks. He smiled at her and a dimple appeared. It made him look less threatening. "Are there more?" she asked.

"Aye. There are more to the south. Not many, but without the fertility problems suffered by the Nordanese and Sudhraian, our numbers are growing."

Raven pressed her fingers to the back of Rue's neck and felt the vibration that thrummed from the contact. So very like what she experienced with Talyn. She broke away from Rue, paced to the window and back again. She put both sets of fingers to her temple. "Wait. I have to think."

Rue fell silent.

She whirled. "That vibration means we're both Aviat, right?"

"Yes."

"Why did you say you had to touch the back of my neck? Why couldn't you have touched just any part of my body?"

He shook his head. "It has to be the back of the neck, unless a man and a woman are tied."

"Tied?"

"It's a little like the Nordanese notion of monogamous mate. Tied means that you and the other Aviat share a bond that goes beyond the normal relationship—you share body chemistry, even compatible thought patterns. Usually two that are chemically tied in this way cannot keep their hands off each other, fuck like rabbits."

She felt her face drain of blood.

He took a step toward her. "What's wrong?"

"I can't even begin to tell you." She went to the window and sat down on the sill. She loved the man who was her perfect mate. An Aviat. She could hope for nothing better. But he didn't love her enough to tell her the truth, or believe she was enough to satisfy him. She looked out of the window to the courtyard below. The sun was going down, mixing reds and orange across the sky, blending into a conglomeration of colors that so closely resembled her own mixed emotions, it brought tears to her eyes.

Rue walked toward her, placed his hand to her head and let it trail down through her hair. "I thought this knowledge would please you. I came her to find you, mate with you, and eventually bring you home with me."

She stood and faced him. Talyn wanted her, but under conditions that were not acceptable to her. Here was a strong, handsome Aviat male in front of her who also wanted her. She raised her eyes to his. "I am very happy," she said. Then she burst into tears.

Rue pulled her toward him and enveloped her in his arms.

* * * * *

Talyn stormed out of the solar, fuming. He'd never trusted Gavin and now the bastard had upset Raven and Talyn didn't know how he'd done it. When Talyn had sought Raven in the sitting room, the ladies had told him that Gavin had arrived and asked her to go riding with him. When she'd refused, Gavin had discussed something with her that had made her leave the room upset and in tears.

233

He pushed a hand through his hair. He had no idea where she would have gone. Perhaps her chamber, or the gardens but...he squeezed his eyes shut. The thought of her in pain stabbed at his heart. Where was she?

Something that felt like Raven flickered in his consciousness. An image of her flashed then steadied. *She stood in one of the tower rooms...in Rue's embrace.* The Sudhraian bastard had caught her at a vulnerable time and undoubtedly held her against her will!

His eyes opened. There was no time to wonder about the strange psychic occurrence, or why it had happened. He wanted only to get to Raven. He ran down the corridor and up the stairs as fast as he could. When he reached the top, the door stood open.

Raven stood by the window in Rue's arms, exactly how he'd seen them in his mind just minutes before. He wasted no time. Talyn strode across the room, broke them apart, and punched Rue hard in the jaw.

Rue staggered back, taken unaware, and slammed against the wall behind him and slid down.

"Did he hurt you, Raven?" Talyn asked, advancing on Rue at the same time. Rue's hand went to his jaw. His already cold blue eyes went frigid and he stood, looking ready to meet Talyn fist-for-fist.

"Stop!" cried Raven. "You misunderstand, Talyn. Rue was embracing me because I wanted him to hold me."

Talyn's steps faltered and he turned. What had she just said? "You wanted him...? Why?" He felt his whole world crashing around him.

"I know about the lies you've been telling me."

"What lies? What are you talking about?" His eyes widened. "Is this something Gavin said?"

"Never mind where I heard it. The point is, I know. You wanted me to take no other man, but you bedded many other women. I know you are not mine to keep, not monogamously. But at the same time, I will not allow myself to be treated that way."

He took a step toward her and she backed away. "Raven, you must believe me. I have not bed any woman since you arrived. It is out of character for me, I know. But it's true."

She shook her head. "I can't believe anything you say right now."

"You would believe a Sudhraian over me? I'm your lover."

She crossed her arms over her chest. "What reason would Gavin have to lie?"

Rue made a scoffing noise. "Have you not noticed the way he looks at you? He wants you, my lady. He covets you." He threw a glance at Talyn. "Almost as much as I do."

Talyn itched to punch Rue again. His hands curled into fists. He ignored the urge to cause Rue pain and concentrated on Raven. "Gavin may have been trying to pit you against me, Raven. Rue may be right about that. If he wants you our...connection...would certainly be in his way. He'd want to sever that."

"What about Saria, then? She told me you visit her bed regularly," Raven said.

Talyn resisted the urge to cradle his aching head in his hands. "Saria," he stated carefully, "is incredibly jealous of you. She would say anything, or use any situation to her advantage if it were to hurt you."

Raven looked to the floor. "I don't know what to think," she whispered.

Talyn walked toward her. She looked so sad and sounded so sorrowful. His heart twisted. She looked up and stabbed him with a piercing gaze. "But you still won't take me to monogamous mate status, will you?"

He stopped in his tracks.

She raised one narrow black brow above a beautiful eye. "That's what I thought."

Rue stepped forward. "Give me one night, Raven. Give me one night with you. Forget Talyn and Gavin. You know you belong with me."

Talyn turned and growled at him. "Stay out of this, Rue."

Rue kept his eyes on Raven. "She arouses me like no other woman in this castle."

"You can have your pick of females here. Go find another," Talyn drawled out. "This one is mine."

"Would another be good enough for you, Captain Talyn? From what I've seen, I think not. Yet even for your apparent fidelity, you are still not ready to take that final step and make her your monogamous mate, are you? I think that's clear enough."

He glanced at Raven. "I...I don't know."

"Then I want her," said Rue. "Just for a night."

"No," Talyn growled.

Rue sighed. "Well, it's not for you to decide, is it?"

"Have you two forgotten I'm standing here?" said Raven. "No one has asked me what *I* what." Her gaze pierced Talyn. "Of Rue I can understand his lack of courtesy. He was raised in Sudhra and things are different there. But not of you, Talyn. You haven't pledged me to monogamous mate status. Even if what you say about not bedding other women is true, you still have the potential to do it. I seem to remember a blond beauty named Saria ready to spread her legs for you at a word. Whether or not she lied to me, you're free to slip your cock into her any time you choose it. Why shouldn't I take another?"

Damn Gavin. Damn him to the bowels of fiery, inner Aran. "I don't want anyone but you," he answered truthfully.

"But you will not take me to monogamous mate status."

Talyn glanced at the floor and then back to her face.

Pain flooded her eyes. She turned to Rue and crooked a finger. Rue followed as if on a string. They walked toward the door.

Jealousy coursed through Talyn so hard it hurt. "Wait!"

Raven halted and slowly turned.

"I'll...I'll share you with him...once, but I will not allow him to come within your passage."

She only stared at him.

"Raven...I cannot bear the thought of another man taking you," he admitted. "Gavin was correct in that, at least." Talyn had to touch her. He stepped forward and drew her into his arms.

* * * * *

Talyn touched her and she knew instantly that Gavin had played her for a fool. All the love she had for Talyn came rushing up and threatened to overwhelm her.

Tenderly, he covered her mouth with his. He cupped her face between his strong hands and kissed her like he'd die if he couldn't. His tongue stroked into her mouth deeply, probing the recesses, like she knew his cock would soon do within her passage.

He released her mouth, leaving her feeling weak-kneed and drugged. "Touch me," she murmured.

Talyn obliged, his hands slipping down to cup her breasts, rub over her nipples through her gown. Then he was slipping her clothing up and over her head. Her gown fell to the floor, leaving her naked to the gentle, warm air.

Rue came to stand behind her. Raven had forgotten he was even in the room. She stood bracketed in the body heat of the two Aviat men, feeling strangely protected and undeniably aroused.

Talyn slipped his hand down, palming her stomach and tangling his fingers in the dark, curling hair of her mound. She spread her legs for him and he slipped his fingers down, then up. Two of his thick fingers slid into her passage and stroked. She let out a hiss of breath from between her teeth and gripped his shoulders.

From behind, Rue ran his hands over her back and buttocks, his fingers delving down to her anus and slipping over her.

Talyn went to his knees and took a nipple into his mouth as he continued to thrust his fingers into her. Her peak built, inexorably, until she could stand it no longer and she climaxed with a series of moans as her vaginal muscles convulsed. Her fingers clenched on Talyn's shoulders.

Talyn stood and guided her over to the table. Rue went to the opposite side, at her head, took her wrists and pressed her down onto the table while Talyn spread her legs. Rue held her arms pinned while Talyn planed her inner thigh with his palm and ran his fingers up to her pussy.

There was something incredibly erotic about having one man restrain her and watch while another fondled her. Especially when she knew she could get away from them at any time she wished. Talyn slipped one finger inside her, then another, and began to work them in and out of her passage. Oh...sweet Goddess...but she didn't wish to get away. Her eyes fluttered shut.

"Do you like that, Raven?" asked Talyn.

She nodded.

He brushed her clit with the flat of his thumb and she gasped. "And that?"

"Yes," she moaned.

He circled her clit with his thumb and her second peak burst in a cresting wave, making her cry out.

He lowered his head between her legs and lapped up every bit of the liquid that spilled out of her. His tongue explored each fold with exquisite care, delving into her passage from time to time. His mouth settled over her clit, not letting go of the sensitized bit of flesh as he laved and sucked at it. She thrust her hips forward and tossed her head.

Still, Rue held her arms. She could hear his aroused breathing over her. For the third time she came, screaming Talyn's name.

Talyn lowered his trews and put the head of his cock to her passage, then teased her with it by brushing up and twirling the tip of it around her clit.

"Come inside me," she begged.

"What my Raven wants, she gets." With one hard stroke, he sheathed himself within her to the hilt. She arched her spine, stabbing her hard nipples into the air and Rue released her wrists and caught them between his fingertips.

Talyn's strokes faltered and he growled.

"I just wish to taste her nipples," came Rue's rasping voice.

"No more than that," Talyn ground out.

Then Talyn began to stroke and Raven became conscious of nothing more than him within her and Rue massaging her breasts, rolling the hardened nipples between his thumbs and forefingers.

She closed her eyes and gripped the edge of the table, immersing herself in the incredible sensations. Talyn gripped her hips and pounded his cock into her pussy. The sounds of their lovemaking were audible as her passage sought to keep him within her on every outward pull. Talyn's murmurings of how good she felt around his cock nearly drove her over the edge.

Rue lowered his mouth to one of her nipples and laved it with a skillful tongue. Using his teeth gently on the hardened peak, he drew a moan from her throat. With his other hand he worked the breast not attended to by his mouth.

When Talyn began massaging her clit, she came hard and fast, overcome by the exquisite combination of hands, tongue, teeth and cock.

Talyn came with her, spilling his hot seed inside her with an agonized groan. After his tremors had subsided, Talyn gathered her up against him, while still sheathed within her, and stroked her hair. "I love you," he murmured over and over.

Raven heard Rue politely take his leave. Undoubtedly, he would go in search of a willing woman. She knew well he'd have no trouble. Indeed, the lucky woman would benefit from his state of arousal.

"I want you—" murmured Talyn into her hair.

"You have me, Talyn." And it was true. Even if Talyn never asked her to become his monogamous mate she would appreciate every moment she had with him.

"No. I mean I want you to be my monogamous mate."

She shook her head. "But you just let me know that you didn't want that."

"I've changed my mind. Raven, I want you for my own. Seeing Rue touch you inflamed my anger. I have never felt that way about a woman, never felt so possessive. Gavin was lying to you, but there was a kernel of truth in what he said. If I cannot bear the thought of another man having you, then I should not have the option to take another female. Our path lies as mates, Raven. You and I and no other."

Pleasure coursed through her at his words. Raven hoped Talyn would be happy to discover that not only was he Aviat, he was tied to her as well. She couldn't wait to tell him.

"Do you accept?"

The words came out with a rush of relieved air. "Of course I do."

He crushed her to him and feathered kisses over her lips, cheeks and forehead. "I love you, Raven."

Pleasure for what was to come coursed through her. "I have something to tell you, Talyn. Something very—"

A scream broke from the courtyard below, quickly followed by shouts and sounds of commotion. Raven and Talyn ran to the window and looked down onto the dusk-darkened courtyard.

Gavin had returned leading a horse. Facedown over its withers laid an ashen skinned and naked blond woman.

"Saria," breathed Raven.

Talyn turned from the window, scooped Raven's gown up from the floor, and handed it to her. Together they ran from the room. Raven slipped the dress over her head as she went.

Her bare feet pounded on the steps as she followed Talyn down the tower stairs and out the door at the very bottom. By the time they reached the gathering crowd, they were both out of breath.

People gathered around Gavin, who had dismounted. Haeffen had pulled Saria from the horse and cradled her limp body in his arms. Her neck was bent at an unnatural angle. Raven could see that life no longer lit her body.

"What has happened here?" roared Talyn as he stepped through the crowd of people and advanced on Gavin.

"One of the breeders!" wailed an old woman in the crowd. "She might have conceived again!"

"She fell from her horse and broke her neck," explained Gavin. "We were riding down the bank of the Grosham River. The rocks we were traveling over were wet and her horse had trouble. She was thrown off-balance and lost her seat."

Talyn took two menacing steps toward the other man, his hands fisting. "Then why are her clothes off?" He ground out between gritted teeth.

Gavin glanced at Saria and back at Talyn. "Because when I pleasured her in the river they got wet. She decided to ride without them."

"Where are they?"

Gavin walked to Saria's horse, pulled a wet gown from the saddlebag and threw it at Talyn. "I'm sorry you don't trust me."

Talyn ignored him and walked to Saria's body. Raven moved so she could overhear what he said to Haeffen.

"She has bruising around her throat," noted Talyn.

"Aye," answered Haeffen.

"Something doesn't seem right."

"I agree," said Haeffen.

The crowd parted as Lord Marken entered the courtyard and approached. He calmly surveyed the scene and sighed. He said in his deep, commanding voice, "When Saria has been given to the women for burial preparation, I want to see Gavin, Talyn, and Haeffen in my receiving room. Everyone else, please return to your activities and give Saria some respect."

"Oh, my dear Goddess!" someone in the crowd cried.

"It's Alia!" cried another who pointed skyward.

Like a wind of terror blowing through the crowd, they all turned their faces skyward as did Raven. Upon the battlements lining the left side of the courtyard, tottled Alia, dangerously close to the edge. Raven gasped and put a hand to her mouth, remembering Alia smiling at her from her mother's feet in the ladies' solar. Had Saria not given Alia into proper care before she'd left with Gavin?

Raven watched Talyn tear through the crowd, fighting to get through the people who all looked skyward, and get to the stairs leading to the battlements. Raven followed him.

At the same time they reached the stairs, the crowd collectively gasped, then screamed. Raven looked up to see Alia's body fall like a rag doll from high above. Her dark hair streamed around her as she plummeted toward the ground.

"Sweet Goddess, no," whispered Talyn beside her.

"Oh, *please,*" implored Raven softly. "Oh please, let it be true." She squeezed her eyes shut, replaying Saria's words in her mind. *I think she's Talyn's.*

The scream of a child in pain rent the suddenly quiet air, followed by a gasp rippling through the crowd and finally a collective sigh.

Talyn uttered a string of oaths under his breath. "She's sprouted the wings of a dove," he said in amazement.

Raven opened one eye, and then the other. Indeed, Alia now flew around the crowd, diving and swerving in the air. Raven listened closely...and she was giggling. Raven smiled. According to Grandmother, most Aviats did not take to the air until they were far older than Alia because they lacked control in flight. However, younger ones did mentally accept flight much easier than older ones, since they had fewer fears impeding them.

She stepped away from Talyn, who seemed as frozen with shock as the rest of the crowd. Walking into an open area of the courtyard, she began calling to Alia in her native language. Alia's blood would understand the cooing, clicking language. It would be instinctive to her, even being a half-breed, without ever having heard it before.

Gently, she called Alia to her, instructed her to slow down, use the airflow, and turn right and then left until she'd guided the girl down into her arms. Raven crushed her to her chest and stroked her hair. Tears of joy pricked her eyes at the wonderful visual knowledge that she was not the last Aviat. They mixed with tears of sorrow because Alia had lost her mother.

Alia's wings refolded into her body, leaving long weals on her small shoulder blades and her gown ripped. The girl whimpered.

"I know it hurts, but it is a small price to pay. You will see that with time. You did wonderfully, Alia," Raven praised.

Haeffen parted the crowd, which hung back from Raven, watching in amazement and curiosity. He'd apparently given Saria over to someone else. All the better. Alia did not need to see her mother's body. Talyn trailed Haeffen.

"Aviat!" Haeffen declared as he reached them.

Talyn covered Alia's head with his huge hand. The child was already falling asleep in Raven's arms, her head tucked between Raven's chin and collarbone. "What?" he asked absently, a smile playing with his well-formed lips.

"In the books you gave me, I found an archive of a race that is said to have once lived in the northern forests of Nordan. They are called the Aviat and are a little known race. Most think they're but a legend. This race sprouts wings, but to do it, they must launch themselves from a high place." His gaze fixed on Raven. "Like a window. And they bear scars along their shoulder blades, from where their appendages rip through to unfurl."

Talyn looked at Raven. "Is he correct, Raven? He glanced at Alia. But how does that explain—"

"She's your child, Talyn," Raven said. "Your seed is likely the only in the castle that could've created an Aviat."

He turned and stared at her. "What do you mean?"

"You...you're an Aviat too. You've just never spread your wings."

Chapter Five

Raven flipped the blankets back and rose from the bed. Talyn had been in conference with Marken, Haeffen and Gavin all evening. It was now well into the night and still Talyn was cloistered with his lord. Raven had given Alia into the care of the loving and very protective nanny in the children's wing of the castle. But still Raven was troubled. The entire castle now knew of Alia's, Talyn's, and her own heritage. Would they covet their wings like so many before?

She walked to the fire burning in the hearth and the table flanking it. Reverently, she touched the hilt of the dagger she'd requested Talyn leave with her. No sense in taking any chances.

Raven sighed. Perhaps sitting by the fire would ease her nerves. She'd been far too troubled to sleep. She'd barely had time to speak to Talyn before Lord Marken had commanded he confer with him about the recent events. Many things had to be tumbling around in Talyn's mind right now. Would he be happy that he shared such a strong connection with her? Raven hoped so.

On the morrow she would seek Rue out and they would have a long talk. Where had he come from? Where were the others and how had they come to reside so far from their native northern forests?

She sank into one of the plush velvet chairs flanking the table. When Talyn came she would be able to sleep in his arms. She simply had to bide her time until then.

The sounds of a key in the door lock had Raven standing up. "Talyn?" she called to the shadow-swathed room.

No response. The door creaked opened slowly and Raven grabbed the dagger from the table. A dark head poked into the room.

"Talyn?" she asked again shakily.

The man entered the chamber, his face still swathed by the shadows. Raven let out a sigh. She could tell by the way he moved, the easy and confident gait he had, that it was indeed Talyn.

Dropping the dagger on the table, she met him halfway. His face came into the light, revealing a black and blue eye and a bruised jaw. She frowned. "What happened?"

"Gavin happened. I confronted him about what he said to you."

She touched his face and he winced. "You brawled again."

"This time it was the other man who threw the first punch. He didn't end up throwing the *only* one, though." He grinned in the way only a man happy with being a man can. "But you should see *him.*"

"I'm sure," she said dryly. "Come and sit by the fire. I'll dampen a rag and wash away some of that blood."

"Stay away from him, Raven. It cannot be proved he had anything to do with Saria's death, but it cannot be proved he did not, either. I don't trust him."

"Nor do I."

He sat down, and she found some clean material and wet it in the basin of tepid water that sat on a table near the bed. She stood in front of him, one hand braced on the back of the chair and the other gently dabbing the blood away from his face.

With one smooth movement, he pulled her down onto his lap so she straddled him. "Better," he murmured.

Her core rubbed against his already hardening cock. "Much," she answered, then continued to clean his cuts.

"I remembered some things this evening, after you told me about my possible heritage—"

"Possible? It's definite, my love."

"I...I don't have reason to doubt you at this point, but how can you be so sure?"

"The vibration that occurs between us at contact. You and I are tied...as" --she stopped her ministrations and caught his gaze— "as mates." She shook her head. "The vibration wouldn't occur with just any person, definitely not a non-Aviat and then with only select Aviats, according to Rue."

"Rue?"

"Rue is also an Aviat, Talyn." She let go of a deep sigh. "This has been a day of many revelations."

"Being tied as mates explains how I knew you were in the tower with Rue. I saw you in my mind—in a sort of mental link. When did you know? About me, I mean."

"After I talked with Rue in the tower. Then I knew for certain you were an Aviat."

Talyn fell silent.

She continued to dab at his wounds. When she was finished, she dropped her hands in her lap. "What is it?" she asked.

"I remember a woman with long amber-colored hair and huge white wings. I remember flying through the air with her as she held me. I have flashes in my mind of people I don't know, but yet...*I do.*"

He gazed at the fire, but Raven knew he wasn't really seeing it. He was looking back into his own shadowed past. "I have memories of being cherished and loved," he continued. "Then a band of men came through, and I have flashes of blood, carnage. My people harnessed by ropes and pulled from the sky, choking. I see wings cut, stained with blood, piled on a cart. I see those same people who cherished me lying in the dirt, dying."

"I'm sorry you remember such heartbreaking things, Talyn."

"No...I'm happy to remember. They are terrible occurrences, but for the first time, I feel like I have a whole life instead of only a part of one—for better or for worse. I feel like I belong somewhere, and I have a history. I have a people," he finished in near awe. He ran his finger down her cheek. "You gave me that."

His finger reached her mouth and she kissed it, then licked it, then drew it into her mouth and sucked. His eyes went dark.

The look in his eyes stirred a familiar response in her. Her clit pulsed and her nipples tightened. She fumbled with the drawstrings of his trews as he raised her skirts. She positioned herself over him and then sank down.

They both groaned at the satisfaction of being joined so intimately with the other. Raven felt whole when he was sheathed inside her. She began to move to meet him as Talyn thrust up into her wet heat.

* * * * *

Raven opened her eyes and stretched. She was sore in intimate places after a night of making love with Talyn. It was a good kind of sore, though.

She rolled over. Talyn lay on his back, one arm crossed over his abdomen. The blanket was twisted around him from the hips down, giving her a view of his muscled chest and arms and the thin trail of brown hair that led to the coarser hair around his cock. A thread of desire heated her blood. She snuggled down into the crook of his arm, and he gave a contented sigh in his sleep and drew her more firmly against him.

She laid like that for a long time, matching the cadence of her breathing to his, before she slid out from the blankets, donned a gown…and a dagger for protection…and slipped out the door.

The sun had just begun to rise in the east and the castle was stirring. She headed for the gardens to enjoy the sunrise. She had no desire to run into Gavin and she knew she wouldn't see him there.

It had rained hard the night before and the world smelled fresh and damp. As she walked through the lush place, she touched the head of each flower lightly before finding a stone bench to sit down on. The mornings were becoming warmer with each passing day. Summer was approaching prematurely from the feel of things. Closing her eyes she enjoyed the weather and the knowledge that Talyn truly loved her.

Could life be any sweeter?

"Raven," said a low voice behind her.

She jumped up and whirled around. "Gavin." One of his eyes was swollen nearly shut and his jaw was black and blue.

"I was hoping to find you here."

She tilted her head at him, simultaneously putting a hand on her waist, near the dagger that was sheathed there. "Why would you be trying to find me after you lied to me yesterday? You must know I have no interest in speaking with you."

Gavin brought his hand up, revealing a small device. She squinted. It looked like the object was spring loaded to emit something. She backed away at the realization and began to run.

"That's of no consequence," she heard him say behind her just as something sharp stabbed her in the lower back and she collapsed on the wet, flower-strewn ground of the gardens.

She moaned softly and tried to move, but her limbs wouldn't cooperate. They were so heavy, and she was so very tired. She heard him kneel beside her. "Hapinstock leaf extract in a dart. I use them for hunting. It's very effective, don't you think?"

Black spots formed in front of her eyes and she forced herself to stay conscious. Her body was completely numb. She couldn't even move a finger. Gavin flipped her over and scooped her into his arms. As he walked her out of the gardens, she saw from an upside down vantage point that he'd tethered his horse near the entrance. The courtyard was empty.

He slung her face first over the horse's withers and laid a blanket over her. Then he mounted and she heard, rather than felt, the horse walk forward. It felt like she had no body. She was merely a disembodied consciousness. Fear flickered through her as she wondered if he'd take her wings while she was numb. She didn't know if they would unfurl while she was in such a condition. But it was possible he could throw her from some high place and her numb and useless wings would unfurl, and she would land in a broken heap on the ground below leaving him to harvest them.

The sound of the horse's hooves on the cobblestone and the squeak of the leather saddle seemed very far away. Gavin said something to the guardsmen at the barbican, and the horse clattered over the drawbridge. Time seemed to come in snippets as she faded in and out of consciousness. Sometimes Gavin sang as they rode, sometimes he whistled.

Little by little she regained feeling in her limbs. She had the sense they'd traveled a great distance because her body, especially her stomach, ached from being jolted by the horse. Her wrists and ankles were tied. She wiggled them. *Tight.*

Gavin began stroking in the general vicinity of her buttocks and she stiffened, almost wishing the poison he'd injected her with wasn't wearing off. "You will catch me many flourentimes in Sudhra, my little winged one," he murmured. "The men will pay well to fuck an Aviat woman. I'll have to clip your wings off first though, of course."

Rage struck Raven hard in the abdomen and spread out. She flailed. Digging her knees into the horse, she caused it to whinny and jolt to the left. At the same time she wiggled enough so that she slipped off and landed first on her bound feet and then on her butt on the grass. The blanket that had covered her slid off and ended up in a heap beside her. All the air whooshed out of her lungs, leaving her without words.

Gavin halted the horse in front of her and sighed. "Raven, do you really think you'll be able to get away from me? Your fate is sealed. The sooner you accept that the better."

She rolled onto her stomach and then fought to sit up again. Using her motions to distract Gavin's attention, she worked the dagger out from her waistband. Thank Aran he'd tied her hands in front. Once she sat back up again, she palmed the dagger and worked the blade unobtrusively at the rope binding her wrists. "Why are you doing this?" she asked in an effort to keep his attention on something other than her hands.

He laughed. "Why? The money, of course. I'll be able to cut off your wings and sell them, then I'll whore your body out to the jaded, bored men of Sudhra."

She felt the rope give, and braced her hands to her chest so the ropes didn't fall, giving the illusion she was still bound. She shook her head. "Don't you know? If you cut off my wings, I'll die."

He stroked his chin. "I've never heard that before. I think you're lying."

"Check the historical records that are undoubtedly kept in Sudhra," she spat, "you'll see right away that it's true. One hundred years ago, during the hunts in Northern Nordan, hunters cutting off their wings slaughtered hundreds of my kind. It has happened since then too, to smaller pockets of remaining Aviat, making the race nearly extinct."

His brown eyes glimmered in the late afternoon sunlight. "I'll check your claim. If it's true, I'll decide which will bring me more flourentimes, your wings, or your body." He shrugged. "You're my first Aviat.

Everyone said how difficult they were to capture. When I heard my number one rival, Cyrus, had gone to Nordan to catch one, and then I heard about the woman he left behind when he'd been killed, I put two and two together."

"Why didn't you take Alia?"

"The last thing I need is a squalling kid. Anyway, I couldn't figure out how to get her out of the castle. You were hard enough with the ever-watchful Talyn at your side. I tried for a long time to be your friend, get you to trust me so I could lure you away from the castle. That didn't work. Then I tried to drive a wedge between you and your lover and make you run. That didn't work either. Finally I gave up and did it the blunt way. " He flashed a white smile. "It was a risk, but it worked."

"Did you kill Saria?"

He shrugged. "I like my women afraid when I fuck them. I got a little carried away and snapped her neck."

He dismounted and Raven tensed, her hand tightening around the hilt of the dagger. He swaggered toward her—a man pleased with himself and confident in his position. "You're too far from the castle now, Raven. We're over the border, in Sudhra. It's far too great a distance for your lover to track you. He'll never find you. Never."

He knelt in front of her and leaned to kiss her. "Might as well sample the wares now."

She smiled and glanced down at her bound feet. "That's going to be a little hard, don't you think?"

His lips skimmed hers and she suppressed a shudder of dread. "It sounds like you want me to fuck you."

She shook her head. "I'd sooner sleep with a dog." She smiled. "Although, I guess that's what I'd be doing."

He stood and withdrew a small blade from his saddle pack, then cut her ankles free. "Let's find out how much you'd enjoy a dog fucking you, shall we?" He threw the blade on the grass and crawled on his hands and knees up her body.

She separated her wrists. The rope fell to her lap and she arched the dagger out and up — straight into his side.

Raven didn't stop to stare at the look of amazement on his face. She backed away from him on her hands and feet, and then began to scramble upright. A strong hand clamped over her ankle and she sat back down hard on her butt. She kicked, slamming her heel into Gavin's forehead.

There was a flash of silver and biting pain starting in her thigh and spreading out. Raven looked down and saw the blade Gavin has used to cut the bonds around her ankles sticking out of her thigh.

The world went black as she lost consciousness.

* * * * *

Talyn paced at the end of the corridor, staring at the floor-to-ceiling window at the end. He'd awoken that morning to an empty bed. Raven often woke before him and whiled the sunrise away in the gardens, so he hadn't thought anything was amiss. He'd gone to the yard to train, as he did everyday. But by midday when he still hadn't seen Raven, he'd begun to become concerned.

A search of the castle hadn't turned her up. Even more unsettling, Gavin was also missing. Talyn had gone to the barbican and asked after Gavin there. The guard said he'd left early with a sheaf of unprocessed arpinseed stalks slung over his horse's withers, saying he was bound for the Sudhraian border because it had been left off the last shipment of supplies.

Lies.

Talyn closed his eyes and searched again for the mental link he shared with Raven. At first it had been blurry and confused. He thought probably because Raven was drugged. At times it was dark altogether.

Now it was positively black. A shudder coursed through him. Was she still alive?

Talyn eyed the open floor-to-ceiling window. Flashes of Raven flooded his mind. In them, she laughed, cried, and moaned out her pleasure at his hands. He thought of Gavin, and Talyn began to run.

He ran faster and faster and the window grew closer and closer. With a yell half of fear and half of hope his feet hit the sill and he pushed off. For a heartbeat it felt like he was flying and then for another it felt as though he hung suspended in the air.

Then he fell.

Wind rushed past him, buffeting his hair, making his shirt billow around him. The ground came up to meet him with a sickening swiftness. He closed his eyes in sorrow.

She'd been wrong and his memories were false. He wasn't an Aviat at all.

A lightening fast flash of pain ripped through his shoulder blades and down both sides of his back. In midair his spine arched and he gave a bellow of pain. Snapping and crackling, bones formed, tendons and muscles stretched and feathers spread. Still, he fell. Wind whistled through his new wings.

Use them, you idiot! Focusing on his newfound muscles, he flapped his wings experimentally, then flapped repeatedly. Now, instead of plummeting, he rose. Experimentally, he manipulated the pitch and angle of his wings and learned how to turn and swoop and dive. He caught a gust of wind and soared up higher than the castle, higher than the treetops and looked down at everyone in the inner and outer bailies staring up at him in awe.

Euphoria surged into him. He felt so free! He felt freer than he ever had in his life. Raven had given that to him. At the thought of Raven, his euphoria vanished and he angled himself to the south. Gavin had to be taking her back to Sudhra.

Deprived of his mental link with Raven, Talyn knew he would have to rely on his own innate tracking abilities to find her. He scanned the ground below him. Treetops, roofs, and livestock sailed past. He used his superior eyesight to search for any traces of Gavin's passing. In the earth soaked from the rain that had fallen the night before, Talyn found fresh horse tracks leading away from the castle and followed them.

He flew a great distance, panic rising within him at the sights that met his eyes. Just past the Nordanese border, Sudhraian soldiers had attacked villages. Smoke rose in plumes from burned cottages and displaced peasants roamed around their sacked homes, searching for things to salvage.

Talyn knew that scouts and messengers had undoubtedly already brought word of the initial onslaught of Sudhraian troops back to the nearby lorddoms. He had to concentrate on finding Raven. Once that was done, he had to get back to the castle.

Finally, he spotted them in a field. Two crumpled figures lay near each other while a horse pulled up grass not far away. Goddess, Raven was so still... He brought himself down to the ground and his wings furled. He barely felt the sharp lick of pain through his shoulder blades. Gavin lay facedown on the grass. Talyn ran past him, focused on Raven. She lay face up in the grass, her skin ashen. The hilt of a blade protruded from her thigh.

He knelt by her and felt that she was breathing. Intense relief washed through him. Her eyelids fluttered. "Raven?"

"Tal..." her eyes opened. "Talyn," she said on a sigh.

He caught her up and pressed her against him, one hand threaded through the hair at the nape of her neck, his other hand went tight around her waist. "I thought he'd killed you," he bit off.

Her hands fisted in his tunic at his shoulders. "I thought I'd never see you again."

He pulled away and glanced at the hilt of the dagger. "That has to come out."

"I know."

He laid her back on the grass. "I'll be right back." He went into the woods at the outer edge of the clearing. Calenweed would work best for the pain, but was hard to find. Yar root would be the second best thing and was plentiful. Talyn was glad he could put into use some of his soldier's field knowledge. At the base of an oak tree he found some Yar root. Using his short sword, he dug it up, then went back to Raven.

He handed her a chunk of the root he'd sliced off using his dagger and held it out to her. "Chew this and swallow the liquid you get from it. Once you've chewed the root until there's no liquid left, swallow it."

She accepted it, placed the root in her mouth, and made a face.

"Aye, it's bitter. But it will act quickly and will numb you to the pain you feel when I pull the blade from your thigh."

She nodded.

Giving the root time to work, Talyn checked Gavin. He was still alive. She'd stabbed him in the side with a small blade. As long as she hadn't hit any major organs, he would probably live. Right now Talyn was far more concerned with Raven's well being. In Gavin's saddle pack he found a tunic and ripped it into long pieces to staunch the flow of blood from Raven's thigh. He also found a bottle of wound astringent.

He walked back to her with them in his hand. "How are you feeling? Are you ready for this?"

"No, but let's do it anyway."

"How is the pain in your thigh?"

"It's numb. I think the root you gave me is working."

"All right. It's now or never, then." He knelt and gave her the ripped tunic. "Bite on that."

Her eyes widened.

"I won't lie to you, Raven. This will pain you greatly. Bite."

She put the material in her mouth and bit. Talyn curled his hand around the hilt of the dagger and caught Raven's gaze.

She nodded.

He pulled.

She screamed. The material fell out of her open mouth.

Talyn threw the blade to the grass beside her and picked up the wound astringent. He poured it over her wound, and then grabbed the ripped tunic. "Are you all right, Raven?" he asked as he quickly wrapped the material around her thigh and pulled it tight to stop the blood flow. She let out a sound of anguish and squeezed her eyes shut.

"I'm sorry, my love," he said, sounding just as anguished as she had. "I'm so sorry this is hurting you. You were very brave to defeat Gavin on your own." He looked at her. "I'll be honored to call you my monogamous mate."

She opened her eyes and gasped. "Behind you!" she yelled.

Talyn's hand went to his sword hilt and as he stood and turned, he pulled it free of its scabbard with a ringing hiss. Gavin lurched toward him, slashing out with his blade. Talyn pivoted and Gavin's sword tip grazed his side, slashing through his tunic and drawing blood.

With an enraged roar, Talyn spun, bringing the wicked edge of his blade along with him. He felt it sink into Gavin's soft belly. Gavin made a noise that was half a yell and half a scream and went down hard on the grass.

This time he wouldn't get up.

Talyn pulled his sword free. He hated to kill. It was his job as captain of Marken's Lorddom to kill and teach others to kill quickly and effectively, but he never took joy in it.

He turned toward Raven. She sat on the grass with her hand pressed against her mouth. Her eyes were bright with tears Talyn doubted would fall...not for Gavin who'd undoubtedly been ready to take her wings. "Are you hurt?" she asked.

He shook his head and sighed wearily. "It is a scratch, nothing more." He sheathed his sword, which was still stained with Gavin's blood, and scooped her into his arms. "If we hurry we might make the castle by nightfall."

"You mean to ride?"

"We cannot leave this valuable mount here. We are fatigued and too tired to fly. I'm prepared to let the horse bear our weight. He has ridden all day, I realize, but he's had a long rest and has gorged himself on grass. I saw a stream not far where he could drink."

She nodded, and he lifted her onto the back of the horse. He gathered the blanket that was lying on the ground, packed it, and mounted behind her. He headed the horse out of the clearing, back toward Nordan.

* * * * *

Raven leaned back against Talyn's strong chest and closed her eyes. The jolting of the horse made the pain of her thigh a dull, thudding ache. Thank the Goddess for Yar root. Without that she knew she'd really be hurting right now.

After the horse had drunk deeply from the stream and they'd traveled a distance, he told of the pillaging he'd seen at the border. They would travel carefully. Now they guided the horse down a little used road from the looks of it, and hadn't seen a soul for miles and miles.

His lips grazed her temple. "Are you hurting?"

"Some. But it's merely a constant ache and discomfort thanks to the root, not true pain."

With deft fingers, he knotted the horse's reins and laid them over the mount's neck. He put his mouth to her ear and whispered, "I can distract you from it if you'd like me to."

She shivered with pleasure and anticipation. "You know you can do anything to my body you wish, Talyn. I am yours to play upon like a musical instrument."

"Mmmmm," he purred. "And how I love the sounds I can pull from your beautiful lungs when I work you just right."

He slid his hands to her calves and caught the edge of her skirt. With careful, deliberate slowness, he drew it up and up until it lay bunched around her waist. Taking his dagger, he slid it beneath the waistband of her thin scrap of an undergarment and sliced through it. The blade felt cool against her suddenly flushed skin. He did the same on the other side. He sheathed his dagger and gently began to pull the material from under her. The back of his thumb teased her clit briefly, a taste of things to come. He tossed the scrap of cloth to the ground and she tipped her pelvis forward to let the breeze bathe her naked, wet sex.

"Are you distracted yet, Raven?" he murmured into her ear. He placed his fingers to the crease where her inner thigh met her hip and caressed. His voice was a dark, silken snare. "This is my favorite place on your body. I wish I could kiss it right now, run my tongue over it. Would you like me to do that?" One thumb grazed her clit as he ran his fingers over those two creases over and over. Her clit engorged, infused with blood.

"I just want you to touch me," she said, squirming.

"I am touching you," he teased. "Where *specifically* do you want me to caress?" He moved his fingers to her pussy lips and rubbed. "Here?"

"Yesss," she responded on a sigh.

He moved to her clit, circling it around and around. "Here?"

"Oh, Goddess, yes."

He slipped two fingers into her passage, finding her pleasure point within, and stroked in and out over it as he circled her clit with his other hand.

Raven made no attempt to hide her vocal response to the pleasure he was giving her. Her moans ricocheted off the trees and through the forests. Her peak built and then crested. Intense waves of pleasure starting at her pleasure point and clit burst and then spread out.

Talyn groaned. "Goddess, but you excite me." He pushed his hips forward and pressed the long, hard truth of it into the small of her back.

The waves of her climax still racked her body as he began the process again. "Come again for me, Raven," he murmured into her ear.

She climaxed three times in a row, but still he didn't stop caressing her. Over and over he made her come. As she came down from one peak, he instantly began building another. He kept her in a state of constant and incredible arousal. She forgot all about the pain of her thigh.

Without a word, he halted the horse and lifted her down. He gently laid her on the grass beside the road, lifted her skirts and spread her legs. With a dark and ravenous look on his face, his head disappeared between her thighs. Making groaning and sucking noises, he lapped up all the juice he'd wrung from her with his erotic play.

She arched her back and moaned as he used his thumbs to spread her pussy lips apart and his tongue delved into her passageway hungrily. Then his mouth clamped over her clit and, making growling noises deep in his throat, he sucked at it. At the same time, his hands anxiously worked at the drawstrings of his trews.

Raven tossed her head back and forth, making incomprehensible noises of ecstasy as she peaked under the onslaught of his expertly wielded tongue.

He lowered his trews and braies and as she climaxed he surged into her with one long, hard stroke, sending her buttocks into the grass bed beneath her and touching her womb with the head of his cock. She called out his name and spread her legs as far as she could without paining her thigh.

He grunted sexily as he thrust in and out with long and slow strokes. Raven could see the pains he took to ensure he did not injure her thigh. Over and over he rubbed against her pleasure point with the tip of his cock and his pelvis brushed against her clit.

She came again, the muscles of her passage clenching and unclenching around his cock, massaging him and milking him at the same time. He released himself along with her, yelling out his pleasure to the treetops as his hot seed burst within her.

Rolling carefully to the side, his fingertips grazed her wrapped thigh. "Forgive me, Raven. I forgot myself. I'm like an untried youth with no control around you."

"I would have it no other way." She felt incredibly relaxed and sated.

"Does your thigh hurt?"

"Not badly, but I think the effects of the root are wearing off slowly."

He stood, drew up his trews, and got another bit of root for her to chew on. He lifted her and placed her back on the horse. "I want to get you back to the castle so the physician can tend you."

Chapter Six

It was twilight when they finally crossed into Nordan. Raven tightened her hands in the horse's mane at the vision that greeted them.

"It's worse than what I saw from the air," breathed Talyn.

Smoke billowed from a small village just past the Nordanese border. The village seemed deserted as they approached cautiously. The Sudhraian soldiers that had attacked were long gone and had left the survivors to the task of cleaning up.

Raven squinted. In a clearing to the left of the burned out and destroyed cluster of the thatched village buildings, was a group of women and children carrying stones to place on cairns. Raven pointed them out and Talyn angled the horse in that direction.

"What has happened here?" Talyn asked an old man at the outer edge of the group. "How long ago did the soldiers come through?"

The old man regarded them with his rheumy eyes. "Yesterday, my lord. They killed some, took none."

Talyn dismounted. "Took none? Not even women?"

Raven knew that meant they were moving with purpose, no time to dally. It also meant they were confident of taking Nordan and believed the women would be there to harvest later.

"They came through fast, my lord. They burned, they pillaged. They could have lingered and done more damaged, but they did not."

A beautiful woman wearing a red scarf over her blond hair came up to Talyn and spat at him angrily. Her blue eyes flashed. "Where are the soldiers to protect us, my lord?"

Sorrow consumed Talyn's expression. "I am the Captain of the Guard of Lord Marken's Lorddom. There are soldiers down the river at the larger town of Satam." He shook his head. "But we cannot protect every inch of the Sudhraian-Nordanese border. It's far too much. The soldiers are moving toward Lord Gregor's Lorddom, if I am not mistaken, and at a fair clip. They will be overtaken by Nordanese guardsmen before they arrive."

Raven was aware that Marken's Lorddom was just beyond Gregor's. Scouts had undoubtedly already warned Marken of the impending threat, but they had to get back, and fast.

"That doesn't help us, does it? You're useless!" accused the woman as she turned away. Quietly, she sobbed into her hands.

The old man placed an arm around her thin shoulders and looked up at Talyn. "She lost her fiancé and her family yesterday," he explained.

"I'm sorry," Talyn said on a heavy sigh. He surveyed the rest of the people. They regarded them with sadness, anger, and hope.

"More Sudhraian soldiers will be through here," Talyn said loud enough so the rest could hear. He spread his arms wide. "You are offered refuge in Lord Marken's Lorddom. Anyone who wishes to go there may do so. It will be a trip fraught with danger, however, as Sudhraian soldiers now roam this countryside, and you will have to travel quickly."

A murmur threaded through the group. "What of the rest of our belongings and livestock?" asked one.

"Gather what is left and bring it with you. You will be safe behind the lorddom's walls. But I need someone to guide you. Is there one here who can lead the way? I see no strong men."

The blond woman turned. "I can lead them."

"But—"

She tipped her chin up. "What? Do you think a woman not capable of it? Are we too delicate to take charge? I suppose we are too delicate to carry a baby within our bodies and bring it screaming into the world, too." She flipped her full skirts aside to reveal a sword sheathed at her side. She grinned at him, reminding Raven a little of Rue. "I can do it," she asserted. "I fought them yesterday and I look forward to fighting them again."

"What is your name, woman?" Talyn asked.

"Lilane."

"Well, Lilane, myself and my companion must get back to Marken's Lorddom quickly. She is injured and I must stand beside my lord and make ready for the battle that has already begun. You will have to lead these people to Marken's Lorddom yourself. Do you understand that?"

She nodded.

Talyn lifted Raven from the horse and let her lean against him, so as not to put her full weight on her thigh. "We will leave our horse with you. You can use it more than we can."

"How will you travel?" Lilane asked.

"Is there anywhere around here from which a person might jump?"

"Ummm...there is a cliff." She pointed. "Over there."

Talyn lifted Raven in his arms and she wrapped her arms around his neck. He walked to the cliff and the people followed them.

Raven met Lilane's confused gaze. "You are a brave woman. I will look forward to seeing you at Marken's Lorddom. Travel carefully."

"We will, but why are you...."

Talyn chose that time to leap.

They fell through the air and Raven felt herself separate from Talyn's arms. With a blessedly agonizing rip, her wings broke through and unfurled. Her back arched against the pain, but at the same it felt so good — as natural as breathing. She rose on a warm wind current, her eyes searching for Talyn. And then there he was, hovering in the air near here, beautiful, strong hawk wings beating.

"Raven wings," he said with a smile. "They're beautiful, black as your hair." He neared her and they embraced in the air, kissing as they fell. Then they parted and side-by-side, they flew straight upward.

Together, they angled back over the top of the cliff, both of them coming close to the edge and making the villagers stumble backward. Raven's wing tips brushed Lilane's cheek like a sigh.

The villager's cries of awe were audible as Raven and Talyn angled themselves away from them and back toward the castle.

Raven relished the wind blowing through her loose hair and caressing her skin. They dipped, dove, and climbed in the air currents together, their eyes either on each other or searching the ground below for some sign of Sudhraian movement.

Raven gasped when she spotted them. They were like a dark cloud moving through the forests, consuming and burning everything in their path. "Down there," she said to Talyn.

"I see them. Look to the east."

She followed his pointing finger. Large groups of what she surmised were Nordan Guardsmen were moving to intercept the Sudhraians before they made contact with Gregor's Lorddom.

"I must get back to Marken," Talyn said almost to himself.

The Goddess was with them when they found a tail wind and they picked up speed. It was twilight when they arrived in the inner bailey of the castle. People bustled all around them. Clearly much had happened since yesterday morning, and it was obvious they'd been notified of Sudhra's attack.

The bailey's inhabitants gaped as Raven and Talyn stood with their wings extended. With a sharp sting,

Raven furled hers. The flesh of her shoulders healed swiftly, as it always did, but her gown would remain ripped.

Talyn kissed her quickly. "I must go, Raven. They will be wondering where I am at such a critical time. Go to see the physician. I will find you later."

Raven watched him leave, a cold knot tightening in her stomach. Talyn would have to fight these savages who wanted to conquer Nordan.

* * * * *

Marken stroked his chiseled chin. "Could there be other Aviat in my lorddom, I wonder."

"Perhaps," Rue answered. "It is possible some do not know they are Aviat. Many of my people were scattered to the four corners of Aran during the bad times of the hunts. Like Talyn, they would have no reason to know of their heritage."

"How do we find out?"

"Raven and I can find out by speaking our native tongue to them. No matter how old an Aviat is they will understand it," answered Rue.

Talyn made a mental note to have Raven speak it to him later.

"Or to test the castle's inhabitants, I could merely touch the back of their necks. There will be a light vibrational response to such contact. Also, there is more than one way for an Aviat to unfurl their wings," Rue continued.

"There is?" asked Talyn.

"Aye. Not all of us can do this, but I can." Rue walked to the center of the room and closed his eyes. With a snap and a rustle, falcon wings unfurled. He opened his eyes. "If Raven's grandmother was not able to spread her wings by will alone, Raven may not be aware it is a possibility at all." His wings curled back in.

"I will set Raven to the task of finding out if there are more Aviats in the castle," said Marken thoughtfully. He turned to Talyn. "For now, Talyn, I need you here. I need you to keep training the peasants and farmers that arrive in bunches every day. I need you here to consult with me and to aid me in strategic planning. But you must be ready to leave at a moment's notice. I have already sent some of the other higher ranking guardsmen out to command regiments."

"I'll be ready, my lord," answered Talyn.

"We will not allow the Sudhraians to conquer us and do what they wish with our spices, silks, and women. They think us weak because we worship a female deity and give our women equal status in society. They are about to find out the error in those assumptions."

* * * * *

Lilane trudged up the road that led to the castle. She'd walked the whole way, giving up the horses to the older people and the children. Right now she was feeling every single muscle in her body.

She steeled herself. But that was good. This was good training for what she had planned. She would lead the villagers to Marken's Lorddom, gather supplies, and leave right away. She had work do to. She had Sudhraians to kill.

She fingered the pouch of coins suspended from the belt of her skirts. All the flourentimes she had in the world. Hopefully it would be enough to buy a good horse, provisions, and weaponry.

Yes, weaponry was most important.

Her hand went to the sword sheathed at her side. She'd had it forged long ago and had trained nearly every day of her life with the light, yet sharp blade. Living close to the Sudhraian border required her to keep her guard up as sometimes lords from the various priestdoms of Sudhra would make kidnapping runs over the border to gather fresh sex slaves.

Lilane was beautiful. She knew that. It was a curse laid upon her by the Goddess herself. Lilane knew she was exquisite in both body and face not only from looking in the mirror, but also because of the number of times she'd had to fend off Sudhraian kidnappers.

She'd give anything for a good set of buckteeth. Oh aye, it would make her lot in life much easier to bear. Instead, she sported hair the color of the sun at high noon, eyes a shade of blue that made men go breathless, and a body that literally dropped them to their knees—full hips and breasts and a small waist.

Aye, she'd made a few notches in her sword scabbard defending herself from Sudhraian slavers, and she'd make a few more before this war was through. She'd make the Sudhraian pay for killing her fiancé, Dal, and her mother and father.

Dal had died protecting her. Guilt rose and choked her. If it hadn't been for her, Dal might still be alive today.

Tears stung her eyes and she dashed them angrily away. She had no time for sorrow. She had no time for any emotion save her rage. She could get her arms around that feeling, feed off it. Rage would sustain her through this.

They neared the barbican and a guardsman stepped out.

Lilane stepped forward, her hand resting on the hilt of her sword. "We are arriving from Gadstone village to the south, near the Sudhraian border. Captain Talyn bade us arrive and seek refuge behind your walls. Our village has been pillaged and burned."

The guardsman stepped aside. "Welcome. Captain Talyn notified us of your arrival. Go into the inner bailey and someone will direct you to food, a bath, and sleeping quarters."

"Thank you," she answered gratefully as she trudged past him with her people in tow. Food and a bed were sounding very good right now. She was famished and dirty from their hard trek. But by tomorrow's first light, she'd be gone.

A murmur ran through the villagers. "There's another one!" gasped one.

Lilane looked skyward. Soaring down from one of the castle's towers toward them was a shirtless blond man with outstretched wings. Shading her eyes against the glare of the sun she studied him. His blue gaze seemed to catch and hold hers as he flew overhead.

With a mighty flap of long, strong wings, he angled himself away from them and headed back over the forest, headed south. She pivoted on her heel to watch him arc up and soar into a smattering of low-hanging clouds.

Her eyes narrowed. Wings not withstanding, he'd clearly been a Sudhraian with that hair, skin coloring, and that clothing.

If he flew back here, maybe he'd be the first to find the sharp edge of her sword.

* * * * *

Rue skirted the edge of a wind gust then shifted his body to let it bear his wing weight and stared down at the group of bedraggled villagers trudging up the path to the portcullis.

The woman leading them caught his gaze. Her clothes were ripped and filthy, traveling dust marred the creaminess of her skin and smudged across high cheekbones and a full mouth. Her eyes held anger, but even at a distance Rue could see the intense pain that glimmered alongside it. Had she lost loved ones recently? It was entirely possible.

That thought made him break his gaze with the woman and angle himself back toward Sudhra. He had to keep his mind on the task at hand — getting back to Sudhra and leading the rest of his Aviat clan to Nordan. They would do all they could to help the Nordanese in return for sanctuary.

He spotted a cluster of low clouds scudding through the sky and soared up and into them. After he gathered his clan, he would set off on his own and do some hunting himself — for Sudhraians.

* * * * *

Talyn watched Raven as she sat on the edge of the tower windowsill and stared out at the stars. Moonlight swathed the curves and hollows of her body and limned her face in silver.

He'd been absent often from her of late. He was busy constantly now that Nordan had been plunged into war. Thus far, the Nordanese were winning, pushing the Sudhraians back toward their own border. But Rue had divulged many of the Sudhraians secrets and it was known that the country had many more men to send. Sudhra was only toying with them now, fatiguing them, giving them a false sense of hope they were sure they'd crush.

That wouldn't happen if Nordan had anything to say about it. And they did. The might of their armies ensured it.

But now Talyn was tired of thinking war, of strategy. He wanted only to hold Raven in his arms, hear her sweet voice whisper in his ear, feel her wet slit consume his cock and milk it of its seed.

He walked into the room and came up behind her. He reached his arms around her and held her tight against him. She sighed and snuggled into his chest.

"Speak to me in Aviat," he purred into her ear.

She turned in his arms, smiled, and began to speak to him.

At first he didn't understand her words, but slowly, as his blood recognized the lilting coos and soft words, they began to make sense. *I love you* she said over and over in a hundred different ways.

As she spoke, his lust for her grew. His cock lengthened and hardened. He brought his hands up and let them catch at her luscious breasts. He stroked her rapidly hardening nipples back and forth with his thumbs. Her breathing caught and her words faltered.

"I love you," she finished in Nordanese.

"As I love you," he replied in Aviat.

She smiled and it lit up her face, chasing away the worry that had darkened her green eyes.

"And I want you," he continued.

She knelt and untied the lacings on his trews. Cool evening air caressed his cock as she freed it and then kissed the tip of it, licking away the pearl of his seed that had beaded there. His body tensed in sweet anticipation as she slipped him into her mouth. Soft, warm heat enveloped his cock as she slipped him down her tight throat. He let his head fall back and a groan escape him. The woman could do things with her mouth and tongue that literally brought him to his knees betimes. She stroked him in and out of her mouth, her tongue wreaking havoc on his control.

He reached down and pulled her to her feet, at the same time pulling her skirts up. His breathing was harsh in the silent room, matching Raven's.

"Come inside me," she demanded. "I want you within my passage."

He slipped a finger within and felt she was as ready as she seemed. In one movement, he picked her up, she curled her legs around his waist, and he impaled her on his rigid cock.

They sighed together in the contentment that being joined so intimately always gave them. "Yes," Raven said on a long, expelled breath.

With her hands braced on his shoulders, he lifted her up and down, creating friction and making them both groan. His cock slipped in and out of her tight, wet heat.

They climaxed together, Talyn's groan of completion mingling with Raven's moans. Not wanting to let her go after he'd bathed her womb with his seed, he held her against him and she tucked her head against his neck. He braced her sweet weight to him and sighed happily into her hair.

"I have something to tell you," she murmured into his ear.

"What is that?"

"I'm pregnant," she whispered.

Happiness and surprise mixed and melded within him, causing him to momentarily lose his words and nearly his very breath. All he could do was tighten his arms around her and bury his face in her neck, dusting her skin with light kisses. "So now we'll have two." They'd decided to foster Alia after returning from Sudhra.

"Aye."

They went silent, enjoying the moment. Finally, with a huge grin, he raised his face from her sweetly scented skin. "I have an interesting trick to show you."

She lifted her head, smiling. "What is that?"

Talyn closed his eyes and concentrated on the area of his shoulder blades, envisioning his wings opening. With a flash of pain, a pop, and a flutter, they unfolded.

"Oh, Talyn," Raven breathed, touching the leading edge of one wing. "How did you do that?"

"I'll show you."

"They're magnificent."

"You're magnificent."

He folded his wings around them at the same time he captured her lips in a kiss.

About the Author:

Anya Bast writes erotic fantasy & paranormal romance. Primarily, she writes happily-ever-afters with lots of steamy sex. After all, how can you have a happily-ever-after WITHOUT lots of sex?

Anya welcomes mail from readers. You can write to her c/o Ellora's Cave Publishing at 1337 Commerce Drive, Suite 13, Stow OH 44224.

Why an electronic book?

We live in the Information Age—an exciting time in the history of human civilization in which technology rules supreme and continues to progress in leaps and bounds every minute of every hour of every day. For a multitude of reasons, more and more avid literary fans are opting to purchase e-books instead of paperbacks. The question to those not yet initiated to the world of electronic reading is simply: *why?*

1. *Price.* An electronic title at Ellora's Cave Publishing runs anywhere from 40-75% less than the cover price of the <u>exact same title</u> in paperback format. Why? Cold mathematics. It is less expensive to publish an e-book than it is to publish a paperback, so the savings are passed along to the consumer.

2. *Space.* Running out of room to house your paperback books? That is one worry you will never have with electronic novels. For a low one-time cost, you can purchase a handheld computer designed specifically for e-reading purposes. Many e-readers are larger than the average handheld, giving you plenty of screen room. Better yet, hundreds of titles can be stored within your new library—a single microchip. (Please note that Ellora's Cave does not endorse any specific brands. You can check our website at www.ellorascave.com for customer recommendations we make available to new consumers.)

3. *Mobility.* Because your new library now consists of only a microchip, your entire cache of books can be taken with you wherever you go.

4. *Personal preferences are accounted for.* Are the words you are currently reading too small? Too large? Too...**ANNOYING**? Paperback books cannot be modified according to personal preferences, but e-books can.

5. *Innovation.* The way you read a book is not the only advancement the Information Age has gifted the literary community with. There is also the factor of what you can read. Ellora's Cave Publishing will be introducing a new line of interactive titles that are available in e-book format only.

6. *Instant gratification.* Is it the middle of the night and all the bookstores are closed? Are you tired of waiting days—sometimes weeks—for online and offline bookstores to ship the novels you bought? Ellora's Cave Publishing sells instantaneous downloads 24 hours a day, 7 days a week, 365 days a year. Our e-book delivery system is 100% automated, meaning your order is filled as soon as you pay for it.

Those are a few of the top reasons why electronic novels are displacing paperbacks for many an avid reader. As always, Ellora's Cave Publishing welcomes your questions and comments. We invite you to email us at service@ellorascave.com or write to us directly at: 1337 Commerce Drive, Suite 13, Stow OH 44224.

Discover for yourself why readers can't get enough of the multiple award-winning publisher Ellora's Cave. Whether you prefer e-books or paperbacks, be sure to visit EC on the web at www.ellorascave.com for an erotic reading experience that will leave you breathless.

WWW.ELLORASCAVE.COM

Printed in the United States
28332LVS00001B/55-609